MERCY

MERCY ALEXANDER

GEORGE TIFFIN

MERCY ALEXANDER

PICADOR

First published 2001 by Picador
an imprint of Macmillan Publishers Ltd
25 Eccleston Place, London SW1W 9NF
Oxford and Basingstoke
Associated companies throughout the world
www.macmillan.com

ISBN 0 330 48115 0

9 8 7 6 5 4 3 2 1

A CIP catalogue record for this book is available from
the British Library.

Typeset by Intype London Ltd
Printed and bound in Great Britain by
Mackays of Chatham plc, Chatham, Kent

For A.H. and C.J.D.

My Brothers and my Sisters dear,
For you we drop the mourning tear.
And from your tombs I hear you say
Prepare for death, make no delay.
The old must die, the younger may.

Nineteenth-century child's sampler

PROLOGUE

The limo smelled of air freshener and she wondered what the sharp scent of pine hoped to hide. She moved from one seat to the next playing with the television set and CD player and flipping open the ashtrays. They had been emptied but not wiped. The arm rest on the middle bench opened to reveal an ice bucket but no champagne and she cursed herself for not insisting on it. She lay across the black leather sofa at the back thinking of 1970s album covers where half-naked women with Amazon bodies and pastel eyeshadow stared at the camera, lips curled in an elegant fuck you.

Mercy Alexander had never ridden in a stretch. She had only sent the contract as a joke but her new agent had honoured it all. Private dressing room. Case of Stolichnaya. Make-up assistant. Maybe he had been joking, too, but right now she didn't care. She hadn't even opened the vodka: just taken a bottle as a souvenir.

The driver opened the door and Rose climbed in, laughing. Always laughing. She pulled a face at the TV cameras standing in the rain but because she was Rose the foolishness was funny and sexy. The door closed and immediately she started the same routine as Mercy: TV, CD, ice bucket.

No booze?

I know.

You want to lose that agent.

They laughed again hysterically as the car pulled away from

the kerb. He hadn't even asked where they wanted to go. Mercy watched the sign disappear in a comet of blue neon.

MONITOR GALLERY

OUT/TAKES

MERCY ALEXANDER

Rose stared at her.
They were all over you. Let me get a look at you.
She climbed over the seat to the back and hugged her. The streetlights washed over them, orange, white and orange again. Mercy was smiling like an idiot and Rose kissed her cheek.
You'd better watch your step now. You're going to make me jealous.

Two girls, nine and eleven, sat opposite each other on the floor by the bed looking at each other's hands. Rose read the labels carefully:
There's Cherry, Dusk, Hot Vermilion and Beige.
Beige sounded sophisticated, Mercy thought. A woman's colour. Not tarty. She's tarty (wrong colour bra under blouse). Very tarty (bare legs with high heels). She should be ashamed of herself (kissing Mercy's father and leaving a crimson shadow on his freshly shaven cheek). And who could ever wear Hot Vermilion?
Rose unscrewed the top and smelled the cellulose, piercing and volatile.
I want to be hot.
She handed the bottle to Mercy and spread her fingers, resting a palm on her knee. Mercy tightened the cap and shook it.
You have to shake it. That's what they do.
I did shake it.
She didn't know where you were supposed to start so she

4

settled on the little finger and the brush covered the nail from edge to edge in a single sweep. She stopped, amazed at how the little stroke of colour brought the hand alive. She could barely imagine lipstick, eyeshadow, earrings, scent. Rose patted her knee, afraid to mark the varnish but impatient for a whole hand to admire. She held her breath as she finished the second thumb, even and perfectly glossy. Rose flexed her fingers, flipping the hands over and over. She stood up carefully and went to the mirror on the back of the door, arching her neck and inspecting herself over her shoulder. Mercy watched the older girl and she did not understand why she turned herself that way but she knew better than to ask. She knew this was how you learned: close, but silent.

They had opened the Stolichnaya. The limo driver slid the glass down to ask where they wanted to go. Mercy was about to tell him to take them home when she realised that this might be the last time she ever rode on a leather sofa.

Venice, please.

She had always wanted to see Venice. The car moved noiselessly along the bed of the canal, the sun refracting through the greenish water as the gondolas idled high above them.

Venice Gardens?

She smiled. Venice Gardens was where her first proper boyfriend had lived. Perhaps he would see her. She wondered if the limo's darkened windows opened or whether that defeated the point of travelling in conspicuous anonymity.

Fine.

Rose lay back. She had kicked off her shoes and was trying to get the CD player to work by pushing the buttons with her toes. She spoke without looking at her:

I wouldn't be any good at being famous like you and I hate all those posh dealers and the others but I'd die to have a car like this every day.

5

Mercy stared at the long bare legs and she felt the warmth of Rose's head on her shoulder and all at once the evening – crowds, alcohol, noise – rushed around her, buoying her up. She sat forward and took Rose's hands in hers and kissed her on the mouth. Rose giggled and pushed her away seeing in her only drink and the thrill of success and Mercy kissed her again, sliding her lips apart but finding only teeth and the taste of her cigarettes. Rose tried to sit up but Mercy's weight was on her and when Mercy's hand touched her belly she rolled away, shocked. Mercy recognised her own blouse in the darkness and the thought that she would seduce her friend in her own clothes was suddenly irresistible. Her hand moved down to Rose's leg and pushed the skirt aside and Rose hit her so hard she fell against the glass and cut her lip.

What's that about?

You're not a dyke and you know I'm not either.

We're all grown-ups.

Oh, Mercy—

Rose could not bring herself to be angry. She knew that even after all these years and everything she had done Mercy still did not see how these things worked. She put a hand on hers.

You don't have to do this.

Mercy was dizzy. After seventeen years of homework, nail varnish and flats all shared could she really have kissed her, undressed her, held her, tasted her? She touched her lip. It was bleeding but she didn't care: she would never have a chance to wear this dress again anyway. No more Out Takes. She let the blood fall on the black silk. The whole evening seemed obscured now. What had she really wanted? Rose was somewhere at the heart of it. Something she wanted to share with her: to make her see it. And then to take Rose herself as the prize. She tried to remember if she had ever been attracted to a woman before.

Rose knocked at the glass partition:

Layton Road and if you pass a garage I need cigarettes.

The car slowed and began its wide turn.

Rose handed Mercy a paper napkin from her bag and they saw the telephone number written in the corner. She shook her head.

Too grand for a paper towel?

She knew if she took it they would hurtle back to where they had started, to a place they both pretended they had left far behind. Good girl, bad girl. Younger, older. Wise and wicked. Nothing without the other. Tonight was meant to be the end of apology.

Rose stared away: too grand.

Not too grand for anyone. Least of all you. I've just sold some pictures.

To a roomful of rich drunk loudmouths who never even looked at them.

Mercy shrugged.

Go and make a pass at one of them. Some bored millionaire wife who can collect your work and make you famous.

For fifteen minutes.

Fifteen more than me.

The end of apology, she thought. You always wanted what I had. You think these things just rain down on me.

I've already said I'll introduce you to Richard.

I'm not an artist.

He knows people in television.

I'm twenty-eight. They don't put people like me on TV any more.

So you can spend the rest of your life in a little black dress at Intimitá hanging coats and keeping the balcony table free in case a soap star pulls up without a reservation? Collecting reasons not to go out and do anything you really want to do?

I'm not a restaurant manager.

Sorry. Maître d'.

I'm a whore.

We're all whores—

Rose laughed. Sweet sixteen and never been kissed. I left Intimitá eight months ago. I'm a whore, Mercy. A prostitute.

Mercy's heart lurched. She was filled with love but fear had overtaken her from somewhere deep inside in the same instant. Her friend. She saw that Rose's blouse – her blouse – had lost a button. She could take one from the cuff, she thought, and match the other sleeve later. She tried to smile at her but when Rose met her eye she had to look away. This wasn't what they had promised each other standing sideways to the mirror in her little bedroom.

But I don't do girls. Sorry.

PART ONE

From where the photographer stands in the river bed the flood walls mask the world above. What few sounds make their way down here are softened by thin fog and dissolve like breath in the cold night air. The tripod settles in the silt. Even now, at low tide, water runs in a thin sheet across the sand, seeping from the timbers and concrete slabs that shore the banks as if the city itself were haemorrhaging.

The basin at the foot of the wharf has not been dredged for over sixty years but when the river runs high a woman will sink a hundred and forty feet before she settles into grey-green mud. If the shock of the fall from the jetty doesn't wind her and if the sun reaches deep into the water and if her eyes are still open she may see the world shimmer as she passes through the thermocline, the silvery mixing of sun-warmed tide with the icy still pool below. And then the cold will take her. If the stream is fast she will make the docks in two hours.

High above, car headlamps wash the orange glare and the flashes of blue. Voices echo, though nothing can be clearly heard. He finds his frame and sets a long exposure to hold each detail of the scene: the wood that never dries and the steel trusses frozen in their own rust and the skies milky with fumes and light and aircraft.

He shoulders the camera and climbs the rungs to the surface.

*

The city is not asleep but it is sleepwalking. Evening absolves the day with a brushstroke of violet that reaches from the columns of the old power station to the fine antennae of the telecommunications tower while night waits in the marshes to the east. Cars crawl along the widened roads as radio announcers deliver familiar traffic news, the litany of contraflows and gyratories like a medical briefing. Ball-point pens tremble on empty desks as the underground trains drag their cargo home to children already asleep and unopened bills and uncleared tables. Triple-glazed terraces ignore four-hundred-seat jets throttling back as they tear microwave suppers from their foil wrap and television screens beckon soft dust from the air just as they suck images from the ether and stare at the empty rooms before them. The capital relaxes, humming like a vast machine.

Mercy Alexander is laid flat on her back on the jetty and her pale dress spreads into the pool of water around her. The material is translucent now and it clings to her long legs and belly and her brown hair is twisted to one side, darkened and thickened by the water. Her face is still, her eyes shut, her lips slightly apart. Her eyelashes have matted together in fine long points. She has not been in the river long. She looks good.

The cameras flash. The press have arrived and they range themselves without discussion on the walkway above as an orchestra takes a stage: stills at one end, the one-man bands, their cameras stripped back, brand names removed or hidden by black tape – video cameras with station logo stickers and sun-guns in the middle – stragglers, amateurs and ambulance-chasers at the farthest end. Behind them an audience has begun to gather, unsure whether they may talk or whether the scene – or perhaps the press – expect silence. A policeman watches from his car, the window raised against the wind and a thousand questions. Behind him a young woman in a silver puffa jacket sits in silence.

Carter Stark stands half a head above the crowd and they stare up at him as he pushes forward. He ducks under the hazard tape and walks across to Mercy. In front of the cameras he is nervous. He kneels beside the body and lays the back of his hand against her cheek, neither intimate nor indifferent.

You'd be paler. And blue lips.

I'm so bloody cold!

You'll never make it look right otherwise.

She sits up and waves for a blanket. The silver jacket runs with a green tartan rug to cover her shoulders. She pulls a lip-brush and palette from her bag and pushes Mercy's head back. Carter shrugs. Don't shoot the messenger. She sees his discomfort but she cannot speak with a mouthful of blue lipstick, not even as a courtesy to a man she has only known for two hours, so she rolls her eyes and hopes he will see she is cold and tired but not angry. Not angry with him.

PRESS RELEASE

L'INCONNUE DE LA SEINE

Colony Wharf – October 9

On this day 100 years ago in Paris the body of a young woman was found floating in the river. She was taken to lie among the hundreds of other anonymous corpses in the city morgue but was never identified. The cause of her drowning was never discovered.

All we know of her is that her smile, even in death,

gripped the imagination of Europe for half a century. A death mask was taken while she lay on ice, and factories in France and Germany produced over 60,000 plaster casts in the following decade.

She was known as L'Inconnue de la Seine. Young women of the time idolised her simple passive beauty, and men fell in love with this extraordinary face without a history – a blank canvas on which they could paint their own vision of femininity.

We see what we want to see.

MERCY ALEXANDER

Carter knows what death looks like because he is an undertaker. He knows there are as many ways to die as there are to live. Drowning is one of the least pleasant, but in this elaborate reconstruction Mercy has been careful to point out that the woman must have been found within hours of her death. No bloating, wrinkling or discolouration, no swelling of stomach gases, no loosening of the hair – just pulmonary oedema. It is still possible, she seems to think, to want to fall in love with somebody whose lungs are filled with river water.

Carter has not heard of Mercy Alexander. He does not know that this is how she earns her living – performing, provoking. He does not know why cameras from four television stations and one from France have chosen to come to this abandoned wharf at the heart of the city to film her for the nightly news. All he really knows is that he will be paid one hundred and twenty-five pounds for three hours' work, which is half of what he would charge for a plain casket that would take him a day to make, not including the timber. And that Mercy's lips are now too blue.

The photographer stands across her, twisting to frame the face without casting a shadow. Mercy stares back, watching him

14

without moving her eyes. She can hardly focus. She is trying to settle into a thousand-yard stare but she is afraid that she looks more like a fish on a slab. She has no idea what it would feel like to be dead. She is not sure you can know. Or if you would want to. What she does know is that if she does not look painfully beautiful and wholly irresistible then nobody will fall in love with her and her performance will be wasted. So she shifts her gaze and draws her cheeks in and tilts her head back to lengthen her pale elegant neck.

When she stands her bones are cold and the wet dress catches at her legs as she walks. Flashguns flutter around her as she tries to leave the jetty. When she was twenty-one they flew her to Paris and she was terrified she would stumble on the catwalk, that it would be narrow and raked, that the photographers would blind her, that she would fall into the audience. That the power of their looking would be like gravity and would draw her down. She was afraid the clothes she wore were more precious than she would ever be and she wanted to take them off and hold them out in her hands so they would look at the dress and the shoes and not at her.

Don't we all have masks? To make life bearable?

How is she a victim if we don't know what killed her?

Doesn't it demean women to say that their beauty is their most powerful tool?

They shout across each other. Getting it. Not getting it. Mercy stops so the cameras will settle.

Use your beauty, says Mercy.

She used it.

She was dead, says Mercy. We used it.

She's just a pin-up.

For undertakers.

¤

Carter did not watch the evening news when he got home because he did not have a television. He walked through the workshop and went up the narrow stairs without turning the light on because although the furniture importer on the cooling board had been dead for thirty-six hours he felt that even a corpse deserved his rest.

The single bare bulb hanging over the table in the kitchen was too bright and its reflection flared on the face of the birch cabinets he had built by the window dissolving their fine grain in a dull cold smear. Carter would never see this because his love for his work lay at the core of the wood and the kiss of the joints. The surface belonged to the world but the heart was his. It was the same with men and women; he never noticed the point at which they touched the other lives around them, whether they got drunk too quickly or scratched their Adam's apple when they were about to ask an awkward favour or argued over the cost of brass screws on an invoice. But he knew if they were square and true.

He made himself the same supper he had eaten at home every night for five years since he left prison: sausages and eggs, warm bread and tea. A pack of six, everything fried in the same pan and the yolks paled with fat tipped from the tea-spoon. If he was hungry he would just have more bread. Too many breakfasts had been left cooling on the low table as the husbands, wives and children pounded on the door in the early hours. Better to enjoy it in the calm of the evening: a little ritual to celebrate safe passage through the day. And the second place set at the far end of the table. Another little ritual.

¤

Mercy's hands were supple from the heater but beneath the thick coat she was still stiff with cold and she had to force herself to climb out into the darkness and lock the car behind her. The scaffolding had finally come down and the red-brick apartments were freshly scrubbed. She saw the gold of the doorman's braid through the double door and he did not turn but she knew he watched her in the mirror. Her car was the oldest on the street by at least six years. This quiet, rich district north of the parks had been residential when she was a child but those who lived there now worked for their money and their houses were not homes but investments. From floor to floor the windows hid themselves behind a soft fall of glazed cotton as if the warm light inside was too valuable to waste on the wet pavement below.

She could feel the bath already. On a night like this the steam would be visible against the black walls, filling the room with its soft clouds, and the tub would be full in minutes. That was the best thing about the old brothel: beneath the rich panels and silent carpets it was like a hospital, practical and indestructible.

In a proper whorehouse everything is built to industrial tolerances. Everything is used and abused. Most of the men have been drinking by the time they take their girl downstairs to one of the intimate anonymous rooms and – being drunk – they drag their heels, kick the skirting, sit on tables, lean on walls and fall on beds. And being drunk and therefore uninhibited, and feeling they have to justify the hundred and seventy-five pounds they will have spent for the pleasure of a girl's company for an hour, they give bravado displays of humping and pounding, bending the girls over chairs and tables and dragging them across the floor.

Not all the men are like this. Those who do not drink or

whose imaginations are more refined leave their own mementoes. The bed-linen is changed every hour and the beds every six months and the velvet curtains have long since been sold and replaced with materials easier to dry clean.

Rose worked here for almost two years. When she played with Mercy at the bottom of her garden where their mothers could not see them together they knew already that they would become television programme announcers. Rose – the older – would work as a waitress while Mercy finished her exams and they would rent a flat with two separate bedrooms in case they found boyfriends they wanted to bring home and they would go to college together to pursue media studies even though neither of them knew what media were. Rose never made it through school and was waitressing by the time she was seventeen, married at twenty-two, divorced at twenty-four and sleeping with strangers for money within a year. Now she is thirty-one and Mercy twenty-nine and they know what media are but they still haven't signed up for the course.

Mercy's house – the only mansion on the block not divided into private floors and the only one not repainted – sat halfway up the rise. She still used the original front door even though it took half her weight to swing it. Buildings in those days were meant to be entered, and she loved to step into the high quiet of the hall with the drawing rooms and discreet corridors leading her off in every direction. By the time she got there Rose had stopped crying and was almost asleep. She lay on the wide stone step with her shoes under her head and her feet tucked under her coat. Mercy hadn't seen her since her birthday. The argument in the limousine three years before had been no worse than their other battles or betrayals and they had laughed about it quickly enough but since that night they had seen each other less than they cared to admit. Something about Rose's confession had drawn a line between them that neither of them could acknowledge.

She opened the door and threw her wet things inside without stepping over her and reached down to take her hand. Rose started again. Mercy laid a finger on her lips and wiped the first hot tear away with her thumb. She stayed kneeling until she was quiet again and then helped her to her feet. She took the shoes and coat and led her in, pushing the door closed with her back. There was a light on in the drawing room with the old bar and they sat there a moment before Mercy got up and went to fetch alcohol. The high shelves were empty but the glasses were clean and there were bottles in the kitchen.

Mercy smiled at Rose as she poured. Rose watched the whisky.

I saw you on telly. Did you really go in the river?

Feel me.

She took Rose's hand and put it on her belly under the coat and fleece and T-shirt.

God, that's as cold as me!

They drank the first glass without water and when they had had two more without talking Rose told her without being asked.

He was going to be the last one tonight anyway. I was watching you on the news when he came in and he just wanted the full service, straight sex, not even a soap in the shower. He was nice, too, an easy talker, not one of the ones who lie there like you've already done something wrong. Asking me about everything. They always want to know everything. Like they get more of you if they know. So I let him peel off and get on the bed and I took my dress off, the favourite, the one they love that leaves nothing to the imagination because they don't have any fucking imagination, and he just stopped.

19

Mercy took her hand again. This time she only cried a little.

What does your tummy look like?

Mercy took off her coat and her fleece and she pulled her T-shirt up above her white bra. She was still cold.

We're not sixteen any more.

I've seen you in that dress. You look fantastic. Imagination or not.

He was forty-five fucking years old! With a belly out to here and hair all up his arse and the worst fucking teeth you've ever seen. And for a hundred and seventy-five pounds I'm supposed to look like a million dollars.

You do.

After four others. He asked me how old I am.

Thirty-one.

Twenty-seven. That's what I said when he called. They like you in your twenties. I thought I could do twenty-seven.

Mercy nodded.

And he laughed, with his fat fucking forty-five-year-old belly and his fat fucking hands all folded over his dick. So I stopped, I didn't yell, I asked him how old he wanted me to be and he said the best girl he ever had was seventeen years old for thirty quid at a hotel on the south coast and he wanted to tell me everything she let him do to her and I just looked at his ring and the wallet and the season ticket on the table and I knew if I opened the wallet he'd have a picture of a wife and a boy and girl who'd be seventeen by now and I just fucking smacked him.

¤

Mercy doesn't worry about her age but she worries about her looks. She has built an elaborate defence against her fear that the cupboards of expensive cosmetics and seventy-pound haircuts are the indulgences of a woman who cares just a little too much about her appearance. They are, she tells herself, her tools – practical and essential for an artist whose body is her work. She prefers to do her own make-up these days, which means that her bathroom – the former Correction Room of the brothel – holds a thousand times more than her sponge-bag ever used to. In her modelling days she had been proud to carry nothing but a bottle of cleanser and an eyeliner pencil which she used as a bookmark.

Now she has exfoliants in more grades than sandpaper and in seven fruit varieties. Her preferred kaolin face-pack is not from the old quarry in China but from the Czech Republic because it contains less iron hydroxide and needs no bleaching (she knows her tools). At the moment she wears Monster Fun on her nails, although hers is actually a pre-release factory tester labelled Bogeyman. She has a bowl full of varnish just for toes and foam rubber dividers in four colours. She has kohl made from lamp-black and sparkle gel with real gold flakes, and secretly she loves it all. Her mother, who feared the crackle of sexual energy between man and woman, taught her nothing about these things and the first she knew about make-up was from an article in the encyclopaedia her father nearly bought:

> The tone and structure of the face is commonly altered with coloured powders applied with a brush or small cosmetic sponge. Rouge is used to empha-sise the cheekbones and the more familiar blusher adds softness and shape. Compressed powder compacts are traditionally manufactured in sizes small enough to be carried in a purse or handbag.

Not that Mercy had a handbag. Not until she met Rose.

*

Her six-year career as a model was launched by a student writing competition in one of the glossies: Beauty is Created. Her calm, bitter commentary on the manipulation of the female image won her first prize and guaranteed publication and the accompanying author photograph got her a good agent the night before the magazine went on sale. Two issues later she was in Prague leaning against a lamp-post on the Charles Bridge in eleven different winter coats and the following April she was on the cover with a perspex halo and mirrored contact lenses. She was twenty.

Mercy was tall and fair but she was not a blonde and on the one occasion she had agreed to be bleached for a shoot she knew it said all the wrong things. Her natural hair was pale brown and fell in soft waves to her shoulders and she never seemed to wear it the same way twice and whether she put it up in a twist or tied it back with the ribbon taken from a bunch of flowers it seemed right. Her skin was not radiant and her cheekbones were not achingly high and her smile was not broad but her quick brown eyes held the world and her look was unmistakeable. No matter how the stylists and photographers reworked her she was still Mercy and no matter how stunning she looked she never ceased to be real. A woman.

She worried that she had never learned to be elegant – ladylike, her mother would say – and she loved to kick her shoes off in meetings or sit on the floor with her back to the warmest radiator. She never looked like a model because she wore her favourite clothes all at the same time, tight-waisted pale blouses over a man's tweed trousers or hand-made leather sandals with her couture silk skirt. And she knew that according to all the rules her hands were too big and her shoulders too broad for editorial work but on the page she was captivating and everyone loved her because she always seemed to be about to overflow the picture as if whatever they asked her to do, no matter how outrageous, could barely contain her. And of course she was beautiful – she had always been beautiful and she had been told it so often now that she almost believed it – but her magic lay at the outer edge of her vision. She would not reduce herself to a bland accommodating presence and she challenged us to go with her. To see more.

By the time she turned twenty-two Mercy was at the top of her profession. She wasn't a household name but she was a household face and she had done the glossies, most of the runways, all of the talk shows. Models are only as dumb as they're treated and she always found ways to keep her head above water. She had friends outside the business, worked a maximum of two hundred days a year and most of the time she said no to the drugs. All models take them some of the time. Speed for the younger ones because they think they stay thinner. Coke for everyone: the mineral water of the industry. Heroin for those who can't face the success and then can't face the failure. Cigarettes, alcohol and dope don't even count.

Last year's favourite rumour was of the supermodel so far gone on everything she was offered that she was unable to stand. She could smile and she could just about sit but it wasn't a pretty sight. Not what the swimwear manufacturer was paying her fifteen thousand pounds a day for. So they laid her on the sand at the edge of the Indian ocean, her legs and arms falling around her, and let the wind blow her hair over her face to hide the staring eyes and the campaign won every major advertising award that season.

When Mercy started as a model she heard plenty of stories like these and she assumed they were fictions improvised by photographers pretending they'd seen it all or by the girls themselves, bored of small talk. She was never sure who they were trying to impress. Only when she'd seen it all for herself did she realise it was all true and they were desperate to impress themselves, to find something to kick-start them in a job where their value was based not on what they knew or did but what they were prepared to put up with.

But she knew all along that the worst drug of all is flattery. Everybody does it to everybody else: a language all of its own. The editors need the girls and the girls need the covers. The make-up artists have to have the faces for their books and the models need to be sure they can be resurrected after a transatlantic flight or a night of partying. The top photographers will only work with the biggest names and the hot girls will only work with their favourites. Everybody needs everybody else and in a business where everything is illusion truth is the most precious commodity of all.

I created Joni and Augusta. Not one of them has what you have. Really.

How does it feel to know every man in the world wants to sleep with you? Me included. Just kidding.

I've always admired your work. I knew, even before you were getting covers.

You'll always be at home here.

It all melted into a kind of flesh-coloured soundtrack laced with Ruben Gonzales and Lauryn Hill and scented with the peppery smell of dope and hairspray. The only voice she could never tune out was her mother:

There's a good girl.

Pretty is as pretty does.

They're all after one thing.

She would teach her daughter how to sit in skirts of different lengths and how to stand without showing her sights. She would move a button on a blouse by a quarter of an inch so that the cleavage was decent. Mercy used to dream of her in the audience at a show staring at the chiffon halter-top that barely shadowed her breasts and the tiny thong beneath the cheek-tight silk culottes.

24

She had never been one of the girls. Not at home, not at school, not half-naked in the dressing rooms waiting for her rinse. The soft buzz of trivial confidences flickered all around her but she could never quite lose herself in it. She had her own little beauty tricks to trade and her own stories about what Jens Holmquist really carried in his holster – her own insecurities and her own victories – but she had never been easy with others, and even though it was a language quickly learned she knew she would never be natural with it.

The other girls stuck together as they always did, finding safety in a united front against the waves of photographers, agents, editors, liggers and party hosts. When Mercy sat in a corner with her book they saw it as a challenge. When they hurried to check the contacts fresh from the lab and Mercy just went for a walk they felt patronised. Mercy saw the anger but she could make no attempt to soothe it. They wanted her to be vulnerable the way they were, little knowing she had ways enough of her own.

What was her legacy of shame and self-doubt? Modesty, or fear? Indifference, or cynicism? She hardly dared distinguish between them but they kept her sane through the hardest years, and when she finally cracked it wasn't so much a break-down as a revelation. She held on to her agent for a year just to put a barrier between herself and the calls. They pleaded and they shouted and they invoked past friendships and then they increased their offers to ridiculous amounts and in the end they just said her time had passed and she was yesterday's face.

The assistant editor who judged her student article had founded *Matt*, a low-budget high fashion independent magazine for the city's *über*hip. As the name insisted, everything about it was anti-glossy. When Eva persuaded Mercy to write a piece about her career and publish the backstage pictures she had taken over the years it caused a media meltdown. Editors all over the city went crazy trying to figure out which way the bandwagon they were leaping on was headed. Shattering exposé of the horrors of the beauty industry, or sad loser tells all? In-your-face photojournalism, or tacky kiss 'n' tell? The postmodernists had a field day and the glossies themselves, with characteristic lack of humour, fanned the flames. Four days after *Matt* sold out Mercy signed with Richard Strathmore and two weeks after that the collected photographs opened at the Monitor Gallery under the title *Out/Takes* and they made it on to the evening news on three channels. The world knew the faces but now there was a story. Mercy saw that, and the same instincts that had got her out of modelling made her promise herself she would never forget: be your art. What they want is you.

With simple enough logic her second show was called *Me*. Years before, after she had finished a six-day TV commercial in a disused paper mill, she had suffered a chest infection and had a series of X-rays to monitor her progress. She hung two of them on her bathroom window and only when she retired from modelling did she notice that they were the only pictures of herself in the whole apartment. She spent the next few months in hospitals and labs across the city photographing herself with every medical apparatus she could find. Ultrasound scans of her internal organs crushed together beneath a corset. X-rays of her skeleton draped with metal jewellery so the bones and the gold and silver fused into a fleshless science-fiction vision. Thermographs of herself in mini-skirt and T-shirt with her legs, arms and belly bare, the heat rippling away to surround her with waves of gold and crimson. Electron scanning micrographs of her hair, shattered by bleaching, dyeing, overheating and a thousand layers of spray: human barbed wire. Magnetic resonance images of the blood flow to her brain as she dreamed of sex, money, death, food. An intimate examination of her own body and what she had done to it in the name of beauty. This show, too, sold out within days. This time even the tabloids were after her, daring her to shock them.

What does it feel like to know your innards are hanging in some rich collector's dining room?

Just say I'm an organ donor. I'd rather let them have my kidneys than my face.

¤

Carter washed both plates in the sink and set them to dry in the rack. He took the cup of tea downstairs to the workshop and turned on the light. The room was long and low, its walls stacked with timber of every kind and lined with benches and racks of hand tools. A printing press stood in the corner. He liked to work quietly, and the only machine was a grinding-wheel he used when there were no bodies to disturb. He had taken the lease not because he wanted an eighteenth-century coach-house but because he needed a yard away from the main road big enough for a hearse to turn.

He checked the spokeshave with the pad of his thumb and pulled the cloth back from the lip of the coffin. The curve was perfect from bow to stern but now the silk had been tacked in place he wanted to soften the inner edge. Everything in his training told him he should have finished the woodwork before pinning the cloth but he had learned that when each casket is a unique commission a different rule must be bent every day.

The man under the shroud at the far end of the room was Julian Salter, a businessman, importer of cheap garden furniture

27

for cheap gardens, and a keen sailor. He was one of the handful of people (exclusively men) who had read an article about Carter's unique coffins in a colour supplement and had had the foresight to commission the work before he actually needed it. The fees and duties would be paid to Carter according to a codicil in the will. He had also asked Carter to put one thousand pounds in cash in the lining of the casket on the right-hand side at hip height. The solicitor who brought the money in small bills had suggested that nobody would know if the envelope was padded out with newspaper and that it would be far better spent by the living. He mimed his impression of a fifty-fifty split and glanced at his client. Carter didn't even look at him so he threw the pile on the table.

Help yourself, then. Dead man's money.

Carter knew by now that his own father had been poor but it had been years before he had noticed. They wanted for nothing because he never learned to need more than he had. Enough was decent – more was dangerous. Death will show you just what wealth can do. Salter had suffocated when a fragment of bone from a casseroled pheasant caught in his throat. Carter knew that it was just as possible to choke on a mouthful of cornflakes but somehow the story was comforting.

He carried Salter across to the hull and laid him in, holding his hand to the envelope to reassure him. He lifted the deck and slid it across until it sat firmly in its place and he checked the pilot holes were true and clean. He had doubled up along both edges because the mast was six foot high and even with a simple fore-and-aft rig a gusty morning might rip an ordinary lid clean off. When he removed the cover he noticed that the setting pressed against the face so he flattened the pad beneath the head and laid him back down.

¤

Lucas Fuller was a thug but despite his pure mean presence he had longer eyelashes than any woman he had ever slept with or put on the streets. His face, though beginning to line, was startlingly beautiful with eyes as blue as cloudless twilight and rich dark curly hair. In any other business it would have been an asset but he had been a small-time crook for twenty years and in this world of nervous machismo good looks were for girls.

At his single-sex state school he had been a pretty boy quickly marked for the attention of the older pupils. He felt their glances everywhere around him in a world where the urgent jostling of early manhood allowed little independence and no intimacy. He survived the worst of the predators – he was never seduced – but he discovered soon enough that the smile they wanted cost him nothing and if it brought him closer to the power then that in turn gave him a kind of energy. Sex – or even its scent – became a tool, a weapon, a trap. In classrooms and playgrounds his role as acolyte was secure but he dropped out at seventeen and quickly found himself adrift. He had grown used to a world where he could reinvent himself according to the gangs he ran with but outside the school gates his malleability left him vulnerable.

He survived for a while running a ring of eleven-year-olds who cracked vending machines. Later he graduated to blackmail but he never really found anyone who could afford to pay what he demanded and eventually he began to be ashamed of hunting through dustbins for hotel receipts and credit-card slips. For the next decade or so he sold bent cars and passed counterfeit banknotes in bars but the one time he did something he could be proud of – he had once robbed a village post office with a borrowed pistol – he had to keep it to himself and eventually he began to see that nothing in his life was really his at all. He longed to be able to say *I am Lucas Fuller and I did this.*

*

All of this changed on his thirty-seventh birthday. He had become a regular at a popular brothel in the city and was known there as a CQNT (pronounced *qunt*: come quick, no tip) – a bread-and-butter client. He had approached two of the friendlier girls about an arrangement outside the club as a present to some financiers in town to look at a restaurant he wanted to buy and Elena, the younger of the two, had ended up moving in with him for a few months. A year after she left him he was sitting alone at home in front of the television as the evening news showed Louise Parrish, forty-eight years old, three previous arrests for keeping a bawdy-house and related offences, being led to an unmarked police car. She was short, pretty, outwardly respectable, tired. One of the detectives held out a coat to cover her face but she pushed it away and walked down the steps out-staring the photographers, less self-conscious than the officers escorting her.

Lucas did the maths as he watched: when a brothel closes the freelance market in prostitutes overflows. If all the girls who no longer have a place to work hit the streets the independent operators lose business and infighting begins. Cards in phone boxes are the first to go: they pay the same young boys who place theirs to tear down anything left by a rival. The best this achieves is a bidding war for the allegiance of the fly-posters. Next come police tip-offs and violence. It wastes time, money and energy in a business where protecting yourself against the client is worry enough. Most of the men who have visited the brothel are regulars but none of them – for obvious reasons – will have left any way for their favourites to find them. Nor will the girls have cared to give out home numbers and now there are hundreds of men anxious to make arrange-ments with dozens of young women who depend on them for their livelihood but nowhere to meet on neutral territory. Supply and demand just waiting for a broker.

By the time the reporter had finished a sanctimonious

piece to camera about the relief of the local residents Lucas had dialled Elena's number and by the time Louise Parrish had finished her six-month sentence thirty-eight of the girls, including Rose, were working for him in a renovated hotel just north of the financial district.

The brothel had been open in its new incarnation for two years when Connor Fairburn first visited. Tonight he had two girls, both new to him. Lisa (not her real name) was naked and had pierced nipples. With her lover she sometimes wore chains but in the rough-and-tumble of sex with unknown clients she kept to simple silver rings. Suzie (not her real name) wore sheer black stay-ups but kicked off her stilettos when she climbed onto the bed to kneel over Lisa's face. Lisa lapped at her noisily and ran her hands up and down her back but judging by their expressions it was more blessed to give than to receive: Suzie looked bored. Fairburn was also bored. He sat in a chair across the room fully dressed. He had only been hard once since the girls started. He looked at Suzie's imitation patent leather shoes and imagined how the plastic must make her feet sweat.

Lucas had spent more on refurbishing the bar and drawing rooms than on the bedrooms, assuming that once his guests had made it that far they would have more on their mind than interior design. Hot water and clean towels were essentials – the rest was a matter of dim lighting and drink. Fairburn drank, but rarely to excess, and never enough to prevent him from noticing the poly-cotton sheets, melamine side tables and smoked glass mirrors. He was a snob, but in this case it was a question of imagination, not of pedigree. In his dreams he had melting ecstatic sex with women he would never glance at by day – they combined raw physical skills with a shatteringly crude imagination and an utter lack of self-respect, and they made him whimper for more. They were filthy. These two, pretty and young as they were, were strictly for the CQNTs. He threw six crumpled fifties on the floor and headed back upstairs.

The bartender brought Lucas his third spritzer. That's what his girls ordered when they were with clients, of course – nobody could possibly imagine he would drink them unless on duty. An elderly man sat on the next stool, resting on his elbows to hide the frayed patches on his blazer.

How are we tonight?

Just a quick glass on my way home.

This was the standard exchange. The colonel was here every night, mannerly enough not to stare at the girls when they were flirting with the others but not really a player. Once every few weeks he would come in with an envelope and approach one of the younger ones – he had no favourite. He lived off his savings and the money he spent here was entirely from his military pension. It's the least they can do, he always said. He was fit and very well-endowed, and even the more experienced girls found the coupling shocking. They did what they could, but youth fears age.

Fairburn watched the bubbles rise in the glass. A shipper at a tasting of vintage champagnes had once told him that the dissolved gases attach themselves to tiny faults in the flute, where they expand and force their way to the surface. Nucleation sites. He wondered what would happen in a glass made so that its sides were perfectly smooth. He wondered whether Lisa was voluntarily bisexual.

He found Lucas in the Red Room. Lucas knew better than to say he was surprised to see him upstairs so soon – a short session was almost always the result of poor staying power. Unless you paid for a whole evening, the house rule was that when you came you went. Some of the girls tried to keep it quick, teasing and rubbing the men as they undressed and washed, playing with themselves to bring them close so that when they came into them they only lasted a few strokes. They never blamed the girl but they usually felt cheated so Lucas tried to discourage it even though it increased turnover.

Don't you have any suites? Smarter rooms?

Lucas didn't understand. He didn't know much about Fairburn. He didn't visit often but he spent well.

It's depressing.

We'll have to fix that. Suzie was taking care of you?

Suzie and Lisa.

They didn't say anything. I'll talk to them.

They're still down there.

Let me get you a drink.

Fairburn still held his champagne.

Fill you up.

I want something special.

We have all kinds of rooms. All kinds of services. Has anybody shown you?

I don't mean those kinds of games—

It was always a difficult moment – a plea, or a confession. Lucas looked around to see who might hear, but Fairburn didn't seem to care.

No uniforms, no toy show, no panting and groaning. Just dirty. I want to be hard like I've never been hard before.

¤

The day after they met Rose asked Mercy if she wanted to come with her to steal apples from the house at the end of the road. They could climb over from the top of the shelter. Mercy said

33

they had apples in a bowl at home. They stood arguing at the foot of the wall when the bus came and the boys asked them what they were doing. Rose knew them. The boys dared them to climb and when the girls hesitated the boys jumped up and helped themselves but they wouldn't share.

Get your own.

They weren't even eating them. It was a matter of pride more than greed: if boys can do it, girls can do it too. Rose and Mercy pushed and pulled each other up and stood on the little roof. Mercy was taller and crouched on the wall to lean across.

The boys shouted all at once:

Blue! Blue!

They threw the apples up at the girls and ran, laughing. Rose was wearing her favourite dungarees and didn't know what they meant. But Mercy – whose dress had ridden up to show her blue knickers – knew at once and she knew too that her mother had been right. Good girls keep their legs together.

Mercy's mother had always hated Rose. Mercy's father David was an archaeological surveyor and Angela was a housewife, a credential that carried more weight under their roof than any of the professional acronyms on her husband's letterhead. Their life was stable to the point of absurdity. Mercy was their only child, and her arrival had so disrupted domestic arrangements that a second was never discussed. David would have loved a son, but even if Angela had agreed the ritual of their marital duties was so arcane as to be virtually contraceptive.

Every month, two days after the end of her period, during which she would not even allow her husband to kiss her, she would cook his favourite supper (Barnsley chop, medium, potatoes sautéed not fried, creamed spinach, two glasses of dry red wine) and light a fire in the sitting room. After washing up silently she would retire for a bath. David had had a reasonable sexual appetite before his marriage, but now he found the process so antiseptic that he brought work home on the evenings he suspected he would be required to perform. At a quarter past nine she would appear.

I've had a lovely long soak.

Papers rustled.

Those papers can wait. It's nice to have a little time together.

Then she would lay her hand on his shoulder in a gesture of rehearsed tenderness and David would ask himself why he dreaded this moment so much. He had no emotional vocabulary to imagine what other path his life might have taken but he was always surprised to find himself here again exactly a month after the last evening. And they would move slowly upstairs, silently, not touching, staring at little things about the house they had not seen before and they would lie across the bed in the spare room because it was a little further from Mercy's open door and the final act would begin. Once Angela had referred to these encounters as the consummation of their marriage and David, half-remembering a school performance of *Hamlet*, had joked quietly that it was a consummation devoutly to be wished. Now every time he lay beside his wife in the modest darkness, his breath slowing, the soliloquy ground through his head again, devoid of meaning apart from its ridiculous post-coital link.

Afterwards, as they returned to their own bedroom, Angela in her dressing gown and David naked with his clothes folded under his arm, she would turn to him and whisper:

You men, you're only after one thing.

There were plenty of things he wanted besides this, and many of them more than this, but he would kiss her because he knew that beneath her fear she still loved him.

*

Rose looked at the bowl of apples in Mercy's kitchen, which had been the laundry room when Rose worked at the brothel.

We have apples at home.

They laughed.

The week Louise Parrish was arrested Rose had turned a total of almost three thousand tricks. Plenty of those had been repeat business, so the actual roll-call might have been under two thousand, but it still shocked her to think of it – not so much the act as the mileage. Four men a day, three days a week, and four weeks off a year just like everyone else. Today the figure was over four thousand. More than enough.

The week Rose reached three thousand Mercy had sold out her third show in a row and had just signed a contract for a small part in a film. Rose was broke. When Rose told her about the raid and showed her the brothel she wrote to Louise and arranged to buy the building before the bank repossessed it. Louise promised to use half of the proceeds to pay off the girls and Mercy moved in a month later.

She hardly needed the space – thirty rooms – but she needed something. A statement about her life, some gesture to herself. Behave like an artist and you will be treated as an artist. Behave like an artist and you will believe yourself an artist. She forced herself to embrace her new home but, like herself, it was a work in progress, not a *fait accompli*.

She slept in one of the rooms with windows from floor to ceiling but when she tried to open the curtains that had hidden the girls from view for so long they crumbled around her. There was no real kitchen so she used the laundry room behind the ornate Victorian bar where she ate at one of the green baize card tables. Two other drawing rooms were filled with boxes of belongings and props from shows and clothes she no longer cared to wear. Only the upper hallway stayed dark, a low spreading space that led to the network of galleries and bedrooms below. Mercy hadn't been down there since she moved in.

Mercy opened her address book and was writing names and numbers down on the back of a postcard of Matisse's *Nude Study in Blue* – friends they could call to try to find Rose a job where she just had to talk to people and help them with something they actually cared about and perhaps even smile and hug them when the deal was done instead of wiping them dry with a tissue and finding their shoes. Rose watched Mercy turn the neatly written pages and she saw that what she wanted from her was everything but help. She wanted her love and tenderness and laughter but she did not want to have to depend on her any more.

Mercy spoke the names aloud and Rose had heard of some of them – minor celebrities and serious collectors – and she felt it was like watching somebody count their money. Mercy saw that Rose drew back but she did not know how to reach her.

They sat opposite each other on the floor in Rose's bedroom and Mercy had pins and needles in her foot. She had finished with the Hot Vermilion and Rose was starting her right hand in Beige (not tarty) but she was overeager and careless with the tiny brush. It was a shoddy job but Mercy was too delighted to care.

You know in the old-fashioned days if you were grand your maid put your hand on a cushion of velvet and you would have silk mittens in bed to keep them perfect—

They ran to the winter cupboard for woollen gloves and they wore them for the rest of the day. When Mercy was called home for tea she borrowed them and when her mother told her to take them off she tried to explain but the story was ignored.

We don't wear gloves at table.

She knew better than to argue about manners. In the soft summer light from the kitchen door the varnish was barely visible but when Angela finally noticed it she was incensed and her disbelieving fury crushed Mercy's harmless excitement.

Your beautiful hands!

It was all she could say and when Mercy cried and asked why it was wrong she could only repeat it again and again. How could she explain to her daughter where this would lead without telling her about the very things she was trying to keep her from? But she knew that Rose had been with her and she told Mercy she must never see her again.

When she told her mother the following day without looking at her that she was going to have lunch next door as usual it was like leaving home. She loved her parents but Rose had beckoned and she trailed unresisting in her wake. She slammed the front door even though she had not meant to and she knew her mother watched her from the bathroom window.

Rose was waiting for her on the steps and when she came running up the drive past the damp bundles of newspapers and the recycling bin and the bicycles dropped on the unmown lawn Mercy knew she was moving toward something she had never dared embrace. An identical house but a life unimaginably different.

Mercy wrote the names with her father's old fountain pen and the level black loops glistened on the card. When she had finished she held it in the flat of her hand and blew it dry and Rose felt her heart had been wrung. They had split their French vocabulary lists and memorised their half and signalled each other silently with the answers in tests and they had repainted the wing of Mercy's father's car after they had borrowed it without telling him and scraped it in the cinema parking lot and she had stood guard for Mercy outside the door at Martina McLoughlin's thirteenth so nobody could interrupt her first kiss with Adam Kennard but now Mercy did not even trust her to hold a list without smearing it.

She took the apples from the bowl and laid them in a row on the green baize. She had known for a while that something had changed between them and she did not blame Mercy for it but she was desperately unhappy and she could not bring herself to believe that the little girl who had run to her house all those years ago had not stayed to wait for her now. It was Mercy who had the spare bed and the loan until pay day and the dress she no longer wore and they were offered with joy but received without choice. A humiliating charity. But the false names and the cold hands and the silent indignities were wearing her away to nothing and the anger was beginning to creep into the most private corners of her life and she knew she must stop it. It should be less painful to accept love from a friend than cash from a stranger but she doubted Mercy saw how much it hurt to sit with her waiting for the ink to dry.

¤

Six men pulled the quarter-size yacht on its barrow with heavy ropes from Salter's chandler. Carter was glad he had strengthened the mast and the lid – he had been right about the weather, though nothing in his childhood could have taught him how the planet really moves and breathes. He had grown up in a two-bedroom flat on a six-storey council estate halfway between the banks and the abandoned docks in a courtyard that spun litter and leaves in blinding eddies. Throughout the war bombers droning high over the North Sea had torn ribbons from the Victorian map and bankrupt local authorities had hired demobilised half-qualified architects according to the number of the city's poor they could promise to house in these random featureless plots. Flushed with a victory that had left northern Europe levelled and smoking, the designers had outdone themselves and the concrete galleries and walkways that were supposed to frame grand vistas of revitalised community life merely delivered sanctuary for muggers and two-hundred-yard detours to broken lifts.

There was no natural climate except for the relentless damp and even the stairways grew crystal mould like coral. Rain fell inside the buildings day and night from neglected plumbing and the rows of staring windows turned the sun back and forth in a maelstrom of reflections. When it was overcast there was no light and when it was bright there was no shade.

Today the skies sat low over the graveyard and the air was wet and cold: funeral weather. Nobody remembers the sunny days with their smell of warm earth and wild flowers. Carter led the procession, ringing the bone-handled bell in an occasional triplet rhythm. He wore his black coat with the high collar and a spray of rosemary in the buttonhole. His shined shoes were leather but the soles were rubber in a pattern of deep grooves for good grip. Lowering the dead weight into the grave was hard enough with six practised men and to drop it would be a final, irrevocable indignity.

The first time Carter had seen a corpse was when an eighty-year-old resident of the same block had fallen from her bed and frozen. Most of these deaths went undiscovered until other tenants called the pest control officer to complain about the smell but it was too cold for the body to rot, and the single pint of milk left outside the door every day was quickly stolen or thrown over the balcony. On the same afternoon that Rose first let herself touch Richard Hibbert's velvety jittery erection Carter returned from school and passed the open flat. The door had been kicked off its hinges and the furniture removed and still the woman lay on her back in the hall. He watched her for a long time. He wasn't afraid of the fact that she was dead – more that if someone found him there they might think he had killed her. Or caused her death by not knowing her until now, not even her name. It was his first experience of the guilt that death brings, the nervous ripple in the level waters of grieving.

Carter's father was sober enough to call the police but he did it from the pay phone in the courtyard so he wouldn't be questioned. Rose and Richard Hibbert were both drunk but not drunk enough to prevent him from coming contritely over her satchel.

When Carter finished his six-year sentence he was a fine carpenter with no references, no commissions and no experience. He no longer even had friends who could have paid him a charitable amount to strengthen sagging bookshelves or plane a door swollen by damp. He was given a council flat with a bed, a stove, a table and a chair. Little different from prison, except that at least there he had had company, food, warmth, books and the workshop where he had been shown the beginnings of joinery. The rest he had learned for himself by copying and reading with the instinct of someone who has an instant affinity for a chosen material.

When there was nothing left but chance he met a man in the rent office who needed a coffin. His father had died at home and the funeral was arranged for the following weekend but it was impossible to find an undertaker who would supply one at any price unless they could house the body in their own refrigerators and supply their own transport and sanctimonious assistants. The family hated the thought that their father would be taken from them and packaged and their last memory of him diffused under a veil of gentility at a time when honesty is already precarious.

Carter came to take the measurements and asked for fifty pounds for the timber and sixteen hours later he had made a casket and carried it on his back to the dead man's house. It was his first and he had not yet learned the trick of the soft shoulders, the deep kerfs cut almost to the outer edge so the sides can be bent to follow the body, but in the workshops he had learned by example and the prison furniture was built for rioting so there was no danger of collapse. He had lost the flat when he was inside and his father's old tools were the only things worth saving. His aunt had collected them and stored them in an old tea chest. For the moment, the excitement of real work quieted the distress he felt at using them for the first time.

He went to the funeral and was shocked. No attempt was made to protect the living or the dead from the tidal swell of love and loss. No man's being could have been more richly vivid than at this moment. The casket lay at the hub of a crowd of two hundred people talking and crying and laughing without fear or shame – an embracing before parting. A small band stood at the head of the grave with accordion, trumpet, clarinet and guitar.

> Just a closer walk with Thee
> Pray to Jesus if you please
> Daily walking close with Thee
> Oh let it be, dear Lord, let it be
>
> I am weak but Thou art strong
> Jesus keep me from all wrong
> I'll be satisfied as long
> As we walk close with Thee
>
> Through this world of toil and snares
> If I falter, Lord, who cares?

Who but Thee my burden shares?
None but Thee, oh Lord, none but Thee

Now when this feeble life is over
Time for me will be no more
Lead me, lead me, just row me
Over to that shore

More powerful than the faith was the love. Carter wept for a
man he had only met twenty-four hours before as he laid him
into a coffin lined with the sheets he had died in. He thought of
his own father's funeral, with its apology and unreadiness and
anger seeping through the greetings and rehearsed consola-
tions. He saw then that true grief is exuberant.

As it neared the open grave the yacht rode the path steadily, its
sails bright against the dark sky. Thirty or forty men and women
followed, all of Salter's age. Some had known about the coffin in
advance and rumours had spread, but plenty were amazed and
quite a few displeased. Carter looked out for those who were
angry: every frown was a small victory.

You are Desired to Accompany the Corpse of

JULIAN SALTER

From his Late House in Stewart Street
To the Church of
St. John the Divine, Leighton Square,
At 11 o'clock on the morning of
Thursday, October 12th.

THE BURIAL AT LEXINGTON CEMETERY

Carter still had the young man's fondness for the bold gesture; he had printed the funeral cards himself from a box of blocks he had bought at auction. He set the type by hand in the workshop and the formal text told those invited that this was a ceremony to be observed with gravitas but also with energy. Salter was dead: mourn him. Celebrate him. Your friend deserves more than your mumbling and your shuffling feet. Tell him how you feel, Carter wanted to say. But he never did, unable as he was to say what he felt himself. All he knew was that the silence was the most terrible part of all.

¤

Mercy took a cab as far as the broad avenue of theatres but the traffic always froze here and she climbed out and pushed a ten-pound note through the window. She enjoyed the apparent carelessness but she knew the meter had shown nine twenty when she told him to pull over and she preferred only to tip the old black Austins with no advertising. She walked through the fruit market where the empty barrows sat chained to lamp-posts and mats of artificial grass lay rolled beneath the wheels and turned into the wider road that led to the lab.

She hated to walk here now that the cheerful bland brasserie chains were driving the Italian bars and French kitchens out of business one after another. Two generations ago the poorest immigrants had opened these stores here with their familiar bright façades selling vegetables and fish that didn't even have names in the language of their adopted city and after thirty years they had become accepted, after forty years adored and after fifty overrun by businesses that could never have existed without them. Death by homage.

*

Mercy reached the lab – The Red Light District – and the assistant fetched the contact sheets. He sat beside her, too close for comfort but not close enough for her to feel she should mention it. He watched her as she moved the chinagraph back and forth, crossing, circling and underlining, tapping the pencil on its point when she wasn't sure. She fought hard to separate her feelings about herself from her judgment of the impact of the image. A dead woman on a deserted jetty. Herself. With fat cheeks and thighs, heavy from lying on her back.

In her modelling days she had promised herself she would never sleep with a photographer on an assignment and she had only broken her vow twice and the first time – with Richard Whitney – he took her upright against the wall of the clapboard beach house on Plum Island where they were shooting. He said the face is only ever meant to be viewed vertically – the weight of the flesh draws the features into their natural proportion and the hair hangs evenly. You fuck a girl on a bed, he said, as he pushed into her, pinning her with his sandy hands, and her breasts look saggy, she has no neck and you're looking up her nose when you come. I know how to make girls look great, he said. That's what I do. Then he did her.

As a model you learn that your body enables the desires of others and you learn how to manipulate that body to provoke their response. Make-up, hair, stylist and photographer work like a team of surgeons and they take you, naked, and rebuild you. The complexity of the operation is staggering and the fragility of the end result more so.

Like most sexual pursuits it is ruthless. It is also shameless, as you sit in front of the mirror and watch yourself become a person you have never met before and whom you did not yourself dream. Your face is stripped, cleansed, covered, powdered, painted. Cheekbones are created, eyes widened, lips fattened or hidden. Your hair is washed and rewashed, toned and brushed a thousand times. Your face is hidden while your fringe is freed, teased and stuck fast with hairspray. More curl. A shadow in the eyes. Less curl. The pale line of your scalp at the parting is retouched with a cotton-bud of skin-toned foundation. Eyebrows are combed, eyes made dewy. The light that gives the sheen in your hair dilutes the pleasing shadow that rounds out your neck. The high-collared dress in deep blue throws a cold tone under your chin that draws too much attention to your jawline. The light bounced off white card to flatten the wrinkles around the corners of your mouth puts a reflection in your eyes that drains them of colour. Turning your head to the right lengthens the line of your face but makes your shoulder too prominent. You look so serious! Smile now. Not with the teeth. More in the eyes. Chest out, head back. Not so stiff! Nothing about it is ever easy or natural and nothing about it will ever make you feel good about yourself. That is not the purpose of your beauty. If your beauty really belonged to you then you would be the most powerful woman in the world.

Mercy learned early on that those who had succeeded in this business had simply forced themselves to master these techniques and endure the indignities and she knew that kind of self-sacrifice came easily to her. *There's a good girl*. The reward – beyond money – was that she might believe in herself as that created and desired object. For three years she let herself be stripped and remade by strangers in studios in Beijing and tents in the Atlas mountains and hotels made of ice in the Arctic circle but one day she saw herself wink back from the shelf of an airport bookstall and she knew she had become complicit in her own reinvention. She had crossed some line and she was no longer a model so much as a performer whose language was her physical self.

*

There were a dozen pictures from the river that Mercy liked. One was as innocent as sleep. One was misframed as if the moment or the act had been botched. Two were startling, even to her. She was by turns beautiful, barely present, transfigured, or merely flesh. In one she looked tired and she made herself include it to prove to herself that this was not about her, even though it was. In another the flash had deadened her features and her mouth was open and her eyes half-closed and her red throat lay like a wound. For an instant it seemed she had lost control of herself and it was more shocking to her even than the vision of herself in death and she pushed it to the bottom of the pile.

By the time she had marked her final choices with a red star she had checked and rejected over four hundred and fifty shots. But what was the difference? They all told the same tale in a single stark frame and any one of them would have been enough to sell the work but beneath the outrageous image she knew there were layers of disingenuous self-censorship. Was she afraid that the versions of herself she did not choose might be traitors, doppelgängers who would rise from the dead to tell a different story to the world – a story of prudishness and doubt and undeserved success? She dared herself to stand before the world like this and as she handed the contact sheets to the printer her heart was racing. He smiled at her.

This is unbelievable stuff, you know. It took me six hours to print it all up the way you like. It's classic Mercy Alexander.

Classic Mercy Alexander. Was she herself classic Mercy Alexander? she wondered. It seemed these days she only needed to have an idea – something dreamed up over a drunken supper – pitch it to her agent or a gallery, set it all up and announce the opening night. The work itself had become just a part of that larger process. And then the responses would come flooding in: predictable acclaim and predictable outrage. The catalogue with academic essays and the slot on the Friday-night chat shows, always just before the first commercial break so they could cut out of the interview if the host got out of his depth. They always asked questions like *What's your work really about?* or *How much are you really in these pictures?* but they never wanted the real answers so she stopped giving them. And the less she said what she meant, the more people went to her shows, the better the deals her agent would cut and the more the coffee tables sagged under the weight of her books.

Like the media attention and the public interest, these questions hovered around her. Her life had become her press release. The lab assistant brushed her leg with his hand as he told her how much he admired her work and she realised with a feeling of sudden exhaustion that she hadn't even begun to answer the questions she had been trying to ask all her life. Without thinking she found herself looking down at the pictures to see whether her nipples were visible, stiff with cold.

¤

Rose could see from beneath her white duvet that the timer on the video read 14:57. She always slept late after an evening shift but even a year ago her life had seemed more manageable and she would get up whether she was tired or not just so she could see the day, do something, make herself feel that she was still living a life that had a normal shape. Now she just wanted to close her eyes all the time, even at work. Sleep was all she wanted: not quite a release but a reprieve. She had drifted off recently when a client had paid to go down on her and Lucas had found out and was furious. She could understand a man wanting to come into her but the idea that he could actually give her pleasure like this was ridiculous. It just increased the obligation on her to pretend grateful ecstasy and she had always been a rotten actress.

She lay there warm and comfortable and still half-dreaming of her sister talking to her through a closed window and she tried to think of a reason why she should ever climb out of bed again. She reached out to the chair beside her and pulled the packet of ginger creams under the covers. She finished them lying on her side and when the wrapper was empty she pushed it onto the floor and blew the crumbs after it.

She tried to imagine how many of her wider circle of friends knew she was a prostitute. She told them that she helped people out, that she waitressed, modelled and worked in a night club, but they knew it wasn't quite any of those. One more month, she kept promising herself, and then everything would be possible. Waitressing, modelling, working in a night club. Her real friends knew, of course. She had told them after her row with Mercy and they had pretended not to be shocked. She had taken them out for a drink each in turn and they had thought she was going to confess an affair or beg them to come with her to the abortion clinic again but nobody had guessed the truth and when they heard it they told her to be careful but what they really wanted to know – and could not bring themselves to ask – was how many men she had slept with and how much she dared charge them. Rose had never wanted to be hypocritical or evasive about these things but she drew the line at telling them that anal sex for an extra charge of fifty pounds had paid the cable TV bill for that quarter or that the new burgundy pumps were bought with the tip from Sandy Harris who liked to hand-cuff her to the shower rail.

Finally she rolled out of bed and tried to remember what a thirty-one-year-old woman was supposed to do at half past four in the afternoon.

*

49

She showered and dressed and as she emptied her drawers for something for the evening shift she found the blouse Mercy had lent her three years before. It was still missing a button so she put it away again unfolded and she thought of that night behind tinted glass. She could imagine a time when Mercy might have kissed her like that and she would have welcomed it because when she was younger the only taboo was taboo itself but by the time of the first show they had been grown women and she wondered why Mercy had wanted it then. She knew she had never slept with a woman – she always told her who she slept with to prove that she too was a modern girl, as free with her body as her mind – but she had never quite got it right. She had never really been free.

When Mercy was still at art school and they shared a converted workshop in the garment district taking turns to sleep in the only bedroom they might have been surprised that the passion of their adolescent friendship had not spilled over into something more sexual. As with lovers no experience had been complete unless they were together and nothing happened when they were alone. It would be too easy to say that they were perfect for each other exactly because they were so different: enough, perhaps, that they wanted the same thing in different ways. They wanted to be women, although exactly what this allowed them was not yet quite clear. At the very least they wanted not to be girls any more.

The shift was more easily made at Rose's house. Her parents taught at the local adult education college and were proud to be known as liberals. Whether this applied to their dinner-party politics, their mutual serial cheating or just the fact that – as Mercy's mother never tired of pointing out – they never washed their front door was never quite clear. They carried their modish sensibilities openly and wept at the right moments at the subsidised touring opera but when their three daughters came to them for comfort after a failure at school or a fight with a boyfriend they could offer advice but never tenderness.

Rose was the youngest and by the time she wanted to wear make-up to her first proper party the battles had already been long fought and the bathroom cabinet was full of half-dried mascara and broken lipsticks.

It was no surprise to either of them that Rose lost her virginity first. Richard Hibbert had moved away when his father lost his job but Jonathan Bailey was the most eligible of those not already taken and when he kissed her in the coat room outside the clubhouse they both knew everyone was looking. She was glad he had taken his hand out of her cardigan before he took her in his arms even though it was just a formality. She longed to abandon herself to his manoeuvrings but at the same time she knew down to the last button and touch how she would let it happen.

Their exit to the garden was as discreet as is possible to make with eighty friends and classmates pretending not to stare. Mercy walked home without Rose that night for the first time in three years, jealous, angry, and only partly comforted by the fact that she would be the first to be told the following morning what had actually happened. Ripples would move outward through the layers of friends in a careful series of half-truths, counter-rumours and confirmations.

Jonathan was confident and co-ordinated and for that Rose was grateful. She had heard enough stories of yanking and bruising, of mismapped anatomy and ignored warnings, and she prayed it would go smoothly. Apparently she was his fourth. She tried to relax but she couldn't help feeling that the acts that were supposed to overwhelm her happened in some way that was untranscendentally physical and that the shocks and jolts of pleasure came only by accident. Jonathan kissed her breasts wetly and she hoped the progress of her sexual technique would be less laborious than her swimming practice. She was fourteen.

The previous year Michael Winterton had fallen miserably in love with Mercy. His life dissolved in that unwanted sensation as every shred of stability he had built up in thirteen fragile years fell away. The unquestioned rituals of the family and the classroom and the uncertain bonding of football teams and playgrounds all collapsed into a shimmer of background noise above which Mercy floated, a mirage of beauty and femininity radiantly unaware of his passion. He could not express any part of his obsession even to himself: it was beyond anything his life had prepared him for.

It was Rose who finally told Mercy but it is impossible to understand another's love unless you yourself have loved and she thought little of it. She had done nothing. She was pretty, clever and independent but these alone do not cast spells. She was not part of any of the more desirable gangs though she longed to be asked. She thought about boys but not yet as a sexual force and only when she noticed she had become more popular with her classmates did she see it had changed her.

She had hardly spoken twenty words to Michael in the past year when she fell into step beside him in the corridor by the dining room. They had both contrived to leave their tables last of all even though that meant they had to pick the scraps up from the floor and wipe the benches down. They stood there, hands smelling of onion gravy and disinfectant, and Mercy curled her toes as tight as they would go inside her approved brown shoes as she waited for him to speak. He couldn't even open his mouth. He was sure he gave off a terrific heat as he stood beside her. Why couldn't she just know, see, feel what he felt?

With a sudden courage Mercy confessed:

I've only done tables twice this term.

Michael so desperately wanted to tell her everything but all that came was a kind of giggle. Mercy turned and ran. She ran from love, and she ran from whatever it was in her that had provoked it.

Years later, Rose would joke that she had to sleep with boys to get their attention while Mercy only had to kiss them. Even so, Mercy envied her for what she saw as her natural sexuality. Rose fucked the Argentine barman at her second waitressing job on a pallet of mineral water in the cellar before he even knew her name and at closing time the same night she still screamed at him for not splitting the staff tips evenly. But the day she fell for Conrad Gardner, her first real love, she held his hand in hers from the moment they woke on the floor of the old workshop to the second they fell asleep in his flat overlooking the boating lake, eating, walking and peeing together.

Mercy chose her one-night stands like a trainer marks a racehorse, and even when she was drunk she was studying the form. She had slept with the poster boy from the ¡STRIKE! campaign because he was beautiful. She had slept with the very first man to buy one of her pictures because he was wise and funny and because he said he understood her. She had slept with the security guard at her first studio because she had never slept with someone who just wanted to sleep with her. She always enjoyed the act, although the word hung in her head like something at a circus: something contrived, to be applauded from a distance. The utter disposability of the encounter made it something to be treasured and when she abandoned herself to the moment it was not a simple pleasure but a sacrament, a giving of herself to herself as proof of her own liberation. And love? Between these selfish totems of freedom and the terrible longing of Michael Winterton where could love settle?

¤

Fairburn was handsome in that shocking way that makes men feel challenged and women flustered: he was tall, dark and slim and his smile had been photographed by the National Dental Association for use in their NOTHING BUT THE TOOTH promotion. As he grew older – he was now forty-two – he had started to use expensive cleansers and creams but they never compromised the lustre of his natural good health.

He hated the convulsion of rising with its sour breath and undigested dreams, the sunlight too bright or the carpet too soft under his feet. The rituals of his morning – the punch of the power shower, the scent of the sandalwood soap, the razor and brushes laid out like cutlery – had started as simple indulgences and had grown into a kind of tactile countdown to the day itself. Now they were touchstones he could not bear to omit.

When he arrived at the office and Eleanor brought him his list of appointments Fairburn didn't actually mind that she had forgotten to remind him that today was his wife's birthday – had he cared about it he would have remembered it for himself – but he had evolved a series of obscure tasks and arrangements intended to test the diligence of his assistants and it always irritated him if they let something slip. Like a cat playing with a mouse it has already caught it was more a matter of instinct than of malice. Two sugars in the morning coffee, one after lunch. His black cashmere coat never to be hung in direct sunlight. Still water in a tumbler, sparkling in a highball glass. It was a baroque sport that ate up huge amounts of time better spent expanding his business, except that the texture of his life itself was the essence of his business and nothing else mattered.

The entire top floor of the building had been set aside for his own office, a vast room with a forty-foot plate glass window watching over the fire escapes and copper roofs below. The walls and the floor and the ceiling were sheer and white and unbroken by mouldings and even the light switches were hidden away downstairs. He didn't need the space but he loved the privacy. His desk and chair sat alone at the far end, an after-thought in the emptiness. Visitors had to stand, and it was a brave arrival who held his ground without starting what his assistants called *the pace*, circling slowly, lost on the floor before him, unable to hold his gaze.

The desk was a single slice of oak from a vast trunk and the timber was as raw as the day it had been felled. A pen falling or a greasy hand or coffee drip would mark its soft face irrevocably but he loved the naked wood – its vulnerability – and he enjoyed the undercurrent of risk that shadowed his every minute at work. Each day he left the surface immaculate was a day where beauty had triumphed over the attrition of the mundane.

A monotone abstract by Hartung hung on the far wall. Two soft rectangles of blue hovered on the coarse canvas, their faces slashed with repeated strokes of a palette knife. The effect was a strange equilibrium of violence and calm. Fairburn used to say about modern art that the less the effort the bigger the bill and he had adopted the formula himself. Most thought it a joke but as in all things trivial he was wholly serious. He knew Hartung's work and adored it and had attended four auctions before making a bid for a piece he considered had precisely few enough brushstrokes.

His father had been rich but Fairburn had made himself richer by buying companies on the verge of collapse, propping them up with his own ready cash and selling their guts piece-meal. Asset-stripping was already an old game by the time he shut down his first factory at the age of nineteen but nobody else had his nose for the scent of decline. At a board meeting at seven in the morning he had announced to the directors that their enterprise no longer supported itself and that he was going make more money selling off the land from their employees' sports ground than from their entire catalogue of patents. If he had taken the trouble to learn about the businesses he had destroyed he could certainly have turned them around and made a larger profit but that would have taken time and energy. Too many brushstrokes.

He had always been jealous of artists because he believed their work was a way to be paid and admired for exposing themselves in public. Their product – whether metaphorical self-portrait or literal line of dirty laundry strung across the skylit sculpture hall of the city's modern art gallery – was less interesting to him than their urge to create. His own drive to perfect and control had crystallised itself in a talent for destruc-tion but his methods were those of an artist, not a businessman – naïve, spontaneous, obtuse, honest, rigorous and witty. But the key to his success, and his signature – the trait that branded every merger and closure as an original Fairburn – was the fact that he didn't give a damn. Nobody fears a man so much as one who has nothing to lose. He had broken up a three-generation family-owned chocolate empire over a lunch meeting as he peeled apart sandwiches on a silver foil tray to find the rarest beef.

It was a question of vision. If you had asked Picasso *Why blue?* he would have shrugged and if you had asked Fairburn *Why sell?* he would have said the same. He was not malevolent but his actions did not filter through the layers of compassion and deliberation that slowed others. His sense of himself was entirely without context: he had never integrated himself, never shared, never given or owed. He did not exist in the world but merely strode through it. He did not judge and he did not care to be judged; he expected no quarter and therefore would not give it. All he feared was the compromise of the self.

That evening he took his wife to supper at one of the city's generic super-restaurants. Michelin could hardly dish out the stars fast enough – there was a campaign among chefs to introduce a fourth – and it was impossible to find a reason to send anything back now. Proof perhaps of human perfectibility, although it was of no comfort to Fairburn, who had already saturated his senses with every bizarre delicacy he could discover. Sashimi of sperm whale. Boiled cornmeal with salted cricket. Squid laksa with chilli that turned his bowels to water even as he waved for the bill. Brains, tripe, offal and organs that farm-reared animals barely had time to use before they were parcelled out to the nearest specialist butcher. The search for the ultimate culinary high – beyond fugu, sheep's eyes, horsemeat tartare – had outdone itself. When an appetite grows to accommodate these barbarities everything else becomes insipid and Fairburn knew he had to step back. The world no longer held any sensation for him. In an attempt to revitalise his jaded taste buds he had sought out the blandest foods possible, and tonight he had found the perfect *Menu Dégustation*:

Tempura of Watermelon

❖

Vermicelli of Daikon with a Lettuce Jus

❖

Ricotta Soufflé

❖

Perrier Sorbet

❖

Quenelle of Organic Veal
❖
Ile Flottante

Sarah had a salad of grilled chicken and a glass of white wine. Fairburn ordered *Dom Ruinart* 1990 – in her honour – and finished the whole bottle himself. Then, despite the fact that she had an unlimited allowance and three credit cards in his name whose bills he never queried, Fairburn gave his wife an unsealed envelope with her name on it containing a thousand pounds in used notes. He blew her a kiss and mouthed the words: *Happy Birthday.*

They talked about their three children and about Eleanor, about the name of the restaurant – Digestif – and about growing older. They did not talk about his work, or her food, or the sexual act that Fairburn had decided he would try later that evening at Lucas's brothel.

¤

It was rare enough for a brothel to have a drawing room and not all of the visitors liked to be seen there. Lucas had spent as much on it as he could afford in the belief that it would remind the clientele that they were not in for a cheap evening. It was a calm, quiet space of greys and golds that suggested simultaneously discretion and opulence. It was dimly lit without being furtive, and thick carpets and hangings brought conversations to a soft hum. The braggadocio that encouraged men to talk to strangers at the bar about their sexual exploits as though they had just played a game of squash made sure they spent well there too, affecting not to care if a glass of poor champagne cost eight pounds. Lucas sold beer only in equally expensive designer varieties but few were brave enough to ask for it. For those who didn't care who knew how they spent their evenings it was a place to loosen up before business, to look over the new girls and to compare notes.

Somehow the talk was more degrading than the acts themselves. What men and women agree to do together in private is their own affair, and many of the girls were smarter and tougher than their clients. But there was something so desperate – so falsely casual – in the way men talked about these moments where women allowed them the most exquisite intimacies and yet remained excluded from the experience. They spoke of cars more tenderly, of wines with more reverence.

The girls dressed in the bathrooms in the basement and if they were on a break they could relax in a small sitting room Lucas had never bothered to refurbish. It smelled like a cheap minicab. They knew better than to wear a scent that might linger on a shirt but the lubricants and disinfectants and air fresheners swirled together in the small airless space. Conversations here were as frank as those upstairs but less brutal: they were no longer surprised at the bizarre requests their clients made.

Tonight was quiet. Tanya (5'7", 35B-24-34, late twenties, long dark hair, French/Italian, evening gown, all services) sat in the corner with her walkman worrying because her boyfriend had turned up at the restaurant she said she worked at and they told him she had left two months before. Brittney (5'11", 34B-25-34, mid twenties, honey blonde, shaven, Australian, leather trousers and white T-shirt, A-Levels) was writing a postcard to her mother in Fremantle to say she would be home for her father's retirement party and trying to decide whether she would find a supplier of affordable heroin back there or whether she should risk taking a stash with her. Carmen (5'4", 34-24-34, early twenties, shoulder-length black hair, South American, blow-jobs without condom at extra charge but doesn't swallow) had been teased by the other girls for choosing such an obvious name even though it was real. She was reading the financial pages of one of the tabloids and writing figures on the back of a pizza menu trying to figure out how much more she would need to save before she could make a down payment on a one-bedroom apartment in Buenos Aires. Three other girls sat around a low table finishing a thousand-piece jigsaw of the city's most celebrated department store. Chrissy, a thirty-year-old woman in a polyester maid's uniform, came in with a duster and pretended to clean the table.

A woman's work is never done.

They laughed and moved to make room on the old sofa.

It's all right.

When she turned away they saw her bare cheeks were still red beneath the apron.

The piece with the doorman's head is missing. I did it three times yesterday.

Rose came in and hung her coat before going down the corridor to change.

Good evening and welcome. Who's in?

None of your sweethearts.

Fuck. I meant to bring a book.

The camaraderie was easy but it was just a way of deflecting the appalling reality of their evenings. The sweat and the drink and the selfishness. None of these women had anything in common outside this room and they dared not even make friends here because they were all fighting each other for the same thing. Lucas made sure they existed only for the men.

Rose stood in front of the long mirror in the bathroom wearing only her shoes. The fluorescent tube on the ceiling threw her reflection into shadow, flattening it into something solid and ungainly. She knew the terrain of her face and her body so well and yet tonight none of it seemed to belong to her. She washed quickly under her arms and between her legs and arched her back, trying to relax.

For years she had fought to keep herself sane, to stay fresh, alive and human. She had made money, kept her house and travelled a little. Most do a lot worse. You lose touch with your friends and family and finally with yourself. You have nothing to anchor you to real life. No reason to go home, or else no home to go to: nothing to help you draw the line between what the men want you to be and what you are. When that barrier is broken the men begin to feel it in you and they wait in the shadows demanding things you swore you'd never let them have and you no longer have anything to hold you back. You have already given everything and now there is no end.

These days it was not the psychological hazards Rose feared so much as the physical attrition. Her lips were tired and dry as she drew them back over her teeth and took a man into her mouth. She could feel the pull of the muscles in her face as she forced her smile. Her thighs were firm and strong but they ached when she climbed on top and spread herself. Her nails broke all the time.

She wondered who she would sleep with that night. None of her regulars had come in and she tried to prepare herself for the worst. The older men were less attractive but they were often more tender and certainly more forgiving. Tonight, with her confidence low, Rose wasn't sure she wanted to deal with an arrogant hard body, a young buck determined to prove his sexual prowess to the world through some tired stranger and expecting the highest standards of perfection and delight. She was skilled in her performance but these youngsters just wanted Barbie dolls.

She patted her belly and pinched her thigh and she thought of the man she had hit. He hadn't told Lucas or she would have heard about it by now. Maybe he did that to all the girls and they all hit him. Maybe that was what he really wanted.

She thought of the first time she had adored her body, a body that every boy at school had dreamed of and some had held. She had taken Jonathan Bailey's younger brother up to her parents' bedroom one New Year's Eve and they had kissed and touched each other through tight trousers and thick jumpers and when she finally pushed her jeans down and he saw the beautiful pale flatness of her belly and the soft fringe of hair above her knickers he came, dangling out of his blue Y-fronts, in great gushing pulses. His mixture of pleasure and embarrassment thrilled Rose in a way that was deeply sexual. To do this without even touching him! That was when she knew her body held a power men could only begin to imagine.

Eleven years later, long after she had thrown Conrad out, she let Rob move in with her. She hardly remembered where she had met him and it was weeks before they slept together – it was as if neither of them had noticed that it hadn't yet happened. They were friends at a time when she had lost her bearings and he knew how she earned her money but he didn't care. She needed that. One night after they had made unhurried love Rose climbed out of bed and Rob was watching TV and as she stood up she blocked his view.

Got to pee.

Have one for me.

Want anything while I'm up?

I'm done.

He shook his head and patted her in a gesture that was fond and absent-minded at the same time. At twenty-six her figure was still fabulous but her bottom moved under his touch, the soft ripple of muscle at ease. He patted her again.

No more ice cream in bed for you, my lovely.

Rose could still recall that instant of feeling shatteringly separate from him. He may as well have leaned over and whispered *Fat bitch* and when she spoke through her tears it was to herself. A kind of plea.

What is it you want?

She looked down at her breasts and her tummy, her smooth thighs and her long legs.

This is it. This is me. What is it that you want?

Neither of them knew.

I live in this fucking body! I feed it, I sleep in it, I walk, I breathe, I shit! What can I do?

She was already too far ahead. The words fell around him, too heavy to pick up. They had made love, they were friends, he was watching TV.

Do you want me to stop breathing? Is that what you want?

It was hard enough to breathe already. He turned the volume up.

Rose put on a black dress, plain white knickers, no bra, stay-ups, black heels. She was proud that men chose her even though she never looked like a whore. She covered a small spot at the corner of her mouth with foundation and finished her eyes. Lips were the worst: they had to be redone five times a night. Everything else she kept as simple as possible. It was amazing how little time you had between one man and the next sometimes. If one of her regulars came in and asked for her when she was busy Lucas and the others would entertain him for as long as they could upstairs. If she had agreed to a longer session or something special she would try to let the others know because a client who has chosen his evening's pleasure does not like to have to wait. He will start to imagine what his girl is doing with another man downstairs and if he finds himself a little jealous he may take it out on her later. Often Rose would be back in the bathroom wiping herself and untangling her knickers and one of the girls would shout through the door:

Rosie? Your little fat bloke's here again with the black shirt. Hurry up, I need a wash.

Five minutes later, lipstick fresh, dress smoothed flat, she would be stripping again in another bedroom, her hands barely dry.

Tonight she waited with the others. When she started with Lucas she would hang around upstairs in the bar because she thought it gave her more control over who saw her, who chose her. Now she didn't care. If you don't care they can't reach you.

She made herself a cup of coffee and sat on the floor by the door with Matisse's *Nude Study in Blue* and the list of names. She was supposed to go to the opening of Mercy's show that night but she couldn't bear to see her and have to admit she still hadn't called anybody. What did she know about working in a gallery? Assisting a stylist? How would she call these people, arrange an interview, win their confidence? She thought nothing of sleeping with a stranger who didn't care to know her name but she was terrified to speak to a human being who might actually want to help her. She had brought a dress and proper shoes so she could go along later but she knew she did not dare. The world she had dreamed of for so long was already too far beyond her grasp.

¤

The invitations to the 'Inconnue de la Seine' show had been sent in sealed metal boxes containing a piece torn from the dress, still wet from the river. On them the words *Dead or*

Alive were hand-written in dark ink that bled and clouded the cotton.

Mercy no longer showed in established galleries. She chose her own settings – an underground car park or a disused mental hospital – places where the work made sense of itself, uncompromised by pale walls and tiny halogen lights that said ART. Tonight they stood in a cold store behind the old meat market, a huge steel room with a low ceiling and doors a foot thick. They had softened the refrigeration but clouds of condensation hovered where they spoke. Meat porters' white coats hung on immense steel hooks for those who were cold, their faded logos brutally clear:

ROCHESTER TOWN KILLED

Farringdon Slaughter

SWEETBREADS, LIGHTS, TRIPE

Jackson & Daughter Chilled Meats

Mercy arrived later than she meant. Recorded fragments of the news coverage played quietly on monitors in each corner of the room and were being filmed by the same crews as before. The press releases were available beside the guest book. She was always relieved when she finished a project and she normally loved opening-night parties because it was the first taste of freedom and laughter after months of meetings and planning and sleepless nights but this evening she dreaded the thought of a crowded room and a thousand questions. She stared up at herself on the steel walls and she was uncertain about the work. She felt she was at someone else's show.

She hurried over to find her agent. Richard Strathmore was an oddity in the art world: short, chubby, balding, cryptic and unstylish, but his stable of artists – and his hit rate – was incredible. He never used one word when three would do and when he was nervous he spoke in quotations. Mercy mouthed a kiss at him.

Sorry I'm late.

Mercy shall follow me all the days of my life.

Richard. I'll withhold my commission.

She picked up the guest list and ran her finger down the columns of names.

I don't know half of these people.

He showeth Mercy to his anointed.

Stop it!

She knew that despite his reputation he suffered a kind of stage fright at these events and she squeezed his hand. It was waxy and damp. He smiled at her and nodded wordlessly. The waiters were still unpacking the champagne at the back of the store so she went to fetch them both a glass just as the team from the evening arts programme came over and she was not sure she should be drinking on camera. Fuck it, she thought. I'm an artist. But she held the wine down by her waist, below the tight TV frame.

Mercy left the invitations to Richard. He knew where to place her work among the complex subsets of punters, pundits, rivals, reviewers, curators and collectors and all he asked was that she was there. If there was somebody he needed her to meet he would take her by the elbow and steer her across the room whispering background information along the way.

Largest collection of site-specific work in the country.

If she buys, they all buy.

Talk about the new stuff.

Don't tell them you hated the Cuba show.

The man they approached was tall, dark and head-turningly handsome. He was one of the few wearing a suit but in the swirl and the colour of the crowd his still grey presence was imposing. People stood in front of every picture drinking and chattering but he looked straight through them at the work itself as if everything else was invisible.

Connor, this is Mercy Alexander.

Connor Fairburn. I'm glad you're all right.

He gestured to the pictures and Mercy felt herself colour. She hadn't blushed since she had misattributed Crivelli's *Coronation of the Virgin* on a quiz show two years before.

I came to your last show but we didn't get to meet. I can only guess that Richard doesn't take me seriously.

Don't you believe it, Connor. We know who bought that Hartung even though it was a telephone bid. You even went to Geneva for the sale and you didn't even blink.

Fairburn laughed.

I play poker.

He turned to Mercy.

Did you try to imagine what it would be like to be dead?

I had too much to think about. And I was too bloody cold. Next time I'm going to do something in the Sahara.

Does it seem strange now?

She looked up at the pictures but the noise and the smoke and the shadows veiled them. Right now they were just pictures, safe in their frames. Art. Richard chattered on.

A dozen pictures was a difficult decision. It's the smallest show we've ever hosted.

They fill the space perfectly.

Mercy found it.

For a woman who doesn't like to be cold maybe you should have gone for a bakery.

Richard laughed too loudly and took their glasses.

Let me top those up.

Mercy was conscious that he had left her alone with Fairburn and that she was expected to sell herself but when it was put like that she could only think of Rose and her nameless men. She could smell him now and she was surprised she could not recognise it – something clean and warm. Maybe he had it made up for him; his suit was obviously tailor-made. She thought she saw him glance down at her breasts and she looked across to the photographs again. Even at this distance her nipples were clearly visible.

Who else do you have?

A ragbag. Nolde. Rothko. Still.

People who like that sort of thing don't normally like my stuff.

This is better than stuff. Not like most of the others are making.

I can't tell any more.

But she was pleased he had said it.

What else is there?

Besides the work?

Of this series. You must have taken hundreds.

They didn't work. You have to shoot so much. Framing, focus, background, exposure. The magic moment.

And the model.

I don't really think of myself as a model any more.

He nodded, allowing the distinction.

I love to see what an artist will tell you about himself. Or what he won't. Did you see the Rembrandt show where the museum hung an X-ray of the canvas beside the original so you could see the overpainting and the sketches beneath?

I missed it.

Too bad. The skull beneath the skin.

She was intrigued.

I'd like to buy one of these but I want to know more about what you threw out on the way.

You should talk to Richard. If he thought I was going ahead and selling something without asking him first he'd hit the roof.

Not hard in here, even for a man of his height.

He reached up to the low metal ceiling and tapped it with his long fingers and she laughed.

Fine. I'll do business with the businessman but I want art from the artist.

There's no magic.

I think you're wrong. I'd give anything to do what you do.

Try saying that the night you open a show.

Fairburn laughed and took a card from his wallet.

If you want to see what I have I'd be happy to show you.

She took his card without looking at it. Come up and see my etchings. Well, maybe she would.

She turned away but a photographer's agent – one of the names she had written on the card – waved at her from the door and she knew she would have to talk to her. As she made her way across the room she wanted to know if Rose had called anyone yet but she hardly had the energy to bring it up right now. It was only ten o'clock but she just wanted to go home and she couldn't believe Rose hadn't come and she wondered where the hell she was.

¤

When Lucas decided to open the brothel he had seen it as a last real chance to legitimise himself – to begin to exist – but he was smart enough to admit he knew nothing about running a real club. Managing prostitutes was illegal but there was plenty else to master and while his sister's husband's decorating company refurbished the third-rate hotel he had leased he signed himself up for a six-week business course.

His principal interest had been the revenue itself because he knew in the fluid worlds of sex and ready cash he would have to keep a firm grip but he also wanted to learn about staff training, customer control and time-and-motion analysis. He told the other students – garden designers and catering managers – that he was in the entertainment line and already he liked the ring of it. The more casually he said it the more impressive it sounded.

Most of the lectures had been dull and he found it hard to reconcile the concepts of economies of scale, information structure and invisible assets with a building full of naked women and drunken businessmen. He left the course after ten days and the only part of the business plan he had completed was the section headed:

7.2 What Do Your Customers Want From Your Product?

21-30 years / younger OK Firm Loud

Inspired by this vision he began to structure his empire but the changes he hoped to make ran counter to all accepted brothel wisdom. He tried to turn the Silk Suite into a laundry room so the maids wouldn't have to go down to the basement between customers. This, he calculated, would cost forty minutes every night – forty minutes during which his clients could not be entertained. The girls pointed out to him that the Silk was already the most popular room in the building: why not just stack the towels on the bar and tell the men to help themselves? That would save another seven minutes. Perhaps he could even ask the guests to change their own sheets.

The accountancy module had bored him – there had been no attention paid to the complex issue of laundering fourteen thousand pounds a night – and when the lecturer began to explain the double-entry procedure it was not book-keeping that came to mind. From the very first day he began to compile a database of girls, clients, activities and fees so he could work out whether he should be spending his imminent profits on a new whipping room or on hiring more oriental women. He told the staff they must enter a full account of the evening's activities before leaving the building but after a week the only entry read:

```
fuck three men and one man and his
gilfriend. my knees hurt >
```

Though the stories the girls told behind the scenes were shockingly frank they drew the line at sharing their lives with a computer. They could accept that they opened their mouths and legs for a houseful of strangers but their modesty overtook them when they were asked to write:

```
Name         Shelley
Client       D 407
Suite        Venice
Activity     Massage, oral (two way),
             intercourse (various
             positions), ejaculated
             on face
Extra time   10 mins
Fee          £175 cash
```

Perhaps it was because everything sounded colder and more brutal in black and white. Perhaps it was because it constituted a diary, a hard copy of all the acts they hoped they would eventually forget. Most likely it was just the thought of Lucas reading it.

¤

Chrissy unzipped the maid's costume and hung it on the back of the chair behind the door. The red welts on her bottom had softened to a warm ache. Angeline's mother ran the laundry like a good hotel: towels on the shelves on the left, sheets in the middle, fantasy outfits in the cupboard. The nurse's kit lay folded on top of the traffic warden and school uniforms. Chrissy stepped into the short blue dress and pulled the starched white apron tight across her bosom. The rest of the kit she had assembled herself from toy shops and chemists: hospital watch, plastic stethoscope, clipboard, thermometer, rubber gloves. Angeline's mother had made a cap from one of the bartender's glass cloths carefully folded and ironed with a triple dose of starch. It wasn't very convincing but it never stayed on long anyway.

Chalcroft lay naked, face down on the white sheet with his eyes closed. His clothes, wallet and watch were laid out on the chair beside the bed. He had brushed his thinning hair. He heard Chrissy come in behind him.

Good evening, Nurse.

Good evening, Dr. Chalcroft. What seems to be the matter?

I suspect it's the same as last time.

Will we have a look?

I think we ought.

Chrissy put on the gloves, snapping the rubber loudly against her palms.

I have prepared myself.

Hospital policy, Doctor.

I see.

He drew himself up into a kneeling position, his head resting on his forearms.

Lucas greeted Fairburn at the bar. A glass of champagne – on the house, a privilege reserved for the twice-a-week men – had already been poured and the bartender pushed it across on one of the new monogrammed cocktail napkins:

$$ L $$

Fairburn was not a regular but Lucas was pleased he had come; he did not usually allow himself favourites but there was something about him that was compelling. He would never admit to himself that he found the older man attractive but he knew he wanted to be close to him just as he had with the bigger boys all those years ago. To walk in the shadow of that power, confident, paternal and predatory.

Most men contemplating an hour or two of unrestrained commercial sex are smug and drunk or silent and ashamed but Fairburn sat by the fire as though unsure why he was there. Waiting for something to be revealed to him. Lucas would kill for this degree of self-possession. He knew he was shifting, restless and too easily provoked and he hated himself for it. The territory of his maleness had been staked on the cornerstones of force, authority and ownership but his sense of himself was irrevocably compromised by the knowledge that men had loved him and that he had allowed it. None had touched him but they had wanted him. Nobody could want Fairburn in that way, he thought, although Fairburn undoubtedly had the looks. Fairburn was one of those who did the wanting.

Lucas crouched beside him, his arm on the chair's smooth leather.

I've been thinking about your little request.

I don't want play-acting.

You want filth.

Fairburn put the champagne down. Too sharp, an overtone of apple, too many bubbles.

I've hung from the chandelier. I've had three at a time. Young and old. I've done everything these girls have to offer and I want you to prove to me there's something in this world worth trying I haven't already tried. I want the fuck of my life.

The bartender, despite years of pretending not to overhear his customers' requests, couldn't resist a glance. Fairburn looked right through him.

I'm going to give you Rose. A lovely dirty girl.

He looked around to see if she was here in the room.

You don't fuck her. She fucks you. She's going to turn you inside out.

Fairburn nodded. Lucas was happy now, expansive.

And I'm going to throw in Mara. She's new to all this. Uncorrupted. But you'll soon see to that—

Lucas wanted Fairburn to laugh with him. He wanted them to conspire together but Fairburn just pushed his glass across the table.

We'll have to carry you out.

I'm ready.

Rose hated working as a team. It wasn't the physical contact – the other girls were always clean and gentle. But she had found her own way of doing things over the years, her own way of reading and handling a man, and sharing the experience with another woman complicated things. Besides which she barely knew Mara. She had walked in off the street the previous week and Lucas had taken her in on looks alone. He signed her up on a beginner's deal, a 50/50 split, and threw her in with the girls who had been there for years. He believed everyone should fight their own corner because it was better for the men that way but a young one always caused a fuss. She was pretty, tall and skinny, with broad shoulders and long, thin arms and legs, deep dyed-black hair and an eagle tattooed on her wrist. Something else on the other arm, done at home with needle and ink, but too faded now to read. Nineteen, maybe twenty. She had a distant look, dreamy. The kind of look men love that says: I don't care what you want to do.

Rose picked at a broken nail as she sat on the bed. She smiled as Mara came in. She was breathtaking in her red dress and heels and nothing else. She could conquer the world. She ran her fingers through her long dark hair and shook it out.

I don't do kissing on the mouth.

Something about her diffidence reminded her of a child: the nervousness spat out like a threat. Christ, she thought. Nineteen. She wanted to run to Lucas, to tell him this was madness. That she would do it with someone else, one of the other girls, even Carmen. Someone stronger. Girls like Mara thought they floated above it all but it didn't take much to bring them down and when they fell they fell all the way.

¤

Mercy stood in the loading bay outside the cold store and her skin pricked as the warmth of the evening washed over her. She stared back in through the heavy steel doors as she waited for her cab. Twelve dead women stared down from the walls at the guests laughing and drinking, voices ringing in the low chamber.

She had called Rose at home but there was no answer. Mercy was livid. She tried to recall the name of the street where she worked. Near the financial district, she thought. She hailed a passing taxi and climbed in.

I need that brothel. The one that used to be a hotel?

The cabbie looked at her in the mirror. Maybe he thought she worked there but she was too drunk to care.

Prentice Place.

She nodded and leaned back in the seat. They probably didn't allow women in. Maybe she should pretend to be a whore. How would she find her? Maybe she'd just gone out for supper with a friend. Maybe she was on her way to the show right now. The city raced past the clouded windows and she knew she shouldn't be doing this.

¤

Lucas said goodnight to the colonel and hurried to the lavatory behind his office. He had only had three spritzers but he was amazed how quickly they went through him. He unzipped himself and took aim into the pan and for a second he saw his face reflected below him in the pale circle of water before it dissolved in the noisy stream. He shook himself three times and switched off the light with his elbow.

As he stepped into the corridor he was met by a group of young men laughing loudly and one of them patted his arm.

Hey there, Lucas. I promised I'd be back with the boys and I'm as good as my word.

They were in their early twenties, salesmen or office juniors, and they had made the effort to dress up a little for the evening: the newer suit, a silk shirt, a pair of real Guccis. They were all wearing too much aftershave. Lucas had seen the ringleader before but he couldn't think of his name. Why should he? He was the busy host of the last real brothel in the city and he reserved his courtesies for the high rollers. The rest of these boys were first-timers and their friend was only greeting him to show them he knew the ropes; first-name terms with the boss. Maybe one day it would be Mr. Fuller.

He walked with them to the bar and explained the house rules. It was somebody's birthday but it quickly became clear that they hadn't known how much the girls charged and now they were thinking of pooling their funds and drawing lots to see who would get lucky. Lucas watched them and he thought of himself fifteen years earlier. Sharp. Cocky. Quick to smile and quick to lose it. Perhaps he would offer them one on the house: he liked the idea that the girls were his to give.

Tanya ran into the room stumbling in her heels and holding the hem of her dress so she wouldn't trip. She stopped by the door, breathless, lifting her hands to clasp them at her chest and then letting them fall. Lucas had told them time and again about discretion upstairs. He excused himself from the group and walked over.

Tanya. Running in the bar.

She couldn't bring herself to look at him. She didn't want to have to tell him but there was nobody else. She thought she was going to be sick but she knew he would take it from her wages if he had to clean it up.

Rose is dead. I think she's dead.

She glanced up as if she expected something to be different now she had said it but the confession had loosed something in her and she started to cry in a kind of hiccough that Lucas found intensely irritating. He stared at her shoes and the tiny trail of prints in the soft grey carpet.

Mara was past crying. She sat against the wall outside the Shadow Suite rocking softly back and forth, her head in her hands and her shoes in her lap. Her dress was wet with tears. Lucas walked straight past her into the room. Rose lay on the bed as though she had fallen forward and tangled herself in her own arms and legs.

Lucas kicked the door shut. He had never seen anybody dead without blood, without a wound or a weapon. He lifted a wrist to take a pulse but he knew he had no real way of telling. She was still warm. She still looked like a woman. The marks on her arms and ankles and around her mouth were still flushed. They had all seen bruising – that was nothing unusual. Even the girls who wouldn't allow spanking or real pain would play along with a little tie and tease, especially if there was another girl there to keep an eye on things.

Mara squeezed her tattooed wrist, tightening the free hand into a fist until the knuckles cracked. Her pale veins ran blue under the thin skin.

Lucas didn't see Fairburn at first. He was sitting in the chair by the basin fully dressed with his feet resting on the table.

She's dead.

Fairburn barely heard him. His desire had evaporated and he was listless in the reprieve of orgasm but he was obsessed. Something about Rose's gaze had fixed itself in his memory like the aftershadow of a camera flash. If he closed his eyes she was there for an instant and then she faded. She clung to him, staring.

What the fuck did you do with her?

He tried to think but all he could remember were the things he had not yet done.

78

Even Lucas's fury was muted by some instinct to reverence in the presence of the body but whatever Fairburn found in himself it was not remorse. The pain that twisted through his gut was not grief or shame or even pity but fear – the fear that he had finally found a woman who knew the pulse of his lust but who had vanished before he could confront her with it. It seemed to him that she had promised everything he had ever dreamed possible and he was certain now that no other woman would ever be able to tempt him with it again. He knew nothing about the person lying dead before him on the tired bed but he felt an intimacy with her so powerful that he was afraid.

Chrissy peeled off the rubber gloves and dropped them on Chalcroft's legs. He lay there with his head buried in the pillow, his silvery hair matted with sweat.

I'll leave you, Doctor. You rest a moment.

Thank you, Nurse.

He was still breathless. She took off the apron as soon as she left the room, unsure if it could be used again or whether it should go straight to the laundry. Lucas and Tanya were running down the corridor.

Where's your doctor? Is he a real doctor?

He talks like one. We're just done.

She laughed. They ran to the White Room and Lucas pushed the door open. Chalcroft was sitting on the edge of the bed looking for his socks in the darkness.

What in the name of Christ do you want?

A doctor.

Then you must call your GP.

Are you a doctor?

That's none of your business.

Lucas took him by the arm.

*

By the time they returned Fairburn and Mara were gone. Chalcroft took Rose's pulse from her throat, avoiding the bruises.

Yes, she's dead. I really don't think you need me any more. I don't think you need a doctor at all.

He stood without shoes or shirt and he was afraid. Afraid for Rose, afraid of Lucas, afraid of Chrissy's rubber gloves in his coat pocket.

Bring the doctor's clothes, please, Tanya.

She drew a sheet over the body.

Did he strangle her?

This is none of my business. Please.

It's my business and you're a guest of mine.

A paying guest.

I need you to help me.

Why don't you just dump her? Who knows where these girls come from?

Lucas closed the door.

Nobody wants to make this a big deal. Did he strangle her?

I'm not a pathologist.

And I'm not a fucking copper.

Fairburn's car passed Mercy's taxi on the corner of Prentice Place but neither saw the other. It was raining hard and Fairburn drove quickly. The world outside the windshield drifted past mixing with the raindrops and melting away as each arc of the wiper blades unveiled a fresh scene. The park, the row of interior design shops, the private hospital. Nobody was on the streets; it was like moving through a map. He lived near here, a residential district that became blander as it became more expensive. He drove on.

He had not killed her. He had not fucked her. He had not

asked her to do anything she didn't want to do. You can tell because they always try to charge more – they think that's what hurts the men when they're giving something that hurts them. Money as a weapon, sex as a tool. What was it about these women whose names he barely knew? Once in a while one would manage to surprise him with a trick, a tongue or a breath or a finger, but his wife was as filthy as the best of them and if he wanted he could have her every night of the week. He had driven her from his bed by his insistent infidelity because what he craved was not sex – not the charge of desire and the deliverance of orgasm – but the blank faces, the engagement itself, the sheer fact of the fuck. And now there was the fact of the death.

He had started one of the nanny's blockbusters in a moment of boredom in the Maldives the summer before and one of the paper-thin characters had broken down in the emergency ward and sobbed that she wished she could turn back time, have it over again, do it all differently. He had laughed; he had never regretted anything in his life. Some know that grief and guilt power them but Fairburn moved unrestrained through his own internal landscape – there were obstacles to negotiate but none cast a shadow – and yet tonight the vision was beginning to cloud. He tried to grasp what it was he was feeling but no single moment or emotion stood still in his mind for long enough to grasp. It was as if he had left some part of him behind in that darkened room, something he could not now retrieve.

Waiting at the traffic signal by the war memorial he was overcome by an insupportable lust. The light turned green and he sat there unmoving, his forehead pressed against the cold window. He touched himself through the silk lining of his trousers. He was sure now that Rose understood. That she knew what he needed to feel. He had let himself be distracted by Mara while she lay there watching him and he thought of

Rose's look and he was hard like he had never been hard before. Lucas had been right. And he had never even laid a hand on her.

¤

The cab pulled up at the foot of the main steps but Mercy told him to drive around the block. There would be a door for the girls, she thought. Rose had talked about the elaborate stage management, of service rooms and hidden corridors. The men must never see their evening's entertainment in jeans and jumpers, hair still wet from the bath and make-up half finished – the girls would appear in the drawing room from nowhere, ready to be unwrapped. She saw a dustbin toppled by the wind, its load of paper towels and torn tights and condom foils and empty bottles strewn across the wet flagstones. She paid the fare and ran into the archway pounding on the door with the flat of her hand. The taxi didn't move. The driver watched, smiling.

Mercy wiped the wet hair from her face and called out:

Fuck you!

He winked. Not on my wages.

The door opened, checked by a heavy chain. Angeline's mother stared out into the alley. She was small and wore a lavender track suit and she held a copy of the city's TV guide. Mercy wanted to go to sleep. She was in the wrong place in the rain in the dark in the middle of the night and her anger hung around her, catching her up in its folds. She needed desperately to see Rose. She despised her. She was going to tell her exactly where she had screwed up her life, why she had sold herself to four thousand men for nothing, why her dreams of a career in television were the dreams of a child, why she would never be able to do anything with her life without Mercy, Mercy's wisdom, Mercy's love.

Suddenly she was crying.

Angeline's mother folded the corner of the day's schedule and set the guide down on the chair. The wind swung the door but the chain caught it. She had no idea who Mercy was or what she wanted but she had seen her own daughter like this and she knew it was best to say nothing.

Mercy was going to tell Rose that she had to get out, that they all had to get out, that their lives were racing past them so fast they could barely tear the pages from the calendar. She wanted to set her free and she desperately wanted to go with her.

I've come for Rosie.

¤

The penalties for providing false information on a death certificate are severe and any doctor knows he will be struck off if caught. Lucas knew this. But Chalcroft's livelihood depended more on his expensive tailoring and bedside manner than on his diagnostic skills and if his clientele discovered his taste for Chrissy's regular check-ups they would soon abandon him. Lucas also knew this. Chalcroft agreed to take the body to his surgery while they found a way to record a death by misadventure.

Lucas gave Tanya his car keys and together they carried Rose outside and laid her across the back seat under a towel. Chalcroft had wanted to put her in the boot but Tanya refused that final indignity. Lucas returned to the drawing room to calm the other guests. Tanya drove in silence. Chalcroft stared out of the window.

Stupid bloody woman. Stupid bloody dead bitch.

*

Angeline's mother hid Mercy in the drying room and went to fetch the girls. They had all heard; Brittney had gone to the Shadow Suite to look for a hair clip she had lost the evening before and had seen them carrying the body. When she screamed Lucas had hit her and told her not to say a word but he knew it was already too late. They were afraid and they were angry and they wanted to know why Mercy had come as if she had known all along that this was going to happen but Mercy was still drunk and she could not believe what they were telling her. How could Rose be dead when she was here to save her?

Mercy had imagined a palace of whores, of irresistible self-possessed women with arcane sexual skills who drew men to them with a glance. Here crouching in this hot small cupboard with seven half-naked bodies she saw nothing but fear. This whole underground world was shoddy and decrepit and a sham and the girls had spun these dreams for the men but they had grown desperate to believe them for themselves too. What else was there for them but hypocrisy and selfishness and despair? Mercy had known she would despise the men in a place like this but it was the women who shocked her.

She felt grief well in her and her whole body shrank to a tiny cold point of pain and she longed for tears but none would come while fury and shame still tore at her. Fury that Rose had not come – that she would rather hide in these rooms than accept Mercy's love – and shame in the certainty that she should have forced Rose from this place years before. These terrible conflicting truths paralysed her and her hands shook in the darkness and she knew she must hold Rose for herself.

¤

The dirty white transit van pulled up in front of the long terrace of Victorian town houses and Ross rolled down the tinted window to check the number. The girls climbed out of the rear doors, cursing in the damp night. Brittney was still in her leather trousers and T-shirt. The blood on her lip had dried. Tanya waved to them to stay away from the wide stone steps.

The light comes on if you go up. She's in the back.

Ross took the tyre iron from the tool kit. They went down the service alley and into the small yard filled with wheelie bins and Tanya pointed to a window above. They climbed up onto the flat roof and peered into the narrow room. The streetlight beyond the garden wall threw the shadow of leaves and branches over the grey striped wallpaper and boxing prints and the body lay on the plastic couch still covered in towels. They could not see the face but the dark hair fell almost to the floor. Tanya pointed to the open door where Chalcroft's shoes lay in the hallway and gestured inside pretending sleep.

He stayed here.

Mercy stared at Rose. At least the alarm will be off.

Ross shook his head. This is more than a big drink.

Brittney slid her hand across his chest and her nail circled his nipple. He shivered. He wrapped his sweater around the tyre iron and began to bend the metal frame back.

The day Mercy met Rose she had hidden herself in fury at the foot of the garden. She was nearly ten and her mother had let down her sleeveless yellow dress to cover her knees but nobody else in her class – she had moved up a year and they were all older – wore theirs long. Rose sat in the lime tree above the leaning fence and watched her pick at the neat hem stitches with childish blunt fingers. When the thread refused to snap and the cotton buckled as she tugged she took the fine loops in her mouth and tried to tear them with her teeth.

My mum did that on my favourite skirt and I tore it up.

Mercy looked up at the shadow in the sunlight that fell through the dark sticky leaves.

Move out of the way and I'll throw you my knife.

She stood and tried to make out the shape on the branch above. To tear up a skirt – your favourite skirt – because your mother had altered it! The little red penknife fell beside her and Rose jumped down.

You're Mercy. My dad says you think you're posh but my mum said you're just pretentious.

What's that?

Rose put her finger to the tip of her nose and pushed it up.

I'm Rose. That's our house.

Mercy had heard her parents talk about it. She felt the end of her own nose and Rose picked up the dress and started ripping the threads free with her blade. Twice she went through the material but Mercy saw that if it was shortened the holes would be hidden so she said nothing.

After a few minutes the hem was free and they argued about how much to take it up. Mercy could see the original crease and she was happy enough to sew it back the way it had been but Rose wanted her to try it on. She wasn't sure she could undress here in the garden even though nobody could see them but Rose looked at her like she was mad. She took her T-shirt and skirt off and hung them on the fence and pulled the dress over her head but she knew she was blushing and she kept brushing her hands down her front.

You look nice in yellow. I don't get new stuff because of my sisters.

I wanted a sister but I'm the only one.

You'll have to give me some of your things then. I don't like your dresses much but your shirts are okay.

86

Mercy had not known there was a difference but she was pleased anyway.

Too long.

She held it where it had been before but Rose shook her head.

Up.

Half an inch.

Up, up, up.

An inch.

It's a waste otherwise. Give it to me and I'll do it—

Mercy thought it was too short already but she did not want to lose this wonderful new friend and she pretended to agree even though she knew her mother would see and she was afraid of what she would say.

Rose lay in her lap as she sat on the plywood flooring in the back of the van piled with tarpaulins that smelled of creosote. She was stiff and her arms were still curled above her head and her hands were cold but her back was just warm where it lay across Mercy's legs. God how she loved her! The smile shook on her lips. The memories of twenty years were beginning to drift, anchorless already. She pulled fragments from all around her. The sound of Rose's laugh when she was angry and the scent of the oil in her hair in the bath. The vast pile of shoes under the bed. She began to cry silently. Sharing a bed the night the heating broke and sleeping under a single duvet in their coats. Rose stealing a make-up bag from Selfridges for Mercy for her sixteenth birthday and Mercy making Rose a skirt for her eighteenth in the same week and both of them loving their present more than anything else they had ever owned.

Mercy's tears fell on Rose's face now. On her cheeks and in her mouth.

Cooking a surprise supper of *chilli con carne* – all the rage, and home-made – for Rose's hen night and Rose announcing before they sat down that she had decided to become a vegetarian but changing her mind when she saw the trouble Mercy had taken and then lying in bed for two days with food poisoning. Both of them falling in love with Ivy Short's brother Steve on the same evening at Ivy's leaving party and confessing to each other on the bus home. And promising for the sake of their friendship that they would both give him up, and discovering two weeks later that they had both had lunch with him anyway.

And they had laughed. They had always laughed. And when they laughed they would remember everything else about how their lives looped and twined around each other and how somewhere within the madness of their difference existed a perfect quiet space in which everything they wanted would happen. And yet without each other there was nothing. Rose's death ripped a thread from the weave of Mercy's life that left every other fibre exposed. Rose was dead but Mercy's life had dissolved into these thousand unbound strands. No longer life but the components of a life.

She wanted so badly to laugh now. To hear Rose laugh. But she stared at the pale waxy wet face with its dull eyes and dry lips and she thought of that laughing and she had to look away.

¤

The street-lamp in the yard outside Carter's workshop had failed years ago. The city no longer replaced bulbs unless residents complained and Carter had never noticed, so the long courtyard of blood-red brick sat in shadow broken only by the harsh light from the kitchen. The sign above the stable door swung silently.

Carter was finishing his breakfast when Mercy rang the bell. He put both plates in the sink, the clean beneath the dirty, brushed the crumbs from his trousers and took his black jacket from the hook on the back of the door. Mercy called up to the window and he opened it and leaned out. His silhouette barely fitted through the narrow casement.

Carter?

Yes.

It's Mercy Alexander. From—

From the river. But it's a cold night for a swim.

She couldn't see his expression and she wasn't sure if he had been asleep. He was still dressed. Perhaps undertakers went to bed in their clothes.

My friend is dead.

Carter took Rose single-handed from the van and laid her on the cooling board. The icy slab of steel would preserve her while the rigor eased and the body could be set out in the casket. He seemed too big for this long, low room crowded with strange tools. Big enough to carry the bodies of all those who lay on that board. His chest rose and fell beneath the white shirt but he did not break sweat.

She thought of the undertaker who had organised her father's burial and everything about the funeral parlour that had been designed to wipe out feelings, to kill sound and smell and light with dark wood and velvet and marble. This did not look like a room for the care of the dead. It was a place where things were made. Where someone lived. Everything in it was alive. He brought a shroud and he laid it over her but he didn't cover the face. As if she might simply be cold.

Ross walked around the body, staring. He opened doors and

picked things up. Brittney took him outside. She was freezing, exhausted and frightened. None of them had any money. She didn't want to have to sleep with him. She climbed into the back of the van. She hadn't been close to Rose. She tried to think of a single time they had really talked. Ross pushed her T-shirt up.

Shut the doors. Please.

When he pulled them closed it was totally dark. He kissed her belly as his hands went to her belt. Why was this so hard for her? Her fourth man today. A month ago Rose had given her a bottle of champagne on her birthday and they had drunk it with the others out of tea cups downstairs. This was her little present to Rose. On the day of her death. She felt his hand inside her knickers and she spat on her fingers and trailed them between her legs to make herself wet. When he pushed into her she slid on the plywood and her head hit the back of the seat. She raised her hands to push herself away from the sharp metal and she stayed that way until Ross had finished.

Tanya sat unmoving in the corner. She had said nothing since they stole the body. She was sure Lucas would know she had taken them back to Chalcroft's surgery and she tried to imagine what would happen to her if she went back to the brothel. Or if she didn't. She thought of her boyfriend waiting at home and his anger that she had lied about the restaurant. He would want to know where she had been tonight.

Mercy knelt beside her. Will you go home?

I can maybe stay with Brittney.

You can stay with me if you need.

She shook her head.

Ross was in the doorway.

You done?

Where's Brittney?

She's ready.

They stood. Tanya looked at Rose again and crossed herself. Mercy hugged her and was surprised to feel her heart beating.

Thank you for—

She drew herself free and walked away without looking back.

I'd offer something stronger but I don't keep any alcohol in the house.

Carter handed her the cup of tea, too sweet.

Was she an old friend?

Twenty years.

I'm sorry.

The words meant nothing. Maybe none of the words meant anything but there was something about him that was comforting. That he said nothing else. That he was not trying to protect her from herself. That he was not shocked to see Rose dead.

What happened?

I wasn't there.

Why was she afraid to tell the truth? Because she didn't know it? Because he might think she was a whore, too? Could he tell by looking at Rose that she had died in a *ménage à trois* in a brothel? She watched him as she said it.

She was a call girl. A good one. She worked in a house in Prentice Place.

Carter understood at once that she had been killed and he thought of the man he had killed.

Can you make a coffin?

He nodded.

Do you know what happened?

Mercy wondered. While she smiled for the cameras with a glass of champagne toasting her own success her best friend was naked in a damp basement living a stranger's angry dreams. Cause of death: neglect.

I was supposed to meet her. She was supposed to come to the show, to the one we did together on the jetty. I didn't even ask you. Sorry.

Carter didn't look like a man who went to many opening nights.

Nobody knows. They know his face, but if he never comes back—

Are you going to tell the police?

I don't know. I don't know what I'd say. Don't they pay them all off, anyway?

Rose had told her Lucas had asked her to entertain a vice-squad officer one night. A favour to keep things quiet. It was no different if you ran a restaurant or a club, she had said, and she could always tell even without the uniform. The officers didn't want the brothel closed down and those who were regulars couldn't afford to get on the wrong side of Lucas. It was an uneasy partnership and even Mercy in her anger knew better than to upset it with no motive and no suspect and no evidence. The new girl there said the man had never even touched her.

She thought about what she would say if she reported it. None of the girls wanted to be questioned. And what about stealing the evidence? Breaking and entering? Who could prove the body had ever been at the brothel now? Grudge matches between girls were common enough. They were far more likely to investigate Mercy than Lucas while Rose was impounded and examined and held in a steel drawer in the city morgue for months until the case was closed.

She touched her hand and she saw the nails were un-painted.

She looks so young.

It happens that way. The blood settles and the skin relaxes.

If you go when you're seventy it's a blessing but at this age it'll break your heart. How old was she?

Thirty-one.

She looked five years younger.

They like you in your twenties. I thought I could do twenty-seven.

The first year we were allowed a calculator for our exams we worked out how many hours we had spent together since we met.

You never forget.

She nodded and she tried to reckon the total today but they only saw each other once a month now. They still thought of themselves as best friends but neither of them had seen how much of the past they had clung to as their lives pulled apart. And Rose had come to her to be saved. She had reached out across that unacknowledged divide and cried for her help and Mercy had helped her but she had not given her love or comfort or any of the things that they had shared in twenty thousand hours.

What do I need to bury a body?

A spade.

She knew he was trying to make her smile. He counted them out on his lined fingers: A medical certificate from a doctor. A death certificate from the registrar. Notice of interment. Disposal certificate. She could hear Rose laughing. *Four fucking departments!*

What happens if you make the coffin and I just take her away?

If I help you and they find out, I lose my licence. If I help you and they don't find out, I just have to want to believe you didn't kill her.

So let's just say I need it for something I'm working on. Like last time. Measure me. We're the same size.

Even in death, she thought. Share a flat. Share a car. Share a dress. Share a coffin.

You can leave her here.

She took his hand and suddenly wished she hadn't. She knew now that she would tell nobody. She would bury the body herself somewhere they had loved where nobody would ever disturb her again. If Lucas and the killer wanted Rose to disappear then she would.

But not Mercy.

PART TWO

The police van had arrived early at the court buildings and Carter had stared up through the steel riot mesh at the pitted stone pillars and the frieze that ran the length of the façade. The charges were aggravated assault and manslaughter and he was to be judged beneath a carving of Leonidas and his fight to the death at Thermopylae. He was nineteen and knew nothing of the history of his own country, let alone ancient Greece. All he saw were men, naked but artfully modest, hacking each other to pieces in a mountain pass.

He had known he would go down for at least five years. There had been more than enough witnesses even on an estate where amnesia was a habit acquired young. He thought of the bar filled with blind eyes staring at them both on the splintered wooden floor and of the statue outside the court: Justice, her chaste robes freshly covered in anti-climb paint and her arms wound with razor wire so the practical jokers would not climb up again to leave what looked like a kilo bag of cocaine in her bronze scales. He imagined Bullen, the arresting officer, questioning her in her blindfold. I just went out to get my fags from the car, Officer. I heard shouts. Breaking glass.

Now that the prisons were privately run it was cheaper to house the disenfranchised at Her Majesty's delegated pleasure than on the council estates but they were equally shabby and brutal and managed with equal indifference. As on the estates, the hierarchy of fear was ruthlessly maintained by those at the top. New arrivals were quickly assessed and shown their place. Those with contacts or resources were courted but contained; those who thought themselves rivals were either assimilated into the power structure or viciously and repeatedly beaten. Those who had nothing to offer and posed no threat were the workers, forced to perform the chores assigned to the leaders. The empire was small and barely profitable, but the territorial struggles were relentless and bloody: the less there was to fight for, the more desperately they fought for it.

Carter had been at school with some of the recent arrivals and since his case had taken longer to be heard than theirs his reputation had already been established. A fresh face with no previous convictions, no allegiances and no assets who kills a man with his bare hands is hard to classify. He arrived at eleven one night in a wing already past curfew and sat on the foot of his bed in his darkened cell breathing the damp air quietly. As soon as the guard had gone he heard a voice.

Carter Stark.

Yes.

How long did you get?

Seven. Seven years.

They don't generally do weeks. My name's Hedge. You're not the restless type, I hope.

I can do eight if I have to.

You'll find it easier if we march in step. There'll be a few favours. Nothing impertinent.

I can look after myself.

So they tell me. Let's hope you don't have to.

*

They talked again the following morning at breakfast. Hedge was a small man, tidy and quick; he had endured three of his five years but this was his second term. A thinker, but wild, Carter saw. An insider, but not an intimate of those who ran the prison: an emissary. He introduced Carter to a man sitting opposite them, fortyish and lean, his thinning hair cropped close. Like all the others he was fitter and healthier here than he ever had been when free. Hedge banged the man's bowl with his spoon.

Show us your yardbird smile, Alan.

Alan turned away from them and Carter saw the scar, raw and ragged from ear to shoulder.

He declined a favour. Six weeks ago.

It looked like it had happened yesterday. He had heard how they did it: two blades from a disposable razor melted side by side into a toothbrush handle. A single cut will heal evenly but a double wound leaves the skin unable to bind or mend itself. It was a mess.

Hedge explained that the guards allowed men to exchange chores among themselves if the tasks were carried out satisfactorily. This was supposed to encourage independence and self-motivation – rehabilitation skills – but there wasn't much the prison system could teach its inmates about a free-market economy and inevitably it supported the élite at the expense of the masses. The tasks Hedge assigned him were simple enough: an extra afternoon refilling the towel dispensers and a second morning of washing up. He was to sign the time-sheets in the name of Lindsay.

Carter was neither bloody-minded nor a trouble-maker, but he was not much given to compromise and he didn't see why he should spend a day mucking out on someone else's behalf if he wasn't going to get anything in return except protection he didn't need. He began to divide the work into two halves: his own days according to the prison rota, which he carried out impeccably, and his delegated share which he repeatedly botched or failed to finish. Eventually Lindsay was questioned. Hedge came for a chat but Carter just smiled at him and said he was doing his best. After two months of complaints they admitted a stalemate and a newer face took on Lindsay's share.

He had freed up four hundred and sixteen days of a sentence that stretched ahead for two thousand, five hundred and fifty-six including two leap years. He realised that even a man of his small ambition was going to have to find something to do if he hoped to stay sane.

When the prison maintenance staff advertised for an apprentice he jumped at the chance. The unit actually consisted of a single supervisor by the name of Farragh who had worked as a carpenter for fifty-two years in factories, sports pavilions, railway stations and schools. Since the former munitions factory had been built with steel joists and pre-stressed concrete and finished with prefabricated industrial accessories screwed to blockboard he farmed out most of the work to independent operators (referred to as the Meccano men) and spent his time keeping his workshop in perfect order in case the management company should decide to put dado rails in the detention cells or veneer the library bookshelves in quilted willow. He was a brilliant joiner. Nobody had ever taught him how to do anything badly and the slow pace of state employment had never hurried him into cutting corners. Even here his work was finished to a tolerance beyond the wildest comprehension of its audience.

The functions of the tools in Farragh's workshop were so specific that they transcended the merely practical. Handsaws, gouges and planes were the heart of it but their distant relatives – blitz saws and offset dovetails, drawer-lock chisels, goose-neck scrapers and double-ended rifflers – seemed so perfectly fitted to their arcane purpose that a man could no longer doubt that the universe had been designed by a higher force. Carter knew no more of teleology than of Thermopylae but he had seen these tools in his father's boxes and in handling them here for the first time he felt he was waking from a strange hibernation.

Carter never understood why his father refused to teach him how to make the toys he loved so much. Yachts with long sloping keels and tapered lead ballasts and cream cambric sails. Nested boxes with interlocking folded sides in tulip, maple and cherry. Cars and rockets, mobiles, fairground scenes with their faceless painted figures bobbing on eccentric cams. He knew every curve, every joint and fixing – even the mechanisms, the pulleys and rockers and pushrods buried deep inside, were perfectly balanced and silenced. God sees the back, his father would say. It was the only time they spoke of God.

Carter learned quickly, though it took longer for his hands to discover the hidden patterns of the wood than for his mind to master them. Nothing in a world of appliance and convenience had prepared him for the sensation in his fingertips of guiding a perfectly set bench plane or the smooth rocking of his body weight behind the chisel. At first he saw the wood as a raw material to be cut and forced to its new purpose but his first pieces sprung and warped and tore themselves apart as they settled and dried. Farragh showed him how to leave the joints room to move – to rebate edges, set panels in grooves and use shrinkage plates so the timber could flex freely. The wood is still alive. By the time he walked free Carter could feel if a table had been overstressed just by sliding his palm across the surface.

*

Now, in his own workshop with Rose beside him as the cold dawn broke, he ran his father's marking gauge the length of the board and tried to imagine how many carpenters ever made a casket. It was the most heartfelt work of all: simpler than a chair, stronger than a chest, more intimate than a bed. To be used only once, but for eternity. Made to measure for someone who no longer cared about the fit. But the making itself was the tribute.

Mercy had asked for something simple – if she was to bury her friend unnoticed she would need a traditional design – but Carter had a stock of clear Weymouth pine he had gathered over the years, timber free of knots and blemishes whose pale simplicity shimmered as he planed.

He went over to Rose to take her height. She had been hurriedly slipped into her black dress and her feet were still bare. He laid the back of his hand against her cheek just as he had with Mercy on the jetty. Her temperature was dropping fast now.

You wouldn't think it but wood's lovely warm stuff. It'll be like wearing a coat.

God, don't let me be cold.

It never freezes that far down. You'll be snug.

He pulled the sheet up over her eyes and he tried to think what Mercy had told him about her.

A friend of twenty years.

A prostitute.

A woman.

What did he know of any of these things?

By the time he finished it was almost dark but he had not turned the light on. He was faint with hunger. He wiped Rose's face and brushed her hair out on the cooling board and took her on his shoulder to lay her in the casket. He held her hand as he settled her, straightening her legs and tilting her head forward on the little wooden rest. He slid the top into place so she might grow used to the quiet but he did not nail it yet.

He took the hand bell from the shelf by the door and stepped out into the evening. The wind came up the river bringing with it the warm wet scent of the breweries and the sharp smoke of the first bonfires. Night had shrunk the city and even the pealing of the great baroque churches to the west had drawn closer, their melodies muffled like voices after a snowfall.

He crossed the yard ringing slowly and went out under the arch to the road. The shops were dark and the blinds above were drawn and shutters folded. Schoolchildren had forced chewing gum into the pedestrian signal at the crosswalk and in the brief strange silence of traffic halted at the lights the city smelled and sounded as it had a century before. He watched the cars slide past and he stepped out among them walking along the centre of the road as he continued the lament in a long easy swing.

Back inside he replaced the bell and took from the same shelf a stone flask and two small heavy glasses. He filled them to the brim with the *eau-de-vie* and set them on the lid of the coffin and went upstairs to make his breakfast.

¤

Chalcroft stood at the bar of the brothel. The cleaners had already started their morning's work ferrying piles of sheets and towels and unloading the freshly delivered baskets. Lucas was in jeans and a jumper, barefoot. He stood behind the counter trying to make a cappuccino.

Sit down, for fuck's sake.

Chalcroft put his coat on the stool but didn't move. He hadn't been home to change his clothes. He was fifty-eight years old and he was terrified.

They took her out the back window.

Who took her?

This is nothing to do with me.

A body stolen from your surgery while you sleep there is nothing to do with you?

Chalcroft saw his life float past him in pieces. A successful practice. A tolerable marriage. A quiet retirement approaching. He tried to recall the reassuring noises he had learned to make when his patients suspected a heart attack but nothing would come. He pictured himself holding the receiver blankly as his own voice echoed down the line.

Lucas burned his hand under the milk steamer and hurled the jug at the mirrored shelf of bottles. Why did this feel like a kick in the balls? A personal affront. He employed these women. Gave them a decent place to work and paid them on time. He expected them to be able to handle themselves. Rose had always been reliable. Not his type – she was one of the few he had not slept with – but a good earner. A little old, but still fuckable.

Not any more.

And with Fairburn. He wondered why that made a difference.

He wanted to smack Chalcroft but he had the terrible suspicion he might piss himself on the newly vacuumed carpet.

The room was pitch dark. Fairburn wasn't sure why he answered the phone. He kept one on the bedside table but he usually unplugged it unless he knew he had to take an early call. His wife was already downstairs with the children: he could smell the toast.

Fairburn?

104

Who is this?

Come on.

How did you get this number?

This is a people business.

Fairburn looked at his watch. Seven thirty.

A twenty-four-hour people business.

Your girl has gone.

Your girl has gone.

The girl who died in front of you last night has disappeared.

A girl you employed who died on your premises has disappeared.

Fairburn enjoyed the game but he knew Lucas thought he had killed her and he was not yet sure if he should be worried.

Someone took the body from Chalcroft's surgery. If he ever comes back in I'm going to do to him for free what he pays Chrissy a fortune for.

What do you want?

I want to know where Mara is.

She's your—

I want to know what she saw.

They met outside the brothel and crossed the paved square with its empty fountain to fetch coffee from Spiccioli on the corner. Fairburn noticed Lucas's steam burn as he slid the coins across the polished zinc.

Caught red-handed.

Lucas was starting to doubt Fairburn was ever going to take this seriously. Fairburn had a lot more to lose. If anyone went to the police it would be handled by officers who were on good terms with his girls. Intimate terms. Nobody wanted to close the place if they didn't have to. Even if Fairburn hadn't laid a hand on her – as he claimed, amazingly – he was the obvious suspect. If they shut Lucas down he could move elsewhere with the same team, but even if Fairburn got away with manslaughter – womanslaughter – he would get eight years.

They took the styrofoam cups and walked out into the tired morning air. A body still slept on the bench beneath a yellow quilt and a police van emptied a crowd of wardens onto the street five minutes before parking restrictions began. At this time of year the sun barely rose above the terraced houses across the road and neither of them wanted to be awake right now. Fairburn took the lid off to smell his cappuccino.

Excellent.

He seemed surprised. As they turned the corner a large brindled dog leaned on the steps of the brothel and urinated for almost half a minute while heavy dark testicles swung beneath the propped leg. Lucas thought of Chalcroft as the liquid pooled and chased the cracks in the paving stones into the gutter. He started to run but the dog looked up and was gone before he could get close enough to kick it away. He stared after it, unsure what to do about the mess. He felt foolish and angry.

I wouldn't call that a big dick.

Fairburn watched it disappear into the park.

I thought a dog like that would be hung like a horse.

Bullmastiff.

Big fucker.

They went straight to the Shadow Suite. It had already been made up and showed no sign of the previous night's agony. None of the rooms had windows and at this time of the morning the glow from the two dim lamps beside the bed was falsely intimate. Fairburn sat in the low chair. The room was cold and the scent of sex had dissolved in a mist of air freshener. Lucas picked at a cigarette burn on one of the night tables.

You didn't touch her.

Fairburn saw Rose there and he wanted to reach out and stroke her skin. He wanted to put his fingertip to her lip and feel her hair on his face.

Why do you want Mara?

Because she works for me. Because she knows what happened and until we find her she can say what she likes to who she likes.

And when we do?

Lucas simply smiled and Fairburn noticed how pretty he was. The eyelashes and the dark curls. He had slept with several men without ever caring if he was gay or even bisexual; the uncoiling of his lust was not bound by the etiquette of skirt or trouser.

What if she says I killed her?

You might want to ask her that yourself.

He could not imagine Rose dead. The obscene epiphany he had pursued for so long had been revealed to him and obscured again in the same instant and it had left him dazzled. His head was unbearably heavy and he could hardly draw breath and he was shocked to realise that his physical self could be compromised by this terrible yearning. By a feeling.

He knew now that it was not raw beauty or carnal sleight-of-hand that would deliver the ecstasy he dreamed of – not a mortal body nor sensation, no matter how rare – but a mirror of his own hunger, some primal response to the desire itself. He had looked at Rose and had seen only himself in those dark eyes. How should he recognise before him the pretty, funny, vivid woman who had learned to give her men what they longed for but who longed in turn to be free of these nights and these rooms? She allowed him his dream but she had snatched it from him before he could awaken and now he was trapped for ever. It was as if he himself had died and he was certain that Rose's loss was nothing compared to his own and for the first time in his life he knew regret.

Who would steal a body?

I don't know. But they'll want to talk to us soon enough.

¤

Mercy wanted to talk to Mara, not Lucas. She needed to know why Rose had died, although she had no idea what she would do when she found out.

When she called Louise Parrish it was the first time they had spoken in over a year. At the time she bought the brothel from her she had still been in jail and the arrangements had been made through solicitors. They had met only once and spoken through glass in the visitor's wing. Now she stood outside her yellow front door in a floodlit corridor on the seventeenth floor of a tower block behind the international train station. Louise opened the door and put her finger to her lips. She was on the telephone.

Oh, yes. Do that for me, lover. I'm ready for you, you know I am.

Her words were smooth and warm. She nodded for Mercy to come in and she could hear the caller's voice, low and despairing.

The flat was small and poorly laid out with cold high ceilings and fat iron pipes that radiated noise from surrounding apartments and it overlooked the trains that clattered off to the south. Every spare foot of floor and wall was stacked with old furniture – from the brothel, she guessed – under dust-sheets.

You know what I'm doing now, don't you? Yes. Oh yes. I'm touching myself. For you.

She moved to the counter and filled the kettle noiselessly. She switched it on and leaned against the wall by the window. She was still handsome at fifty. She did not dye her hair and the silver strands shone in the bluish light from the October sky outside. She wore an old track suit rolled back at the cuffs and ankles.

That's it. That's it. Do that for me now. That's good now. Good. Good.

She whispered the words as if soothing a child to sleep. She waited until the line went dead and she put the phone down in the cradle on the wall. She scribbled a note in the pad beneath it and then she picked up the phone again and wiped it with a cloth from the sink.

They pay a fortune for it and they still want to do all the talking.

Sorry. I didn't know you were still working.

Louise laughed and did a little pirouette in the track suit.

I don't even have to brush my teeth. I haven't worn lipstick since they let me out. All that stuff I taught myself about how to be a lady. Finishing school crap. The only kind of finishing they care about is whether the girls swallow. But I did once double-book a bishop and a baron for the same girl and I knew enough to keep his Lordship talking downstairs with me while his Reverence took first bite at the cherry. It know it's just fucking for money but we did it better than anyone in this city.

She saw Mercy look around the tiny room.

I bought a little house across the river. My daughter lives there now with her kids. This was hers.

She shrugged.

I'm not very good at sharing. I learned that.

She brought a pot to the table. Milk and sugar were already in the two mugs.

Brickie's tea. We used to open twice a week in the afternoons because our married callers couldn't visit in the evening. Seven years I forced myself to drink Earl Grey with milk and no sugar. Only good thing about losing it all is I'll never have to taste the filthy stuff again.

She wasn't unfriendly, Mercy thought. But distant. Too used to second-guessing, double-checking, never quite being able to trust. Mercy wanted to ask about life in the old brothel but it was already a thousand years in the past. So she told her of Rose, and of how she had died and of how they had been friends. About little things like the apples and the pile of shoes under the bed. And she told her that she was going to take her away the next day and bury her in the woods behind her uncle's house.

I know Rose.

A thousand years ago.

She was always going to be all right. With some of them you worry.

She had never lost a girl.

I didn't think she would be with us that long. She signed up straight away when they went to the new place. To Lucas.

What else could they have done? She was going to be inside for a year at least. None of them wanted to go back on the streets, she knew that. But still it hurt.

I'm not coming to see her buried.

It's fine. I haven't told anybody else.

The afternoon light was gone. The railway tracks laced away from them in the blue shadows below and the distant suburbs melted into the fringes of the evening and the world had no edge. The city looked old and tired.

Do you know any of the other girls?

Most of them were mine. They tell me how things are. Who's around. They come for tea and try and get me drunk.

Tanya said Mara was with her.

Mara. We never had a Mara.

Louise went to the door and switched on the light above the table and suddenly the room seemed smaller.

Nobody saw him?

Tanya saw him. She'd seen him before. She described him to the others but nobody knew.

He won't be a regular. They know the regulars.

Tanya said you keep a book. I know you have to be careful. Know who people are. Rose told me about it, too.

Louise blinked.

She trusted you.

She stood up to refill the pot.

If I could see the book I could help them tell me who he is. I don't know everybody.

They might recognise a name. That's all I need.

From eight thousand names.

It doesn't matter how many—

It's not a fucking jigsaw, my love! Not Cluedo.

She picked at a fingernail and rubbed it with a pan scourer. She shook her head again.

You wouldn't even be able to read it. It's just my notes, a little scrapbook, nothing. It's not going to help you.

If Tanya says she saw him before then he's in there.

That's not how it works.

She saw she would have to twist the knife.

One of your girls is dead.

What do you know about my girls?

She sank her face in her hands and forced herself not to cry but her whole body rocked.

I don't do this any more. I don't.

Mercy knew she should comfort her but she felt only anger and she wanted to seize her and shake her and make her tell her where the book was. Because she knew he was there, waiting for her.

¤

They left the city at half past five in the morning and drove north for three hours to the heart of the eastern wheatlands where great unbroken fields lay beneath a featureless sky and bare trees choked with ivy leaned over abandoned farmhouses. Autumn had already given way to winter here and the flash of frost lay on the dull turned earth. Finally the road began to climb and the hedges grew around them until they were in the twilight of a wood. Mercy had camped here with Rose once thirteen years before and she couldn't think if Rose had even liked the place; she had chosen it because it was her uncle's land and she knew if he ever found out he would keep it to himself. It was strange, she thought, to know something that must never actually be told. For so long her secrets had just been facts with hidden value, tools, investments.

She had come with two friends from the years when they lived above the tailor but they no longer had anything in common. Sara knew Rose had been a call girl but Emily thought she worked in a gallery. Mercy no longer really knew either of them but she didn't think she could do this alone and she wasn't sure she would ever really believe Rose was dead if she was the only one to see her buried. She told them she had been knocked down by a motorcycle courier and she begged them to come because she hadn't been able to reach anybody else and she wanted to tell Emily the truth but she couldn't. Because the past they had shared was too distant to retrieve and because she had never quite believed it herself.

The car pulled up and the engine died and as she faced the silence she was suddenly afraid that she had gone too far – that she had lied to too many people and that the truth and the death and the secret burial would all be discovered and she would be blamed for it all. She had not foreseen how complicated it would become and she realised she had no idea what the penalty was for stealing a body and she wanted to climb back into the warm car and drive away to a place where no one knew her but she saw she would not because she could not abandon Rose now.

When they had stolen apples together and let the tyres down on Phil Kempton's convertible and gatecrashed the opening night at Incognito they had stepped outside the world Mercy knew and she had gripped Rose's arm to whisper *We can't* but Rose had laughed and said *We're here now* as if the decision were no longer theirs. She had taken Mercy to the threshold and shown her what lay beyond. And so Mercy put on her coat and gloves but as she clapped her hands to hear the echo roll back from the trees shadowed in mist she wondered whether she would be allowed to carry on her work in a prison cell.

They met the others at the gate to the quarry. The grave-diggers had prepared the plot the night before and they were asleep in the car when Carter arrived but they were already dressed and five minutes later they crossed the footbridge together and started up the hill. The edge of the wood skirted a field too steep and narrow for anything but hay and it was utterly overgrown now and not as pretty as she had remembered; trees had fallen and lay undisturbed and brambles shadowed the soft trunks. The bluebells and the sudden dappled sunshine were long gone.

It had rained heavily before daybreak and even though the men had cut a path beside the old railway line they still had to crouch to clear the low wide branches as they carried the coffin. Carter wore his high-buttoned dark coat but no tie and carried in the crook of his arm a small cross of the same pale pine as the casket, simply bevelled and carved with the date of Rose's death. The women talked quietly as they followed him and they stared at their shoes and trousers soaked with melting frost. They were not ready for any of this.

God. It's incredible.

She would have loved it. I hate those city cemeteries.

We'll come again next year to clear the path and lay flowers.

But when they thought of her they did not see her peaceful in these misty woods but yelling from the open window of a taxi or drinking unlabelled beer on a deafening dance-floor.

They reached the clearing. The grave was neatly cut but it was oddly ordinary as if unaware of its purpose and the earth from which it had been carved was dull and heavy. The bottom lay under an inch of water and Mercy was afraid the coffin itself would fill as the level rose.

God, don't let me be cold.

The air moved in long low gusts that trailed fallen rain from the trees. Mercy had wanted to speak but her feet were wet and she was hungry from the early start and she had hardly slept since the night of her show. What would she be doing today if her friend had not died? She had no idea. Her grief was softening into something deeper and more shapeless and everything that had brought her to this point in her life seemed suddenly irrelevant: courage, fear, ambition. Someone else's life.

She looked at Carter to ask *How shall I do this?* But he mis-read her and he signalled for the assistants to swing the casket into the void. They let the ropes slip through gloved hands as they struggled to keep it level and then in an instant Rose was gone. He handed her a spade and she copied his wide-footed stance as they began to replace the earth. Would there be a pile exactly the size of Rose left over when the pit was filled? The wet soil fell like a bruise on the unvarnished pine and with her next swing she tried to fill the space at the sides. She could not bring herself to bury the box itself. Carter watched her and she saw him and felt foolish but he understood. They all did it.

It took twenty minutes to fill the grave and tamp it down. The shallow neat mound made no sense in this careless wasteland and Mercy knew it would only be a matter of months before the brambles reclaimed it. Carter asked her if she wanted to place the cross and she took it and set it at the head. She was afraid to splinter it by driving it home with the flat of the spade so she leaned into it and twisted it home.

¤

The van had a radio but no cassette player and there was no reception here so they drove in silence and Mercy watched Carter's hands on the wheel. He barely touched it but the empty fields flew past unendingly until slowly the city grew around them in a patchwork of forecourts and playing fields and artificial lakes and then for no apparent reason the highway was a high street and she was staring into shop windows and paved gardens with cars under tarpaulins where flowers once grew. Young boys leaned on their bikes against the window of the video shop and a bus driver called across to a woman in a passing car. They were in the capital and yet this was not the city she knew. It was its flesh but not its blood and suddenly she was desperate to be back at the heart where doors stay closed and nobody knows his neighbour and nothing quite means what it promises.

When they arrived at the coach-house it was mid-afternoon. Carter switched off the engine and swung the wide doors open and pushed the van in backwards as the tyres squealed on the wet cobbles. Mercy had never been here by day. From the court-yard she could see only the broad gable of the old hospital and its blind windows and the darkening sky and she thought she had come to a place that did not belong to the larger world but the sounds of air-brakes and steel shutters and scaffolding poles falling in empty trailers echoed under the arch. Moss grew between the stones and she tried not to crush it as she walked.

She went to the sink under the stairs to wash the earth from her fingernails and caught a flash of herself in the small triangular mirror and she was surprised to see herself there at all. She wiped her hands on her trousers. Carter stood at the foot of the stairs picking pine needles out of his turn-ups.

Have you had lunch?

She nodded but she meant the day before. In another life.

In the car just now. Fish and chips. Pizza. Sushi and soup.

They laughed.

I mean I know you haven't. You must be hungry.

She didn't know. She just wanted to sit down. She could try, at least.

Sure. Thanks.

They went up the narrow stairs. Mercy's experience of men who lived alone – and who were not homosexual – warned her that every surface would be buried beneath packets and pans of meals not yet finished or begun but the room was as bare as the workshop. Could he be queer? Some lingering instinct of political correctness wagged its finger at the stereotype and she wondered why she cared. She saw the table was already laid for two.

Am I that predictable?

It wasn't for you.

He hadn't meant it to sound like that.

Don't let me steal someone else's lunch.

No, there's no one else.

He hadn't meant it to sound like that, either. He was happy she was here but her presence in the room had thrown something out of balance. He tried to think where he kept the pan although he had put it away in the same place a thousand times. It no longer felt like his kitchen but he could not say what had changed. He went to the fridge for eggs and sausages and Mercy

116

moved around the room touching the shelves and opening the perfect cupboards with nothing in them.

It's so beautiful. Can I look around?

He nodded. He had never thought of it as beautiful and as she stood in the doorway he realised that no one else had ever been in the bedroom.

The walls were panelled in beech and where the sun fell across them at the end of the day the grain had darkened. There was a chest of drawers, a table beneath the window and a narrow wardrobe all in wood. Nothing was painted. Mercy stood at the foot of the low plain bed which stretched almost the full width of the small space. She reached down to touch it and found it softer than she had imagined. The room was silent.

Beyond it a simple bathroom lay in shadow. This was the extent of the house. She came back and stood in the doorway, suddenly starving as she smelled the eggs in butter.

You don't have any pictures.

Pictures of what?

Anything.

He sounded surprised.

I don't know anybody who makes pictures. Except you.

I really feel bad I didn't ask you to the show.

She tried to imagine what he would have thought of the cold store and the drone of voices.

Where are your pictures?

It's still on. They'll be there for a month.

Then I can see them.

She liked the thought of Carter looking at her quietly instead of the drunken restless half-recognised faces. And then Connor Fairburn smiled at her from nowhere and she tried to think where she had put his card.

He slid the eggs onto their plates and speared the sausages – four for him, two for her – and wiped the pan with the heel of bread. He cut it into quarters and put it in a separate bowl.

When Mercy cooked for herself it was usually vegetables but in some odd way the fry-up seemed perfect. Meat and death, cried the dim politically correct voice. Freud and sausages, she thought. Was Carter attractive? He was if he would let it happen. He was handsome enough and manly, too, though it sounded old-fashioned. She wanted to know who had shared that bed.

When she left she asked him how much she owed for the burial.

I gave the boys eighty each.

And for the coffin? For you?

I had the wood.

And now you have none. And your time.

He shook his head. He knew he couldn't afford to turn down the money: two hundred and fifty pounds in cash would last him nearly two weeks. Mercy counted out a hundred and sixty for the grave-diggers and wrote her address on the back of a cab receipt.

Invoice me for whatever you need.

He nodded but he knew he wouldn't. She took her coat from the back of the door, still wet. He held it for her.

Thanks for coming this morning. I assume it means you believe me.

Or I need the money.

She laughed but this time she remembered not to hug him and she went down the stairs without looking back.

When Carter took the plates to the sink he could still smell her. Something floral, female, tender, tired. Warm. He imagined that was what it would smell like to share a life.

¤

Mercy hailed a cab and asked for Prentice Place. This time she knew the address but she was still afraid the driver would think she worked there. Rose would never have given a damn but Mercy felt his eyes in the rear-view mirror. Her mother watched from the bathroom window.

It was still just light when she arrived and she felt less nervous as she walked up the alley but when Angeline's mother opened the door she slammed it again without a word. Mercy knocked for a while and then she sat on the ledge by the door to wait. Another cab pulled up and Brittney climbed out in her leather trousers and a thick jumper. She had just left Tanya at the hospital.

Lucas knew Tanya had helped take Rose's body. Even though he knew she was going to leave him and even though she was already too scared to tell anyone else what she had seen or done he beat her badly enough to break her jaw. He hadn't meant to but as he drove home from her flat he saw it was oddly appropriate. There was something satisfying about a silent woman, he thought. Maybe that was why he loved a blow-job above all else: because a girl can't talk with her mouth full.

Brittney sat with Mercy in Spiccioli but neither of them noticed how good the coffee was. Brittney was frightened. Lucas knew she had seen the body and she didn't want to be caught talking. She had already risked her life and slept with a stranger for a woman she barely knew and who was already dead when she did it.

I have to find Mara.

She's gone. She was freaked.

Lucas must know.

He'll have a phone number, that's all. She won't be there any more.

Brittney turned to sit with her back to the window.

I don't think he'll kill her. But he'll beat her worse than Tanya and when he's finished she won't have anything to say to you. Or anyone else.

These women were being harmed for what they knew and as soon as Mercy found Mara she too would be on the list. When Mercy had first seen Rose's grave she had been afraid but the fear of death is different from the fear of violence. She wondered what Lucas looked like and whether she would recognise him when he came for her.

Will you ask the others?

She looked at Mercy for a moment and then she looked away.

We should get on.

They walked back to the brothel without speaking and Mercy turned south through the winding streets where the new banks and broking-houses gazed down at the elegant stone arcades from their icy bright towers. The streets were named for crafts that these institutions had driven to extinction but they bore their legacy without irony: Copperbasin Alley, Plume Blind, Last Row, Squirrel Hair Square. The arms of the illustrious guilds hung like a reproach, a circus of leaping fish and dogs with daggers in their mouths and twisted serpents, and as she passed beneath them she daydreamed a Worshipful Company of Street-Walkers with its livery of gilded legs beneath a hoist skirt and three johns couchant, tongues lolling. The oldest profession.

But maybe Brittney was right. Maybe nobody knew where Mara was and maybe it was better that way. At least it would end the violence. But now that Rose was dead and her own life had been torn from its mooring what else remained but this? She knew she had no choice but to push on but she wondered why she had to do it alone.

¤

Carter stood in the courtyard of the estate where he had spent seventeen years of his life. The flats were officially abandoned now and notices at every stairwell warned that the structure was unsafe but nothing had really changed and from the lines of clothes strung across the balconies it was still a home to some. The stench of urine in the disused lifts was as strong as ever. It must be something in their diet. He could have come here blindfolded and known where he was.

He walked up the concrete steps to the third floor. Behind him he heard a metal latch close but he saw nobody. The blue door was one of the few that had not been kicked off its hinges or burned open but it was easy enough to see through the broken window that there was nothing to steal. His father had sold the furniture gradually to pay for the alcohol and sometimes for clothes and food. He was a drunk but never less than pragmatic. Carter oiled the lock and turned the key and stepped into the hallway. The kitchen window had been opened and the room was filled with the sounds of the streets below. He went to close it and on the ledge he found the old beer glass etched with its imperial measure and filled with rain.

They water it, I know they do.

When it started he would walk to the pub every evening and drink a pint alone and order another and take it home. It became such a ritual they gave him his own mug.

*

Carter's mother had given up when he was three. She told her husband that she no longer loved him and that she had met someone who would make her happy but she hadn't left the flat for over a year and everyone knew the lover was a dream. She went in the middle of the night and she had put out clean clothes for them both and laid the table and finished the ironing as if it would last them for ever and as if she could leave them now knowing she had acquitted herself of all her maternal duties.

She sent them a card every year on her birthday telling them that she had married and found a good job but the postmark was from a different town each time and she had always been a rotten liar. She wrote once when Carter was eight that having a child was not what she had been led to believe and that she hoped he would forgive her for leaving him but he saw that she had already forgiven herself and that was all she needed. Carter felt that having a mother was not what he had been led to believe but he never wrote back. In any case the return address would have been another lie.

He stood in the doorway of his old room with its yellow walls and green carpet. They had never sold the bed or the chest of drawers but he kept his toys in cider crates from the off-licence. His father's toys were kept out of reach on the narrow shelf that ran the length of the corridor. He started with the boats when he was sacked from the factory that made reproduction furniture. Last decent job in town, he had said. For a decent man. He was a wonderful cabinet-maker of the same patient generation as Farragh but he liked to know where he stood and he was lost without a foreman and a card to punch himself in at nine and out at five. By the time he had spent his redundancy pay he had made dozens of cars and trains and old-fashioned aeroplanes but the painstaking work was just a way of keeping his skills in escrow until the klaxon sounded again and the freshly painted factory gates swung open for him and all the old friends he never saw any more.

One day while his father slept off his lunch Carter had taken the sleekest yacht to the paddling pool on the common and set the sail to run before the wind and chased it as it arched across the filthy water. The rudder could be moved but he could not fix it to hold a course and he raced all the way back to the flats to ask his father to tighten it or tie it back. His father knew he had taken the boat and when he saw that he had also sailed it he was incandescent. He would never hit a child but he sent him to the little yellow room and he sat in the corridor with the yacht on his lap and he wept. He had not been promised anything in this life, nor expected much, but he had made his peace with what he had earned and now he saw he had nothing. Only a son he loved but to whom he could give nothing that would not in turn be taken from him.

Carter could hear his father crying helplessly and he wanted desperately to go to him and make him come with him back to the pool but by the time he found the courage to open the unlocked door he had taken his glass to the pub and the yacht was in pieces on the floor.

¤

Mara climbed the steps from the station underpass and headed up the road towards the shunting yards and gasometers, the last shards of the city's industrial infrastructure. The lights and signs faded behind her as she made her way up the hill. Everything was hidden here – chained or shuttered, turned away from the world – except the girls themselves who shone coldly under the sodium street-lamps against the carbon-darkened walls. She opened her coat and undid another button on her blouse. This was no work for winter. She had not understood why the others persuaded their johns to take them in the back seats of their cars where they could never lie flat or straighten their legs but she saw now that at least they would be warm.

She had been at the brothel barely a week and she had made no effort to get to know any of the girls. Some of them had told her she should be softer. Tall Nina had said she should smile for her gentlemen friends and she had screamed at her to shut her fat mouth. Her anger and her pride and her vulnerability had fused into this bitter mass. She longed to be tender towards herself and the world but who would allow her that luxury now? She had ached for the same love that the world aches for and she had given herself as a child gives herself but she had known only taking and blaming. The only warmth she had ever felt was in the arms of men who would say whatever she needed to hear once they were sure she would allow them into her bed. And why should she disbelieve them if she no longer believed herself? If you say I am a whore then I am a whore.

At school they called her Lippy. She rarely laughed but others did when she told her stories or slipped her quiet jokes into the conversation. She would write books, she hoped. Nobody from her school had ever done that.

At fourteen the awkward rituals of courtship were at full tilt and she was kind to the boys in her life at a time when they needed confidence. The first afternoon she slept with Ryan was everything she had wished but she soon discovered she was pregnant and the hurried abortion put her in hospital for three weeks. She had wanted to hide it but the school found out and she was suspended. She was in a home at sixteen but her care officer played with her under the blankets and she sold herself to the older boys when they promised they would break his fingers if he did it again. They paid her with cigarettes; they never even took their clothes off. At seventeen she was released but her mother's new boyfriend came into her room and tried to kiss her. The following day she ran away and six weeks after that she found she was pregnant again. She went back to the boys at the home just to raise the money for the abortion but she miscarried in bed with Nicky Richards in the third month. Her old bed.

She had fucked her way in and she fucked her way out but at least she earned a living now. She lived alone on the outskirts of the vast city and she spent what little she had after rent and food on a thousand cosmetic treatments: body buffer, eye mask, leg wax, bikini cream, pore clarifier, skin-firming serum, foot-energising gel, cuticle softener and nail strengthener. On her days off she would sit in her room in her tumble-dried dressing-gown and purify herself. Heal the body and the mind will follow.

She had been paid nothing for her time with Lucas but she knew that what she had seen meant she could never go back. She owed a month's rent and she had neither money nor food and tonight she was on the same streets she had worked in her first week in the city. Her life was unspooling, running backwards, accelerating, unstoppable. Soon she would be in custody again. Then fifteen again and pregnant. Then twelve and back in her brother's bedroom with Simon Moffatt, holding her tummy in while he unbuttoned her brand-new jeans.

Tonight she wore nothing under the blouse and skirt and her legs were bare. She had used the last of her shampoo and she took her hair between her fingers and smelled it, enjoying the warm synthetic scent. She hated it when the men ran their sweaty hands through it, twisting and yanking as they came.

The others watched as she moved among them. She didn't recognise any of them from her time there but she knew turnover was quick. She knew, too, that territory was hard-earned and viciously guarded. She had hated the false cama-raderie of the brothel but here girls were knifed for working another's patch.

Rush hour was just starting – the busiest time – and she walked in the gutter sidestepping the cars as they wound through the one-way system. These roads went nowhere. Women from fourteen to fifty circled slowly on the old bridge beneath billboards selling financial advice and mineral water to those who cared to be neither prudent nor healthy. Some pretended respectability, hiding satin and lace beneath long coats that fell open as they leaned down to talk to the passing trade. Others risked arrest and hypothermia by exposing all they dared, the boots covering more than the clothes. A few dressed in jeans and jackets, relying on the walk and the level stare to mark them out from the innocent. And the men came in the dark cars, faces hidden behind reflections in the curved glass, driving one-handed, ties loosened, jackets hung on the back of the passenger seat. Windows were rolled down and the litany of transactions began, no different from any other trading floor.

Busy, my lovely?

What did you have in mind?

Company?

Do you go bareback?

Couldn't do it for thirty.

In the car?

I know somewhere near if you got another ten.

*

By the end of the evening the road was quiet. Most of the girls disappeared as the traffic died and Mara found a stretch where she could walk openly. Cars passed and slowed but she saw nothing, not the men nor the bridge nor the other girls as they stared. She thought about her book and she saw herself reading it aloud to the two girls she had lost sitting on her lap in pyjamas, their hair washed and brushed. She would find a job at a nursery so she could work in the afternoons. It would take time, but what else did she have? She would make fifty pounds tonight if she took two cars and as soon as she had paid her debts she would buy a notebook and proper pens – not like the ball-points from the clinic, but black fibre-tips – and she would begin her new life. Her real life.

When he slowed and pulled over he called out to her twice before she noticed. He was in his thirties, small but broad-shouldered, thinning. The car was clean but old. She didn't know the make but if she got in she would memorise the licence. He looked angry, probably because work had kept him late and he had arrived at the tail end of the evening when the best girls were gone.

Busy?

What are you after?

Nothing funny.

Thirty.

He shook his head but he waited.

Twenty-five.

He shook his head again and Mara turned away.

Get in then. But for twenty-five you better be sweet.

Mara looked around at the other girls to make sure someone had seen her leave but they were all so far away she couldn't tell.

He drove her quickly back over the canal and past the rows of workshops under the railway arches into a cul-de-sac filled with sheet metal and sleepers, braking too hard and skidding on the wet gravel. He took the folded notes from his back pocket and dropped them in her lap and climbed out of the car without even looking at her. A goods train passed, lurching noisily across worn points on its slow journey north. When it had gone the silence settled again and Mara could hear the change sliding in his pocket as he waited.

She walked around to the front and sat on the bonnet, enjoying the warmth through the thin skirt. She slipped her coat off and leaned back on her elbows. He had already loosened his belt and he stepped forward, arms crossed, waiting for her to come to him. She sat up again and slipped his trousers down around his hips and took him in her cold hands. He watched her without appetite or compassion. When he was almost hard enough she stretched the rubber over him and lay back, rolling the skirt up to her waist. He entered her quickly and pulled her down towards him to come deeper into her and he thrust raggedly as she struggled to stop herself from slipping. She reached out and pushed against him and he took her hands in his and crushed them to his chest. The car rocked and the gravel cried out softly beneath the tyres.

When he came he seemed disappointed. Her wrists hurt. He threw the condom into the darkness and wiped himself with a tissue folded in quarters like his money. She sat up and he ran a hand over the paintwork. When he was sure nothing had been harmed he pulled the coat from under her and held it open. She slipped her arms in and buttoned it tight. He climbed into the car and started it but by the time Mara had walked around to the passenger side he had thrown it into gear and dropped the lock on her door. She didn't try to follow him as he turned and pulled out into the side street and when she felt in her pocket to check for the money she knew already that it was gone.

¤

Carter walked the mile and a half from the estate to the meat market in twenty minutes, passing the button wholesalers and the jewellers and the refurbished warehouses with their fresh-painted freight gates and loading cranes that no longer swung because nobody needed to lift anything heavier than a card-board packing-case. A hundred years ago the managers and the clerks and the porters hurried to the suburbs at five every evening but now the sugar and the wines and the bolts of cloth had been sent to industrial estates at the mouth of the river and the merchants had moved in where their goods once belonged. Everyone wanted to live at the heart of the city.

He didn't know why he had come to the cold store to stare at Mercy's pictures any more than he knew why he had risen at dawn two days before to see Rose buried. He hadn't been to a gallery since his school trip twenty years before to see the por-traits of the kings and queens of England. He turned into the long colonnade as the first deliveries of the evening arrived in great articulated transports and the porters threw the doors open and the dark red ribs of the carcasses stretched behind them into darkness. He watched as they swung the bodies across their shoulders, no longer animals but not yet food. He remembered the first time he had hefted a corpse and struggled to balance the peculiar lifeless mass. A man unconscious is still easier than that dead weight.

*

The young woman gave him a pen to sign the visitors' book and offered him a porter's coat but he declined.

Do you know her work?

He nodded. Work. It wasn't the way he used the word.

We see it as more challenging than her recent pieces.

She meant it wasn't selling well but Carter had never learned to read between the lines. She looked at her watch.

We close at six.

He was the last visitor of the day. He stepped into the low silvery space and felt at once its coldness. His blurred reflection floated around him in the polished walls and he thought of his bedroom with its warm wood panels. He looked at each photograph in turn. Could he imagine her dead? He understood that she wanted to be provocative but he had no idea what he was supposed to feel. Now that the arts were the property of the media the world was saturated with images and everyone was familiar with Matisse and Rothko from the ads for shoes and emulsion paint even if they couldn't put a name to the palette. Carter had seen pictures he liked and pictures he didn't and he had a sense of what each was trying to show him but when he looked at Mercy he just saw Mercy – nothing transfigured and nothing revealed – and he didn't understand why the pictures were better in a steel tank lined with racks and hooks than they would be in a room with lights and a picture rail. Some part of him knew that these pictures had not been meant for him but he saw too that the woman in them was not the woman he knew.

The jetty was five minutes from the cold store. High tide was just past and the far bank was strangely close across the black water. Wind rippled the surface back towards the old cathedral, hiding the deeper currents as they ebbed east to the saltings. The soft swell lapped at the timber footings beneath him. He sat on the old steel ladder and thought of the crowds who had come that night to watch Mercy lie there in silence. And he thought of his own work, the measuring and marking and carving. We make because if we do not make we have nothing. We shout in caves and scratch our name in the rock. He thought of all the coffins he had built and how they would now be rotting, crumbling around the bodies in their soft silk linings, parched or waterlogged beneath six feet of mud and stone, the wood softening and falling away from nails and screws and glue. What would be left? Handles and bones.

The river at his feet seemed darker and more distant than the sky above, pale with the bloom of the city and streaked with satellites. He saw Mercy in the loose dress floating in the winter water, forcing her face down to drain the blood from the skin. She hung there like a child in a pool who has lost something she can no longer see and gropes for it blindly. Because she did not feel beautiful? Because she did not deserve to feel beautiful? Because she did not dare to feel beautiful? He did not know but he was beginning to see that her work was a question, not an answer. That she was not so sure of her life as she wished.

There was a telephone at the foot of the bridge and he found her number on the cab receipt in his wallet. She answered but she didn't recognise his voice at first and he wanted to say *You are beautiful* and hang up.

I saw the show.

When did you go?

I was there just now.

He wasn't sure why he had called. Mercy wanted to know if he had liked the pictures but she didn't ask him.

They're only letting us have the meat locker for a month.

It must have made people talk.

He was pleased she believed he understood these things but

he didn't know how to say what he thought about the work. That it hid her. They stood in silence for a moment.

I saw Brittney. The guy that owns the brothel broke Tanya's jaw.

Carter felt the anger surge through him.

They don't know where Mara went.

He thought Mercy might be crying but he couldn't tell.

This is so fucking ridiculous. They killed her. They killed a person and I can't do a thing.

Maybe it's time to tell someone.

They'll dig her up. They'll think it was me. There's no proof of anything any more.

She was crying. He had no idea what he could offer her.

What can I do?

Thanks. Nothing. Thanks. You took care of Rose for me. You did the most important thing.

Do you need me to come over?

It's OK. Thanks. I'm OK.

He could hear her breath slowing.

I liked the pictures.

When he rang off he asked himself why he had lied but it didn't feel wrong.

¤

The radio was playing Schubert's F minor *Fantasy* for four hands for the second time that week. Fairburn stared out of the kitchen window at his youngest son and daughter running in the private garden that linked the houses in the square, yelling soundlessly as they circled the chestnut tree. Something in the concord of the music and the slanting sunlight and children lost in their own laughter sent a wave of delight spiralling through him. He had known many kinds of pleasure in his life – the first kiss, the first bottle of La Mission-Haut-Brion '64, the first million – but these were material accomplishments. What shook him in these moments of joy was the possibility that the world might actually be a place worth embracing. That happiness was not a fiction and that goodness might endure.

He was a decent father but a rotten husband; his wife was a kept woman in that he paid for the privilege of not sleeping with her. Before they married they had been rapacious and he had taken her in her underwear in the changing room during the final fitting for her wedding dress. By the time they returned from the honeymoon they were down to once a week and within a month he had slept with one of the new girls in the legal department. He never made any attempt to cover his tracks or make excuses. The first time his wife had found a credit-card slip from one of his midday liaisons in his trouser pocket she had asked him what it was and he had replied without looking up at her: a hotel bill.

When she realised he had no intention of remaining faithful she had begun a series of affairs. She had a few lovers she cared for and enjoyed and with these she was discreet but there were some she slept with to provoke her husband and in these cases she made her adventures as obvious as possible. She gave herself to his chauffeur in the back of the car while they waited for him outside a restaurant and she made him keep his cap and gloves on. She had no trouble persuading executives whose companies Fairburn had dismantled to restore their wounded pride by bedding her and she always paid for the room on his credit card. When she finally saw he didn't care either way she gave it up and concentrated on screwing his bank account instead but he filled it faster than she could drain it. Fairburn himself was immune to the charms of reckless spending because he knew that the love of money is like any lust: once we possess it the attraction fades.

He didn't want to be rich any more than he wanted three perfect children or a baroque sex life – he simply wanted. He would order his walnut oil from three shippers at a time and use only the best pressing. He sent his brogues back to his shoe-makers once a month to be stripped and polished. His colognes were composed for him four times a year as the seasons changed. He saw that these were senseless rituals but he didn't know where else to look for purpose in his life. He found him-self driven to conquer, assimilate, expand and perfect everything he touched in the hope that something he did might tether him to a world which was otherwise random and sterile. He hardly existed at all except as an incarnation of his own desires, and every day those desires were satisfied they grew greater and more arcane.

Fairburn arrived at Bruno Cale's studio at exactly six that evening. Of the sculptors he admired he had chosen one who needed his money more than most for this commission, a man no longer young who knew his work was good but who had never toured his pieces in the cunningly-marketed art circuses that launched or crippled a career. The disused schoolroom was bare in a way that suggested poverty rather than fashionable asceticism: blocks of stone arranged by country of origin along the wall, unopened bills between the old radio and the kettle, milk on the ledge outside the window. It was in itself a perfect work of quiet desperation.

In the middle of the room stood a life-size study of a naked man in black Spanish marble, his weight thrown to one side as if staggering under some intolerable burden. His eyes were open but they stared at nothing. It was terrific: heroic and futile. Fairburn walked around it, trailing his fingers across the stone.

I may make the belly rougher.

He was right. There was something fluid about the texture of the surface that undercut the force of the piece.

You wanted him leaner but I don't think he should be skinny. But I will make the belly rougher.

He tended to repeat himself when he was nervous and Fairburn said nothing. They had agreed a deal where he would pay three times the going rate for the figure but only if he approved it; Bruno would have to gamble that he could deliver something spectacular. The work was already excellent and the details were academic now but he enjoyed the man's anxiety. He knew it wasn't the sculpture he wanted so much as the artist himself. To own his sweat and grief. He wanted him to have invested every ounce of his passion – the very thing Fairburn knew he lacked himself – in this tortured figure before he wrote the cheque and set it in his garden under the jasmine arch. The vision of agony would be the focus of brain-numbing small talk from the neighbours at their next summer party and he would invite Bruno to meet them and confront their inanities.

Bruno handed him the toothed chisel and a mallet still damp from the afternoon's work. How on earth did he work up a sweat in a room so cold? Most of the base had been carved away in a series of jagged waves but one corner sat untouched and Fairburn reached out to feel it rough and cool beneath his fingers.

How the hell am I supposed to knock this off?

You'll see. Hold the claw at the edge.

He turned the tool and laid it against the stone ready for the blow.

You don't have to grip it so hard—

He touched his white knuckles.

It's not as solid as it looks – just chalk reformed in the heat and force of the earth's movement. You're looking for the tiny cracks from where it was crushed. Planes of fracture.

It tripped off the tongue. He must have said it a thousand times to his students on their first morning. Fairburn lifted the hammer and brought it down on the burred crown of the chisel and the room rang with the metallic impact. The marble fell away easily and he felt a wave of pleasure at an action perfectly executed. An unspoken collaboration between himself and the stone.

You know what the Eskimo said when they asked him how he carved a polar bear from a block of ice. You just take the block and cut away all the bits that don't look like the bear.

Another story told a thousand times. Fairburn stood in front of the statue and looked into the vacant eyes and Rose stared back at him and his heart began to race again and he felt the chisel slip in his hand. He tried to remember if he had known she was dying in front of him breath by breath but it was not that pain that had seared itself into his memory. He knew men who loved to hurt and some of the girls made good money that way but that was not what drove him. He was mad for her now. She waited for him in that room and she alone could make his life complete because she understood his desire. He had made her his own and his dreams were her dreams and whatever he needed her to do she would do and she would want it more than he could believe possible. She had abandoned herself to him. This was his vision, and it haunted him.

It flickered at the corner of his mind in dull meetings and taunted him as he lay in bed with his wife but now Rose was with him every moment of the day and she was beginning to disorient him. He found himself trailing off in the middle of sentences and trying to remember why he had asked Eleanor to place calls for him. Twice he had forgotten the day of the week and once even the name of his own company.

He wanted to ask Bruno if he had ever fucked a woman like Rose but Bruno didn't look like he ever really fucked anyone and if he did it was probably just one of his rich provincial pupils, girls who never made it as far as university but who knew they would have to add a dash of artistic credibility to their conversation in an age where a modest talent for interior design was no longer a marriageable accomplishment. He imagined Bruno on the futon on the floor of his flat at midnight, lazily naked and smoking his pupil's last cigarette while the girl lay on the rug with her blouse still on trying to decide whether she had given herself with sufficient artistic integrity and whether she could legitimately claim the encounter as the inevitable collusion of two creative souls or just a drunken mistake.

You're a lucky man, Bruno.

Bruno thought he was going to pull out the cheque-book and his heart leaped.

You've nothing to worry about but your stone and your time.

And eleven manila envelopes over there by the kettle since September.

Fairburn tried to work out what the rent was on a place like this. Seventy-five pounds a week? Even with heat and light and materials and the flat and food and clothes it barely mounted into the hundreds. When he paid him these worries would fall away at once and Bruno would sit at the folding kitchen table already drunk on proper Russian vodka and fat from a steak with garlic bread and no vegetables and tear the bills open and write the cheques without a second glance at the disconnection notices. And the next morning – hangover notwithstanding – he would be free, solvent and ready to start again on whatever magnificent work he cared to dream up.

I'm jealous.

Let's swap.

Fairburn laughed for longer than he meant to. The thought that he might spend six months of his life hacking away at a five-hundredweight cube of Carrara with a mallet and punch in a freezing schoolroom for twenty thousand pounds struck him as surreal, as did the vision of Bruno at a boardroom table with marble dust in his hair cadging cigarettes from men who spent more on pressing their suits every day than Bruno did on food.

You just call me when that belly's right.

¤

Carter sat at the table in the kitchen to fill out the form. His handwriting was crude but he had taught himself to draw in order to plan his work and everything he wrote now was like a caption on a blueprint: artificially legible. The time of death he knew – or had been told – was shortly before ten in the evening. The place of death was a well-known club in Prentice Place. The cause of death was asphyxiation. Under the section that declared the death was from natural causes he wrote:

Not known.

Under the section for next of kin he wrote:

Not known.

Under the section stating the name of the deceased he wrote simply:

Rose.

He knew that as a licensed funeral director he could be fined for professional misconduct and that if Mercy were ever suspected of the murder he would automatically become an accomplice. But he thought of her and her strange brave pictures and of how she had already risked her life because she loved her friend and he signed and dated the certificate and fetched his coat to take it to the registrar.

It was nearly four in the morning and the city was in its deepest sleep. A few cars passed too fast in the deserted streets and he walked quickly, feeling the cold. He could not believe he was doing this. For five years he had struggled to build a life he could rely on, a life that owed nothing to anybody else for its comforts or its pain. He had established a business which paid his few bills and kept him occupied in a trade he loved and which allowed him to put aside his own lingering disquiet by easing the grief of others. He had achieved a measure of peace by retreating from the world into these reassuring routines and now he was about to deliver a document that would surely bring that world tearing back into his life. 'Convicted Killer Reports Mysterious Death'. He knew it would destroy everything he had salvaged but he knew also that he had no choice and he saw now that it was not for Mercy that he did it but for himself.

¤

Lucas sat at the bar in the middle of the afternoon cleaning his nails with a wooden cocktail stick. When he was satisfied he wiped the tip on his trousers and put it back in the glass on the counter. He was in a foul mood because it was Wednesday and he had forgotten to cut his fingernails the night before and now he would have to wait until the weekend. Like many who believe the world conspires against them Lucas was superstitious. His grandmother would sit him down with her sewing scissors each Monday evening and sing to him:

Cut them on Monday, you cut them for health;
Cut them on Tuesday, you cut them for wealth;
Cut them on Wednesday, you cut them for news;
Cut them on Thursday, a new pair of shoes;
Cut them on Friday, you cut them for sorrow;
Cut them on Saturday, see your true love tomorrow;
Cut them on Sunday, the devil will be with you all the week.

He no longer feared he would actually go to hell for it but the routine itself endured. Most people outgrew these beliefs when they accepted they had no basis in material fact but Lucas continued to cross his fingers if he passed someone on the stairs and he would never pick up a coin if it fell face down. If one of his extraordinarily long eyelashes fell out he would put it on the back of his hand to make a wish and throw it over his left shoulder. He cherished the irrational because in a world floodlit by logic he took a greater comfort in rhyme than reason. He had never loved the truth and he wanted to believe there was more to life than met his twilight-blue eye. He wanted to believe in a god of nails.

Frank Mayman called him on the private line, a privilege reserved for the big spenders or for those whose public profile meant that visits must be discreetly scheduled. The registrar had passed Carter's certificate on to the violent crime squad and it had landed on Mayman's desk. The last thing to arrive in his office with Lucas's name on it had been a stunning black girl of nineteen in a traffic-warden's uniform – a present to celebrate his promotion to detective inspector – so he had more than a professional interest in Lucas and his club.

The registrar asked if we needed to take a look at her but he doesn't know where the body is.

Christ. I can't believe you say she died. She seemed fine. A little the worse for wear.

More than worse, according to this.

I thought the girls had taken her home.

Witnesses?

One of the other girls was there. We're still looking for her.

And the john? Your man?

Lucas smiled apologetically even though he knew Mayman couldn't see his expression.

I'm pretty sure the name was made up. You know how it is with our visitors.

We'll have to send someone for prints.

I'm afraid our most enthusiastic maid cleaned the room when we closed. If I'd known it was this serious –

Was Carter there?

Carter?

Carter Stark, Coach House Lane, Oak Hill. The undertaker. He filed this last night.

Give me that again?

Lucas took a ball-point from his trouser pocket and reached for a cocktail napkin.

But he's stuck his neck out with this – he's already done six for manslaughter. And now an undertaker.

He laughed lazily and Lucas smiled politely.

Maybe I should talk to him.

I sent two of my plain-clothes men. I filled them in.

He could hear Mayman close the door to his office.

Without a body or a witness I might not be sure a crime had been committed at all, especially if the only evidence is a piece of paper from a convicted killer. If you think you can make some progress with your other girl I can try to hold the file in my desk for a while.

When he rang off Lucas drummed his fingers on the counter for joy: Mayman hadn't even asked to take a statement. But he knew now that he would have to kill Mara. As he crossed the landing to his office to call the traffic warden he was careful to tread in the middle of the broad oak floorboards. Step on a crack, break your mother's back.

¤

Carter was still in bed when the officers came, sooner even than he had thought possible. He dressed quickly and went downstairs, knowing that the fact that he had slept through the afternoon would count against him somehow. They stared around the workshop as they questioned him and he knew that the quiet dark space would count against him too.

Did you know the woman?

No. She was brought here by three friends.

Do you know any of their names?

They wouldn't tell me. They wanted a coffin and they paid me in cash. All I know is that Rose – that's what they called her – worked at a club in Prentice Place. It's a brothel.

Organised prostitution is illegal.

So is killing people.

He knew he shouldn't be flippant but something about the questions made him rise.

Why didn't you report it?

I reported it when I filed the certificate.

You must have known at the time that the death was suspicious.

It's been on my mind.

You accepted payment from the women without knowing who they were.

I made a coffin. I'm an undertaker.

You're an accessory to a murder.

To a suspicious death. I'm not a doctor. It looked to me like she had suffocated and I thought you'd send her to the coroner.

We would if we knew where she was.

When they drove away they didn't leave a number where he could call them and he realised they had never even identified themselves. They had made no effort to learn anything about

the circumstances of Rose's death. They had come to find a way
to Mercy.

¤

Mercy knew the night would be cold and she had no idea how
long she would be on the streets so she had opened all the
boxes in the small drawing room to look for the old army great-
coat she had bought at art school. She hardly ever came in here.
Even with the curtains tied back with heavy tassels the light
died as it fell through the thin window-panes. The dim chandelier cast its warm glow but it never chased the shadows from the
furthest corners and even though she stood twenty feet above
the pavement Mercy felt herself deep underground.

Most of the crates had never been labelled and she opened
them at random, finding clothes, books, tax records, old invitations and photographs. She reached for a picture taken with
some friends in the college bar and she tried to summon the
feeling of that long hair on her cheeks and shoulders. She stared
at herself across eleven years and she could not imagine that
young Mercy could have foreseen these dark rooms and this
shuffled mass of history – her future – and Rose's muddy grave
in the woods.

She looked through her first portfolio trying to recall the
names of photographers and girls from studios and hotels and
beaches long forgotten. The hair was already shorter and she
was beginning to grow into herself but she still saw the fierce
quick wit and the challenge in the eyes. At the time she had
been so vibrant and they all said she leaped off the page but
the pictures were fading and now she saw only anger. She had
been so desperate to make it all work on her terms and at every
step she had fought stylists and editors over trivial details that

compromised – so she thought – her hard-earned womanhood. Some admired her for it but few followed her example and she never won the battles without losing work.

Years later when she finally accepted she would never break the system from inside she could not see why she had felt the need to fight so hard. Her whole life had been a struggle with herself, an attempt to exploit her beauty without ever enjoying it. In the summer before Mercy went to college they would go to parties in Rose's sister's car and take turns putting on make-up in the rear-view mirror and Rose would stare at Mercy and wish for those full lips and dark eyes. All Mercy ever needed was lip gloss and eye-liner while Rose layered powder and blusher and eyeshadow and mascara and lip-liner. And yet when they walked together into rooms too dark to show their careful work every head would turn and Rose would laugh with delight and Mercy would look away because Rose knew how to be a woman and she drew men to her because that was what they loved.

What neither of them knew then is that we all mint our own emotional currency and what each of us pays or gains in love or in bed bears no relation to the deals struck by others. Nor did they know that Rose would earn her living for six years by sleeping with men for money and that on some days she would wake up and feel as free and vivid as she did the morning after her kiss with Jonathan Bailey but on others – worn to nothing by the queues of men who had slipped the folded notes under her pillow and groped her and looked straight through her – she would wonder if it might not be better to have had a mother like Mercy's who told her *Good girls keep their legs together*.

Mercy closed the book and moved the carton to the floor and opened the next. It was incredibly heavy and she thought it must be more photographs but it was part of her old collection of records. She flipped through them remembering parties and projects and deadlines when she had locked herself in her studio and unplugged the phone and played the same favourites over and over again. Elvis Costello's *My Aim is True*. Rose's father's original pressing of *Otis Blue*. Gluck's *Orfeo ed Eurydice* in a mono recording from 1947. She pulled out a handful and set them beside the door. She found videotapes, shoes and vases wrapped in newspaper, Christmas decorations and her favourite tarot cards but no more clothes. By the time night had fallen she had opened and closed every box but she never found the coat.

She stood on the bridge beneath the billboards as the cars weaved from girl to girl. She had asked some of them about Mara but few would even look at her: courtship here was urgent and their coy negotiations easily disturbed. She was an unknown quantity – not on the game, not a copper, not a slighted wife, not a social worker – and therefore unwelcome.

Mercy had built her career on the belief that everyone has the right to establish the terms of her own sexuality and she was careful not to judge these women as they walked from corner to corner under the gaze of the circling headlights but what she saw angered her and when the cars pulled in beside her she could not help herself:

Seems a shame to waste a lovely car like this on a fellow without a lady friend.

Seems a shame to waste it on you at all.

Want company, love?

Only human.

Do you do Greek?

If you want Greek you can fuck a kebab.

There was neither dignity nor eroticism – only sex parcelled out by the minute and the position. Brittney and Tanya and the others she had met at the brothel sold themselves with a skill – a degree of elegance – that made the act less overt but here the transaction was shameless. These women were not courtesans or call girls or ladies of the night; they were whores, and she was afraid of them.

It was the same awful unbelonging she had known at her first runway shows in Paris and Milan. She was intelligent and keen and her confidence was not swayed by flattery nor shaken by competition but there was something about these girls as they stared, naked but for their cigarettes and the champagne drunk from the bottle, that crushed her. Assistants ran from rail to rail dressing and undressing and redressing them and rushing them to the stage but she knew then that nothing will make you feel more vulnerable than a naked woman who looks right through you.

The night Mercy first slept with a boy – Anthony Stone, and enjoyed it – she cried with relief that this promised land was open to her too after everything her mother had warned. He thought he had hurt her and he held her tight and said *I'm sorry, I'm sorry* but she took his face in her hands and kissed and kissed and kissed him.

She was seventeen then but as she grew older and more confident she came to love her sexual freedom. Sometimes she would find herself in a strange kitchen cupping too-hot unwanted coffee and the old shame would begin to whisper but she would drive it away by dragging her date into his bed with an aggression that even she found shocking. She knew that the kind of pleasure promised in teenage magazines and Hollywood romances was a fiction but she played her roles with a knowing enthusiasm and although she never confused sex with love she asked herself where in all of this love might find room to grow.

There was a vogue among her student friends for copying

scenes from films but their confessions sounded more like reviews:

David and I finally did the bubbles scene from One and One. *With real champagne. We have to get another bottle before his parents find out.*

Have you tried it with your arse in the sink? Don't bother if he's not six foot.

You want to warm the butter first in the microwave.

It was a consumer Tantric sex, a coupling hallowed by the sacraments of luxury ice cream, designer underwear and silk sheets, and she loved it because making love and laughing was the greatest intimacy of all. But she doubted Mara had ever known these pleasures and she saw she feared these women because they could take a man into themselves and feel nothing. Did they have so little? Did they need so little?

She watched the cars climb the hill. Perhaps Rose's killer had been here. She tried to imagine his face behind the shifting gloss of the windshields but nothing resolved itself into any kind of physical presence and she realised it was not a man she wanted to find so much as a reason. Maybe not a man but all of these men.

¤

The lift doors opened and Lucas stepped into the vast white office. Fairburn was on the intercom to his managing director but he was too far away to eavesdrop. While he was still a teenage blackmailer he had invested some of his profits from the parking meter scam in a lip-reading course so he could keep an eye on victims when they slipped out to call their lovers from the old enclosed telephone boxes but he had never made it past labials and plosives. The story of his life.

He walked over to the window and stared down the world but it seemed to move infinitesimally slowly. The grand proportions of the surrounding buildings had been shaped from the vantage point of the squares and gardens below but anybody with money now lived and worked high above the noise and fumes and all they ever saw were incomprehensible inverted façades laced with pigeonwire and heating vents and burglar alarms. Only the poor – who stayed at ground level and walked everywhere – lived in the world these architects had dreamed.

He turned to the Hartung and saw the two long slashes in the canvas. He glanced at Fairburn to see if it was some kind of trick but he ignored him. He stared at the painting for as long as it took him to form the thought *They do those in the mental homes* but he was close enough to hear the conversation now and he put his hands on his hips in an attitude of hopeful appreciation.

What do we make if we go in with Balgowan?

Two three.

Fairburn didn't bother to write the figures down.

And they keep?

One five.

Just over fifty per cent.

Balgowan make one four on point eight. Seventy-five.

So we cashflow them and they open the fizz.

We'll get our share. Fifty's pretty good.

What happens if we say no?

House of cards. They'll never find anyone else by six tonight.

Fairburn glanced at his watch.

I'm not interested.

He released the button. Lucas had skipped the financial strategy section of his management course but he was fairly sure Fairburn had just turned down an instant profit of eight hundred thousand pounds on a no-risk collateral deal simply because he disliked the idea that their partner would make a greater return on a smaller investment. Instead of jumping ship he sank it. Lucas wondered if Fairburn still slept with his wife. He knew women found themselves aroused by men as they watched them bark orders to waiting staff or finesse negotiations between aggressive competitors and they longed to offer themselves as a reward for this manliness. He flushed as he imagined that marital intimacy. To the victor go the spoils, as his P.E. teacher used to say, with a mysterious wink. He told him of Mayman's call as casually as he could.

Somebody blew the whistle.

Fairburn nodded.

They know a girl was killed and they know it happened at my place.

Have they found the body?

No. And I don't think they're going to look too hard. Mayman's a client. He knows which side his bread is buttered so he'll keep it under his hat.

Fairburn supposed that mixing metaphors was an occupational hazard for those who lived by the euphemism.

Have you found Mara?

We found out where she went. I'll go over tonight.

Fairburn didn't know what he was supposed to say so he just smiled and Lucas felt fury rise in him. Didn't he see that he could throw him to Mayman if Mayman wouldn't bury Carter's certificate? That if Mara's death were ever connected with Rose it would point straight to Fairburn? He had come here to let him know that Mara was about to disappear but now he threw it out as a challenge, not a promise.

The only way Mayman could ever get to you is if Mara decides to talk.

But you said you were going to see her.

I thought maybe you'd like to come with me.

Lucas was delighted with his quick thinking. Maybe he could even make Fairburn kill her. Why not, since he had killed already? He would make sure he did it properly and he would help him dispose of her but that way they could never touch him.

I'm going to the opera and you know they always start at seven.

Lucas could hardly believe what he was hearing.

When are you going to fucking wake up to what's actually happening here?

Fairburn noted the split infinitive.

Don Giovanni, or *Il Dissoluto Punito*.

You killed one of my girls and I'm doing everything I know how to save your pretty arse and you're going to go to the fucking opera while I sort out your only witness.

Dell'empio che mi trasse al passo estremo qui attendo la vendetta. I await my revenge on the . . .

He shaped the phrase in his head, measuring the cadence as he translated.

I await my revenge on the wicked one who sent me to my death. Auden and Kallman give it as *assassin* but that's really just for the singers. They have quavers for two bars. I'm not making you go.

Too right you're not.

They stared at each other across the wide oak desk and suddenly Fairburn felt they were back in the playground. Lucas's hysterical garbled obscenities were no more a part of his life than Rose's death had been. He wasn't sure why he didn't care what happened now – all he knew was that he would never have Rose back and he would never find another way to the heart of his longing. Killing a woman who had seen it all changed nothing.

Lucas broke his gaze and turned away. He was wrestling air and he knew anyway that he would go to Mara. He had had enough of this madness and he was beginning to see that a man who could walk away from eight hundred thousand pounds and who would rather risk prison than disrupt a pleasant evening was probably not the most reliable accomplice in a murder. But even the unpredictable have their uses and Lucas knew that Mara would not be the end of it.

¤

Mercy swam through the corridors. The bulbs had been taken from the chandeliers and the dim shapes of the archways and carved columns appeared around her from nowhere. The cold glow of winter skies through white muslin bloomed softly at the windows but the brilliance only threw the rooms into deeper shadow. She stood for a moment and stared at the patterns of light and dark while far behind her in the bar Orfeo wept for the death of his bride.

She had never really believed she would find Mara but now she had tried and failed and she no longer had even that shade of hope to draw her on. A week ago her life had been so full she hardly had time to finish a pitta wrap in the back of a taxi while she checked the messages on her mobile and now she couldn't think of a single reason to leave the house. Her identity had been stripped to its barest components and there seemed no way to reassemble them. The world had called her many things:

Millennial icon.
Ball-busting spinster bitch.
Dutiful daughter.
Limo lesbian.
Bitter loser.
The voice of a generation.
Prissy little missy.
Best friend.
But none of them added up to anything she could describe

as Mercy and she recast herself as an alchemist siphoning gas from a great bell jar as she tried to discover which invisible elements of her being had been consumed by the noiseless flame inside.

She climbed the stairs again and she saw the thick wisps of dust rise and float in the darkness like seaweed in the swell of her passing and she felt a wave of revulsion. She knew that the tiny drifting clouds were strands of carpet and sheet torn free and flakes and scraps of human skin and she was suddenly surrounded by all the men and women who had ever met and undressed and sweated and cried out in these rooms. They pressed in on her, rising and settling wherever she stepped.

She went to the kitchen behind the bar but all she found was a bucket and a sponge and a broom and a bottle of spray detergent. She took them to the drawing room where the boxes lay and she forced the windows open in their heavy casements and began to beat the curtains with the broom. The heavy lined silk took the rage of her blows in slow motion and the dust spread in a grey haze, twisting in wild eddies about the lintels and cornices. She swung and swung again in her desperation and the dirt caught in her hair and her eyes and she smelled it sharp in her nostrils. Everywhere she was surrounded by death and she would beat the old walls and carpets until the whole place fell around her. She would obliterate her home as she had been obliterated and perhaps then when there was nothing left – no fighting or fear or dreaming and dissembling – she would know what remained of her. She beat the chairs and she smashed the chandelier swinging blindly and finally she stood before the mirror over the fire and she brought the broom down and watched as the space around her collapsed cupping her in its falling fragments and then she too was gone.

152

At first she thought the ring of the telephone was the echo of the glass on the floor and she was surprised it hung in the air for so long but there was nobody she wanted to talk to and she sat by the open window watching the light die in the sky. It rang again and then again and soon it was dark and she was stiff with cold and she listened to the sound of her breathing like the wind in the leafless trees. When it rang for the final time she answered it just to end the noise. It was Louise Parrish.

I found your Mara. She's in a squat in Albany Road.

Mercy was going to ask her why she had called – why she had changed her mind – but she had already hung up.

¤

It wasn't hard to tell which was the house. The terrace was respectable though the gardens were overgrown and most of the lower windows were barred. On the corner by the video shop was a double-fronted building set back from the road in a yard full of construction rubbish. The door had been reinforced with steel plates but the padlock had been smashed with a sledgehammer and the latch was a loop of wire and a stick.

Mercy wished she had brought a torch but she had never owned one. She heard footsteps on floorboards and she was going to call out but she was afraid she might startle her so she beat on the door with the flat of her hand and then again louder with her elbow. Now she could hear nothing but she pushed her way in and stood in the dark hallway. She hesitated to go further in case any of the planks were missing and she put her hand to the wall to feel her way along. It was wet. As her eyes grew used to the shadows she saw she was in the skeleton of a house stripped of doors and plasterboard and all that remained was a mass of pipes and beams and joists stretching away to the roof above. Only the ground floor was really there at all and it was so cold she might still have been outside. She saw there was nowhere for Mara to hide here and she realised she had been mistaken about the sounds but as she turned back towards the door she walked straight into her. Mara hit out at once with her fists, cursing her in a wild whisper and trying to push her against the wall. Mercy tried to tell her she had come to take her somewhere safer but Mara had her by the hair and forced her to the ground. Nails tore at her legs and she slipped sideways but Mara grabbed her and she could taste filthy fingers in her mouth. She was going to gag and she knew she should bite her to loose her grip but she dared not hurt her so she curled into a ball and cradled her head and as Mara kicked and kicked at her she shouted:

I know Rose. I took her.

She's dead! She died on the bed—

She kicked again but in that brief pause Mercy had rolled sideways and she forced herself up with her arms in front of her face for fear that she would run into a door frame or down the stairs. Mara threw herself at her again and Mercy felt the nails graze her neck but she could see light in the street through the open door now and she ran.

Mara watched from the doorway. She knew they would come for her but she had not expected a woman.

I'm not going back.

I'm not going to take you back.

Mercy waited at the gate.

If you tell me what happened we can find whoever did this.

She did not tell her she had no idea what they would do.

We can get you some kind of protection.

Mara thought of the protection she had known in the home and the hands under the bedclothes.

I'm going to leave you my number and some cash for a cab.

I live about half an hour from here and you can stay as long as you need.

She shrugged.

I was a friend. Her best friend.

Mara tried to remember what she knew of Rose. They had met in that room sitting on the bed and an hour later she was dead. Mercy left the note and the money under the tarpaulin on a pile of bricks.

You should come with me.

I'm OK. I can look after myself.

She watched Mercy cross the street and climb into the car without looking back. It wouldn't start straight away and in the stutter of the motor she ran down the steps and through the gate and she caught her as she was turning out into the main road.

She spent the journey playing through the cassettes on the floor of Mercy's car. She was strangely relaxed. She said it was a classic collection but Mercy didn't dare admit that they were the most recent albums she owned. She wanted to know how much older she was than Mara and when they stopped at the next intersection she turned to look at her under the red glow of the traffic light. Nineteen? Twenty? She thought of herself just starting to model, full of the self-certainty of a woman who knows what she thinks of the world but who knows nothing of the world itself. She thought of Rose and she wanted to ask if they had been friends. She rubbed at the scratch on her neck.

Sorry. At least I never keep them long.

She kissed her fingers and reached out to touch her.

¤

Mercy had made up a bed in the first room off the hallway and she ran a deep bath while Mara undressed. She already knew she was in a brothel but when she saw the Correction Room full of soaps and oils she giggled. She carried the towel and the old dressing gown but she came naked and she sat on the side of the bath as the steam curled up around her and Mercy saw that her body was even younger than her face. And yet she used it. Her lack of self-consciousness made Mercy blush and she told Mara to climb in while she fetched something to drink.

Do you know what I love?

Mercy shook her head.

Whisky and Coke.

I've got whisky.

Ginger ale?

Sorry.

OK.

When Mercy came back she was submerged and her heart leaped but her eyes were open and she winked at her beneath the surface. After a moment she rose up and took a gasp of breath as the water slopped over the sides.

Sorry. I used to do a minute and twenty seconds. How long was that?

I wasn't here when you went under.

I love this bath. I saw one like this in a magazine and we rung up to see what it cost but they said seven hundred pounds.

She took the glass and dipped a finger in.

Do you know what they call the lines on the sides?

What?

Legs. The same with brandy. I knew a man who sold whisky. He was older but he taught me a lot about drinking. They're all older.

She looked at Mercy, unsure if she should say it.

I mean, you don't pay for it if you're my age, do you?

She drained her glass.

Will you wash my hair?

What do you like?

She opened the cupboard.

Fuck sake! How often do you wash it?

I was a model.

Are you famous?

When I was your age. Maybe. What's famous?

When people know who you are.

Do you know who I am?

Mercy.

So I'm not famous.

But you were.

I was on a few covers.

That must be so fantastic. You choose.

Mercy asked about her hair and Mara said she wanted something that wouldn't fade the colour because she had only had it done two weeks ago. She could usually last two months between appointments because she was dark anyway. They chose something with fruit in it and Mara lay back while Mercy washed it in silence.

Mercy put her in bed and said she'd leave the light on and to help herself to whatever she wanted and Mara asked if she could have another whisky. She brought it and Mara told her she could sit while she drank it. After a while she put the glass down on the floor and she asked Mercy without looking at her:

You must really love her if you let me hit you like that and you let me stay.

Mercy nodded.

We were friends since we were nine. She was older.

How old are you?

Twenty-nine.

That's not old.

She began to cry. Mercy took her hand and stroked it.

She didn't want me to do it.

Mercy said nothing.

I thought he was OK. He wasn't old. Older than you. In a suit. I know he was rich. We asked him what he wanted – Rose asked him. She was nice with him. He said he didn't know so she went to him and she started to try to take his tie off but he didn't seem that interested. She kissed him and he closed his eyes but it wasn't really working so she whispered to him but I could hear.

Do you like to see two girls play?

Do you like to play?

And she said she did and she looked at me. It was fine by me. I was going to get a hundred and fifty. So we played, girl to girl. I never know why they like that so much but it's better than having them in you so I never mind. And she was good. She put a lot into it but I knew it was for him really. She asked me one time when he couldn't see if I was OK and I said it was fine. But then he took out his wallet and he got the money and he crushed it into a ball like he was going to throw it away and he dropped it on the floor but I could tell it was a lot. He said he wanted to see something he'd never seen before so we stopped but it was hard because Rose and I didn't really know each other and we didn't know what we were both happy to do. You don't want to do anything the other girl doesn't like but you can't really talk with them there. And the whole time he just sat there in the chair. And he wasn't even looking at us. So he picked the money up off the carpet and put it on the table and he opened it up and made it flat with his hand and I could see there was the three hundred and he still had his wallet there and he put out two more fifties.

She looked up at Mercy and shook her head because she just didn't understand.

Rose went to him and she sat across his lap but he didn't even touch her and she asked him again:

Would you like us to tie you to this big old bed and have our wicked way with you?

And he looked at her and I thought that's what he wanted but he just said:

Do you like to be tied?

And she looked at me and then she kissed him and said:

Let's do it, mister.

And I know she just wanted to get it finished and she only said that because she knew she was safe with another girl there.

She rolled away.

So I tied her. With my stockings and hers and she was kneeling on the bed and I made sure nothing was too tight. I made sure.

Mercy nodded. She was looking at Mara but all she could see was Rose naked on that bed.

And I thought he wanted me to go to her or else he would come too but he told me to come to him. He stood and he opened his trousers and he wanted me to take him in my mouth.

She hesitated.

Why do they love that so much?

She had no answer.

And I did it. I can do that. And I looked at Rose and she nodded at me and I thought if I can get him off like this then we'll be done in ten minutes. And he was watching her and he felt as if it was good and then she started to talk to him. Because I couldn't.

What did she say?

She was trying to keep him hot. You know the thing. Come and get it, that's how I like it. Like giving a big old dog his dinner. But he kept looking at her and I didn't know what was wrong because it was like I wasn't there. I gave him everything I knew because I wanted him to be done but it was like he wanted me to be her. And she kept on talking to him, all the hot stuff, and then he said:

Make her shut up.

And I couldn't talk if you know what I mean but he said it again.

Shut her up.

And she looked at him like he was shit on her shoe but I knew he was so hard. And I looked at her and she was OK. Just angry. If she hadn't been tied she'd have smacked him, I know it.

What did you do?

Mercy could see it now.

I used my dress. There wasn't anything else. I just tied it round her mouth. And I went back so I could finish him while he was still close. I was going to finish him so we could go home. And he was standing again and he put his hands in my hair and I looked up at him and he was staring at her and I was getting tired but I tried to keep going.

Mercy had let her hand slip free.

I heard something from her and I was worrying she was hurting but I couldn't look round and he twisted my hair and he said:

That's good. She's good.

And I thought if I can bring him off soon we can all finish. That's all I could think about. He knew I was worried about her and he kept saying in a slow voice:

She's OK, she's good.

And I believed him. I believed him because I just wanted to go home and Rose said it was OK. She said it was OK.

She had no more tears now.

And finally he was done and he sat down and I went to her to let her free. I wanted her to be proud that I had done it and we could go. I went to her and I put my arms around her but she wasn't breathing.

She put her arms around Mercy and she could feel her shake as the tears fell on her soft hands.

They sat there for a long while and eventually Mara slept. Mercy knew there was nothing to forgive. Right now she had no more feelings – anger and grief and love had exhausted themselves in the struggle to claim her – and in the silence they left her mind moved slowly trying to make sense of what she knew.

It had taken her so long to find Mara and learn what had happened but now she had listened she could not bring herself to believe it. Death was so careless and thunder did not roll and yet that empty room still rang with fear and confusion and guilt. No death without guilt. But she was sure she had not heard the truth and would not know it until she had seen it in the face of the man who had watched her friend die.

Perhaps now she had brought Mara here they would take his description to the girls and one of them would recognise him. Perhaps the name they knew him by would not be an invention to protect his private life. Perhaps they would find him and the police would bring charges despite the fact that there was no proof of any crime and perhaps some remarkable piece of evidence would be discovered on his clothes or under his fingernails and he would be brought to trial and punished.

Except that he had not touched her.

And the rainwater sinking through roots and stones was swelling the joints of the unvarnished coffin and even now Rose was melting back into the earth.

She took the whisky and went to the drawing room she had destroyed. Already she sensed she was calmer there and she sat in the dark among the broken chairs and fallen curtains and drank from the bottle. She lay back on the floor and watched the lights from the cars arc across the ceiling. The window was closed and the room was still but the fragments of the chandelier turned slowly in the moving beams. The glass hung above her in its shattered constellation and she closed her eyes and the bright points merged into soft circles hovering in the darkness and she longed to float free with them.

¤

The bar at the opera house was overflowing and Richard Strathmore held the drinks above his head as he forced his way to the balcony overlooking the piazza. The cigarette in the corner of his mouth uncurled its bitter smoke and his eyes watered.

Fairburn leaned on the balustrade as he watched the tourists drift in and out of the bright shops lining the old market galleries. These people – this city, this theatre, these painted sets – were the backdrop to his life but he did not feel connected to them in any way. He had never felt connected and he was sure he did not feel the same things as they did. He shifted his weight on the cold curve of the stone and he was suddenly aware of a space between himself and the ground forty feet below exactly the shape of a falling body. If he leaned a little further out and felt himself slip to the carefully relaid cobblestones his life would be over in a second. All of our most piercing pleasures are brief, he realised. Perhaps that was why we chase them so desperately.

Richard arrived with a single whisky and too much ice.

Why do they come in their herds to visit a world capital that has everything from Duccio's *Maestà* to the *Latex Lobby* when all they want to do when they get here is wave their credit cards in shops that have branches in their own high streets?

Why do they spend two hundred million pounds refurbishing the grandest theatre in the country and still serve quarter-pint bottles of pasteurised orange juice that tastes of brass polish?

He took the glass.

Serves you right for sticking to the soft stuff.

The production is terrible.

I just close my eyes and listen to Sardelli's Zerlina.

Who could blame the Don for trying to drag her into the summer-house to have his wicked way?

I've been thinking about it all evening. *Batti, batti, o bel Masetto—*

Richard finished his cigarette and dropped it in the empty bottle where it died with a hiss.

I want to buy one of Mercy's pictures.

Terrific. You could have had your pick if you'd told me sooner.

The last I heard of it there were still six going.

We don't sell to just anybody.

Who are you hoping to flatter – me or you?

Richard laughed.

I don't want any of the ones from the show.

There aren't any others.

Mercy told me she took hundreds.

I've still got them. But they're not for sale. They're not even in the catalogue.

What do they sell for?

To you, sir – ten thousand.

To me?

Museums and foundations get favourable terms. Madam insists.

Ten is fine.

He shook his head.

You're turning down ten thousand pounds for a picture that's already been taken that nobody else is ever going to see?

That's what I do.

If you let me take my pick and print it just as you did with the others I'll write a cheque for ten times her asking price.

Richard said nothing. He knew she trusted him and a sale like this would push up the price of everything else in the show.

Are you trying to make me an offer I can't refuse?

Let me choose one before you tell her.

What if she says no?

To the deal or the picture?

Either.

Fairburn shrugged. The bell for the second act rang again and they walked back to the stairs.

The deal's a deal. She doesn't get to see the picture until it's mine.

I'd need to let the press know. If we can use this I think I can persuade her.

I don't want to do publicity.

How shalt thou hope for Mercy, rendering none?

¤

Lucas lay in the whirlpool bath in his flat above the brothel washing his hair. He always followed the instructions on the bottle carefully and he let the foam sit for two full minutes before rinsing. He had asked the bar to send up a vodka and tonic and he fished the ice out with his fingers and dropped it into the water as he waited. Usually he preferred a shower – to wake himself up – but tonight as he waited for Mara the cold had crept into him and he needed to settle himself before he went downstairs to welcome Mayman.

He had found the door to the squat open and Mara's bag was still there but he was sure she was gone. Somebody must have known he was planning to pay her a visit. He mistrusted his girls as he mistrusted all women – how can you rely on what you cannot fathom? – and he had been careful not to let them know he had found her. He had only mentioned it to Fairburn and the idea that he had been betrayed by a man whose crime he was trying to cover up angered him beyond imagining. His life in its various incarnations as a crook had been based on the idiotic idea of honour among thieves, largely because it offered a measure of bonding in a masculine world where he already felt himself marginalised. But everything he had built to shore his sense of self – redeemable favours, lazy threats, mean displays of power – collapsed in the face of Fairburn's indifference to the rituals of territorial aggression. The man had no sense of debt or even of fear and it left Lucas impotent.

He thought of the dog pissing on his steps, balls swinging lazily. Even the word mastiff sounded obscene. He looked down at himself in the cloudy water and spread his legs. He was not a small man but he was surrounded by clients who boasted of their size and stamina and the girls liked to confirm their outrageous claims to discomfort him. The cold and the alcohol coursed through him and he suddenly wanted to urinate but he found himself too lazy to climb out of the bath and to his surprise he let himself relax in the warm water and he watched the soft yellow cloud loop and billow. So different from the noisy directed stream he loved in its tumble into the china bowl.

A storm in a teacup.

He could hear his grandmother's voice across thirty years.

Do it on the side. And put the seat down when you've done.

Tina called up on the security radio to tell him Mayman had arrived. He reached for a towel and wondered if he should ask him what his men had learned from Carter but he knew Mayman would want to know about Mara and he decided it would be better to ignore it and offer the evening as a simple gift. Claudine – the traffic warden – was already waiting in the Silver Suite.

Anger still swelled in him. Who had stolen the body? Who knew about Fairburn? Who had beaten him to Mara? He thought of Carter and he knew he would have to find his own answers now. Either the undertaker was a cheeky cunt or he was too dim to see that Lucas had tamed Mayman. Either way, he needed a little loosening up. Certainly more than Mayman's men would have been able to do. He knew that visiting him was risky but he needed something now to restore his confidence and violence was a way for him to place himself in a world that was changing faster than he could comprehend. The thought of hurting Carter calmed him and when he greeted Mayman at the bar he ordered a bottle of the good champagne.

¤

When Mercy woke she was frozen. It was late morning and she felt guilty she had slept so long even though she had no reason to rise. The carpet was damp and she thought it was because she had lain on it all night but when she went to her room to fetch a sweater the smell was stronger and the hall was filled with steam. She remembered Mara and there was so much more she wanted to ask her and she could hear the running water and she went to the Correction Room. The heavy gate was closed and she could not see her at first and she thought she was holding her breath again beneath the surface. Mercy called out but Mara did not turn. She lay in the tub with the taps open and the bath was overflowing onto the floor in a cascade of crimson and beneath the bubbles Mercy saw the water too was darkening. She began to scream and her cry was full of fear and anger.

She shook the gate but it would not open and she saw the hairdressing scissors on the floor and beside it the key. Mara tried to move her head but she had slumped down too far and she just lifted a hand out of the water and Mercy saw the appalling slice from thumb to elbow. She had never imagined the blood could be so bright. She ran to the cloakroom and the thick wet carpet was like paste under her bare feet and it sucked at her as she went.

She found the cabinet where they had kept the keys and she saw the neat rows of numbers printed on the ivory discs but the list inside the door was gone and she had no idea how to make sense of them. She pulled up her skirt to make a pouch as she had when she and Rose had taken the apples and she dropped the keys into it one by one, hardly breathing as she slid them round the brass curve. Death watched her as she twisted them free with agonising slowness but she dared not break her concentration to turn and curse him now.

She could hear Mara talking and at last she had them all and she ran back cradling her load, surprised at its weight. She spread the keys on the floor and tried them one after the other, sliding them home and twisting them in the old dry lock waiting for the tumblers to lift.

He said she was OK.

Her hair trailed over the edge of the bath and the dark strands clung together as the water flowed around them. The deep-dyed black had been softened by the blood to a dull brown.

He wanted me to leave her be. How could he know? I didn't know.

Her voice was almost too quiet to hear.

You know some of them hate you. You can tell. I feel sick if I hurt someone. He didn't seem like a hater. We would have known. Do you think he knew?

Mercy stared at the lock and it filled her vision, a massive cylinder of brass with its lightning-strike cleft. She saw herself deep inside it throwing the levers and rolling the barrel as the latch drew back.

They're all married, aren't they? They have a girl. You can tell. He was rich and good-looking. He was very good-looking. I know he had a beautiful wife at home. Sorry darling, I had a meeting. Why would he want to fuck me? I'm not a meeting.

She fell silent and Mercy was desperate to hear her voice again like a heartbeat. She let her hand hover over the pile, willing one to choose itself and leap to her.

If I loved someone I wouldn't do this. If I had someone who loved me they wouldn't let me do this.

Mercy's heart lurched at the words. The hall shimmered with the keys she had tried and thrown aside.

I wouldn't waste my body if I had my children. I'd keep it for them.

She could hardly hear her.

They don't make love, do they? They don't make anything. They just bash and grind at you. I don't feel it now.

Mercy didn't know whether she meant the lovers or the gashes in her slender wrists. She knew her blood would not clot if the wounds were in water and she would lose consciousness slowly but Mara's words did not soften. In her death as in her life her tenderness destroyed her.

By the time Mercy found a key to open the gate Mara had fallen sideways and her face had slipped beneath the surface. Her heart had ceased to pump the blood from her pale arms and the water was already clearing. Mercy shut the taps off and reached for a towel as she pulled Mara up and cradled her in her lap. She was warm from the bath but her face was white and Mercy stroked her hair with her fingers until it lay straight again because she knew she was proud of it.

She took her to the bed she had made and laid her on her

back and drew the covers up but she did not want to touch her eyes to close them so she rolled her onto her side and brought her hands up to her chin. She looked calmer like that. This time she did not sit with her but when she went out into the hall she left the light on and the door open and when she went to fetch her coat she walked on a path of golden keys.

¤

Carter had just finished breakfast when he heard them. It was nine o'clock in the evening but he often had callers now. Sometimes the knock was patient, sometimes full of fury. Who knows how to announce a death? He took the plates to the sink so the table would be clear for them to sit in silence or to tell him what they needed or just to cry. Then he put on his black jacket and went down through the workshop.

It was exactly twelve years since he had found his father in the stairwell. All Souls' Day: *Pray for the faithful departed.* He was eighteen and every morning after he had called in at the employment agency he would take off his tie and roll it and put it in the pocket of his father's jacket and walk for miles across the city. That day he had set out north past the locksmiths and the antique forgers towards the marshes. The blue sky was icy but the sun was warm enough and some sat on the broad pavement with lips pursed full of upholstery pins while others punched seat-rails with needle files to create the heritage of woodworm. He passed the factory where his father had worked but nothing had changed. The wide brick building with its tiers of shattered skylights had not been modernised nor torn down nor refurbished as a complex of studio apartments but simply

abandoned and he did not know how eight years of mere emptiness could destroy a building that had stood a century of sweat.

As darkness fell and curtains were drawn he felt the world
turn away from him and he retraced his steps to the flat. The
door was open but his father was gone and he went to the pub
to bring him home again but the lift was out of service and he
took the stairs at the far end and he found him lying at the
bottom beside the refuse chute with the beer glass in his hand.
It had not broken in the fall and he did not look hurt but he was
already too stiff to carry without help. Nobody had seen him
and nobody knew if it was an accident or suicide or whether
somebody had wanted the change he carried to pay for his pint.
His pockets were empty. The police asked Carter if anybody
could have wanted to harm him but he knew his father had not
been killed nor had he taken his own life. He had simply worn
away to nothing like an old blade.

Carter switched on the light and stepped out into the yard. He
hadn't noticed that it had rained. He saw the car parked with
the engine running and the doors open and he turned to look
down the alley but the first punch hit him before he could tell
who was there. He fell against the wall and tried to run but his
legs were pulled from under him and he landed in the gutter. He
felt a boot on the back of his head and the metal heel-plate cold
on his neck. The voice was close and quiet.

Where's your girl?

He didn't know whether they wanted Mercy or Rose.

They took her away.

Where is she now?

I don't know.

That's the last time you'll tell me that.

The foot pressed down harder and his jaw slipped in its
socket.

Who took her?

Who needs to know?

A second man swung a kick at the base of his spine and his body arched in a reflex of pain. Adrenaline raced through him and he was already light-headed. His forehead was open from nose to temple and the blood poured into his eyes. He raised his free hand in defeat and they hauled him up with his hair. He let himself go slack and they stumbled under his dead weight and as they lost their grip he kicked upwards with his legs and caught one of them on the side of the head and he rolled away. He brought his arms down just in time to block the punch and trapped a hand between his face and his shoulder and he could smell sweet soap. He spun the man and let him fall as the other took him by the arm. He kicked backwards and caught a kneecap and the man behind went down screaming and he dropped at once with his knee to the first man's throat. He was older than Carter and heavier but he was slow now. Carter leaned down.

Who needs to know?

He heard the door slam behind him and the car began to move. It rolled towards them and they tripped over each other as they struggled to stand. The headlights swept across them and Carter's vision dissolved in a crimson halo of blood and sweat. He crouched by the wall as the car shunted the kerb and leaped at him and he was surprised at the smoothness of the metal against his chest as it forced him to the wet brick and then it crushed him and the fender tore his shin and he fell in a cloud of exhaust and spray and he heard his head hit the ground.

The bar was silver with smoke. Carter was nineteen and he was drunk. His father had accommodated himself to the steady corrosion of beer in the day and whisky at night but his own young liver was buckling under the shock of malnutrition and alcohol. In the nine months since he had found the body in the stairwell his skin had become smooth and yellow and he could feel his teeth moving in his mouth if he ate anything tougher than toast. Every time he raised a glass he thought of his father and every time he drained it he hoped he would obliterate the memory. Not the memory of the man he had loved but the memory of living with a ghost all those years before he died.

He knew some of the faces. It was the only bar still open and everybody from the estate drank there while they still had money. Beside the cigarette machine was a hatch to the pump room where the landlord's daughter would cash social-security cheques for a five per cent cut. They took the other ninety-five per cent over the counter and the only concession they made to their customers was that they served the cheapest alcohol in the city. On Thursday and Friday, when pay packets were running low, they brewed the house cocktail – the *Sugar Shot* – from fermented molasses and sold it at a pound a pint. It was seventy proof without the lemonade or Coke. The walls were the pale green of a police cell and the windows were barred on both sides and the floor was unvarnished wood and the beer that was spilled every night swelled the grain in long splintered ripples. Carter still had the scar on his cheek.

He didn't start the fight and he didn't understand why he had walked into it. It blew up around him like a storm but perhaps he had been waiting there each night for it to come. He sat on the low bench by the door listening to the others talk but there was nothing but noise. He held his beer in his lap. A girl in a long white coat threw her cigarette on the floor and ground it out with her shoe. Her belt was looped behind her and when she turned it swung in his face. It was Wednesday now and he wouldn't have money again for two days.

He heard the shouts and the crowd stirred as the men stood up and he climbed on the bench to watch. He could see their backs dip and sway as they struck out at each other but they were drunk and one of them toppled a table and soon there were five swinging and ducking. The chairs were chained to the floor so they couldn't be thrown but they lay sideways and upside down and everywhere the men moved they were snarled up in them. Some of the drinkers put their glasses in their pockets and left at once and the others moved back to make room. The landlord had called the police but brawls here were pretty regular and the squad cars rarely bothered to switch on their sirens if they came.

Carter stepped down from the bench and walked to one of the tables in the middle of the fight. His glass was still full and he put it down carefully. The men raged around him, dim and colourless in the haze of heat and smoke. Their anger had outgrown whatever slight had fired it – some late paid debt or jibe – and now they fought simply because the momentum of violence was irresistible.

The smallest of them had a knife and he moved to cut one of them from behind. Another saw the blade and he called out and a third took a screwdriver from his pocket. Now there would be winners and losers. The last onlookers had disappeared but Carter was transfixed as the men moved quickly now, skittish. The biggest of them was caught in the centre and he backed away and when he saw Carter's glass he picked it up and smashed it on the edge of the table for a weapon of his own. The beer fell in an arc of gold and Carter reached out by some instinct and he felt it wet on his fingers as it curled down to the floor. He was up in a second and had the man in an arm-lock while he hooked a leg around him to bring him over but when they fell together Carter was underneath and he fought to catch his breath. The glass lay beside them and he rolled on his hip and kicked it out of reach and it spun away under the tables. His hair lay in the remains of his own drink and there would be nothing now until Friday when he brought the cheque directly here. He would start with beer again but he would order two so the second would be ready as soon as the first was gone. The man hit him open-handed and Carter caught the fingers and forced them back and he felt the knuckles separate. He screamed and Carter kicked him between the legs but he had Carter's foot and twisted him down across the fallen furniture. Carter struggled to stand again but he was caught in the chairs and the chains and whatever he held to steady himself made him stumble again. They were separated by the table and they watched each other for a moment.

Carter still had his coat on. The man wore chinos and a white shirt and beneath the beer and sweat Carter saw the freshly ironed creases. The face was heavy with alcohol. Carter was almost as big but he wasn't thinking about winning. Just fighting. He realised he had no idea of this man's name and instead of asking he told him his own.

I'm Carter Stark.

Good night, Carter.

They threw themselves in the same moment and he took Carter down and they fell with their arms pinning each other and a shocking pain burst in Carter's shoulder and raced out through his body. They could do nothing but bite as they lay face to face and when they found each other's mouth it was like a wild sinister kiss. Teeth ground against teeth and Carter caught the man's lip and the man rolled back and tried to break free but his head was between the chairs and neither of them saw the chain. He couldn't stand and he brought his hands quickly to his throat but Carter was already up. His arm hung useless by his side so he landed a terrible kick to his belly and as the man rolled away his head jerked back and his neck gave a dry crack and Carter saw the urine darken his pale trousers.

¤

174

Fairburn's driver double-parked at the foot of the steps to the white colonnaded church beside the city's celebrated art gallery. He put his cap on and opened the door and as they climbed out Sarah trailed her gloved hand across his crotch. She had laughed at how ridiculous he had looked with the tight-cut grey trousers around his ankles on the back seat panting like a dog and calling her *ma'am* at the same time. Fairburn saw her touch him and he was tempted to do the same but he doubted the man had the humour to appreciate it.

He hated charity galas. It wasn't the donations – which he made happily – so much as the inanity of the hosts and the philistinism of the rich who were invited. His wife had joined the committee of a dozen good causes to appease her guilt about his wealth and he referred to her fund-raising activities as Fawning and Yawning. He looked around the balconies at the rows of dazzling young women on the arms of expensively tailored, poorly maintained men with nothing to offer but their wallet. Certainly not their packet, as the girls in the office would say. It was a decadent mutation of the mating game that these women had slept their way to a fortune and now they were persuading their husbands to give it away to strangers; proof, he saw, that sex and money were instinctively partners, tools in the same exchange of energy and rooted in the same well of desire. And these women were more ruthless and skilful than any of the girls in Lucas's stable. They were hardcore.

He stared at the backless dresses and the silky scented golden hair everywhere around him and he found his mind flashing with fragments of sexual encounters free of court-ship or foreplay. Some of his most powerful memories were of women he had never even met, faces shadowed in taxis or shoulders turned away across a crowded lobby. The girl selling programmes below had her hair pulled back from her forehead and her eyes were too big but it gave her a willing, open look and Fairburn imagined her on all fours on her bed with her legs wide apart and her dark skirt thrown up around her waist. The woman in the high raked seats behind them reached for something in her bag and as her skinny legs uncrossed themselves he saw her naked at the foot of the stairs with arms outstretched, her body awkward and attractively angular. She begged him to come to her. These women were everywhere in his mind and he wanted to ask them if they knew how men dreamed them into worlds they knew nothing of. How their identities were no longer their own.

The candle-lit concert closed with the Mozart requiem and as the strings began their lilting dead march he scanned the programme notes. Nowadays every performance was marketed as a *tour de force* of scholarly reinvention as conductors battled to carry the true flame of a composer's vision to a public dazed with a hundred recordings of every work. He noticed tonight that although the players went uncredited the makers of the instruments were listed according to their desks:

FIRST VIOLINS:
JACOBUS STAINER, VIENNA, 1665
JOSEF LEIDOLFF, VIENNA, 1709
VINCENZO RUGGIERO, CREMONA, 1699
JOHANN CHRISTOPH LEIDOLFF, VIENNA, 1748

The pointless erudition and the pomposity of it all delighted him and he laughed out loud during the soprano's first entry. He only ever heard Latin at funerals now but he still had the ear for it and as the chorus fumbled their way through the *Dies irae,* the perfect rabble-rouser for a godless age, he began to translate the mass to himself.

Requiem aeternam dona eis, Domine.

Everlasting rest give unto them, O Lord. Even as a child day-dreaming through interminable chapel services he had been captivated by that promise of peace, of freedom and release. *This is my rest for ever; here will I dwell; for I have desired it.* He wanted not to have to care about anything ever again. He craved silence.

The *Tuba mirum* always brought a frisson to the hall and he looked up to see that the trombone solo was given by a tall blonde woman in a sleeveless black dress. Rows of wives suddenly found blemishes in their nail varnish as their husbands shifted forward to study her embouchure. He thought of Rose on her knees staring up at him as he heard the words:

Oro supplex et acclinis –

On my knees in submission I beg you. It wasn't that she had been tied. It wasn't the hair hanging loose and the curve of the belly as it drew his eye to the parting of her long legs. It was just the look that said *I'd rather die than fuck you.* And the knowledge that he would fuck her. He did not hate her and he did not want to harm her but the lust itself had been self-sufficient and quite separate from the woman on the bed before him. He remembered that pitch of excitement, the electric charge in every cell in his body. Desire is not a judgment but a condition and he saw that it drew him inexorably back to the physical world and fixed him here when all he craved was oblivion, an effortless emptiness without the grinding after-effects of alcohol or cocaine or sexual self-indulgence. He wanted to dissolve himself in the anonymity of eternity but the instinct of desire constantly overcame him. It filled him like his own breath and as soon as he could exorcise it it filled him again. He had been destroyed by his own

hunger and he wanted to feel nothing and to want nothing ever
again.

¤

Mercy rang the bell several times but there was no answer and
she was jealous. If Carter wasn't here at this time of night he
must be in another bed. She walked round to the alley and
the kitchen light was on so she shouted up and he opened the
window.

Mercy?

Yes. Sorry. Oh, God.

How would she tell him? She had not had the courage to
come straight away but at least she was not bringing a body –
just a death. He threw down his keys.

He met her at the top of the stairs and he was shirtless. They
smiled at each other and he kissed her on the lips but so
lightly that she had no idea what it might mean.

Come and sit down.

A pool of melted water spread across the table from a
wet towel so she pulled a chair into the middle of the room.
He went to the sink and she saw his body was simple and
strong and oddly fine without the slightest hair but his right
shoulder was lifted and the bruise was already darkening.
He was cracking ice into a plastic bag and he spoke without
looking at her.

What's happened?

She stared at his arm. She had a guilty feeling it was connected to her.

What happened to your shoulder?

I did it once before. In a fight. The only fight I ever had in
my life. If you've done it once it comes back.

She stood up to have a better look. She could see the swelling under the skin. He pressed the ice to it.

Shouldn't you see a doctor?

The living have to wait. It's only undertakers who get visitors in the middle of the night. It's not broken.

It looks pretty bad.

It's dislocated.

But you can't move it.

He twisted his torso.

Upward motion is limited because the head of the humerus is no longer correctly supported in the glenoid cavity of the scapula.

He smiled. She seemed impressed and he was pleased.

I was wrong about the doctor.

I smoked for twelve years and when I was inside I earned enough for tobacco but not cigarette papers. I found some volumes of an old encyclopaedia they were throwing out and whenever I wanted a roll-up I'd tear a page. I'm pretty good on everything between *Gnosticism* and *Malagasy*.

It's a good thing it wasn't a fracture, then. Or your radius or your ulna.

They laughed.

Do you have anything to drink?

Carter shook his head.

I can't. I used to.

I'm turning into an alcoholic.

You're not yellow. And you're not paranoid.

I think I am.

She started to cry as if she were laughing and her shoulders heaved. She spread her hands in a gesture of defeat and then she hid her face so he could not see the tears. He stood over her and he stroked her neck and he felt the fine hairs under his fingers.

Mara killed herself. In my bath. She was safe—

He leaned down to hold her and he kissed the top of her head. It smelled of wet carpet. He kissed it again.

Mercy. Oh, Mercy. I'm sorry. I'm sorry.

He wanted to say so much more but it was all she needed to hear. He let his touch slip gently and he went downstairs to the shelf by the door where the bell stood silent and he took the stone flask and the two heavy tumblers. He wiped the melted ice from the table with his good arm and put them down but he saw the glasses were clouded where the alcohol had evaporated and he fetched a mug from the cupboard.

It's *eau-de-vie*, like a white brandy, he told me. I buried a Polishman two years ago and his son gave it to me. I've no idea what it's like.

She took a sip. It was cold in her mouth and hot in her throat. She wanted him to drink too but she knew she shouldn't ask. She told him about Mara and what had happened in that room and she spoke slowly, measuring out each word as though telling it were her punishment. Carter thought of Rose and how her life had just floated away from her and he thought of the man he had killed in his ironed white shirt and it frightened him to see how close we are to death at every moment.

Mercy saw his hands were raw where he had been crushed against the wall and suddenly she understood.

How did they know it was you?

I signed the certificate.

She took his hands in hers and stared at the torn skin and the grit ground deep into it. Why did everyone who tried to help her have to be hurt?

Thanks. I'm sorry.

I wish it had done some good.

He closed his eyes.

I'm so bloody cold.

You should lie down.

180

He stood carefully and went to the bedroom and sat to unlace his boots with one hand. He tried to free his belt to take off his trousers and she came to help and he stopped.

Go on. You can't sleep with them on.

She turned down the covers. He switched off the little table lamp but the light from the kitchen fell across the bed and he knew she would see him naked and it felt odd that they had never even kissed. He managed to undress by himself and she pretended not to see as he lay himself down but he could not pull the blanket up and she leaned over to help. He smelled the brandy on her breath and he wanted to kiss her to taste that warmth.

She lay beside him in the shadows and she knew she would be happy if she never left this room. Her elaborate building with its debauched history was distant and insincere.

Neither slept and soon she was cold and she took off her jacket and her shoes and she climbed under the covers. She kissed him on the mouth and now there was no doubt in their minds and nothing more to be asked about why she was here. He was still cold and she climbed onto him as gently as she could and wrapped herself around him. They lay like that for a long while but she wanted to feel his body against hers and she climbed out of bed to take the rest of her clothes off and he circled her waist because he was afraid she wanted to leave. She put her hand to his mouth and he waited in silence and she climbed on him once again. She lay her head on his good shoulder and he put his arms about her once again and she drew his heat and hardness to her belly and Carter held her tight and it was as if he held the world.

¤

In the morning Mercy woke early and she helped Carter dress. The city was quiet and they drove easily through streets undisturbed by crowds and traffic as the first rays of the sun warmed the glassy towers high above them. They passed the museums, compelling monuments to a certainty of knowledge long discredited, and crossed the park with its great deserted lake. A band of guards in grey coats and bearskins paced the carriage road with their instruments glinting and Mercy rolled her window down to listen to their elegy for the day but beneath the skittering snare they were playing a brisk arrangement of *Eleanor Rigby*.

When they arrived at her house the sun had risen through the bare trees but down here where they climbed the steps the air was cold and blue and their figures cast no shadows. Carter had imagined she was rich and he was not surprised to see the ornate façade and the heavy oak door but nothing had prepared him for what lay inside. Mercy had fired up the old boiler to dry the carpet and as she opened the door the hot sour air spilled around them. There was only a single light left in the long panelled hallway and the floor was covered in keys like fallen leaves. It was like a passage to the centre of the earth. Mercy stopped by the iron gate.

She was in the bath.

The water was still in the tub and Carter went to pull the plug. He saw the chains and the bars and buckles on the walls and when he turned to Mercy and she saw his face she just laughed.

Oh my God! Did I not tell you?

For a second he feared the worst.

It was a brothel. I bought it for a joke.

She shocked herself. She had bought it because she loved it

and because she thought her life should be filled with grand gestures but now she saw she was right. It was a joke.

Carter walked into the drawing room and he heard the crystals from the chandelier grind beneath his boots. The curtains hung in rags and the chairs and cushions were toppled and split. The boxes in the middle of the room had been torn open and thrown aside and on the mantelpiece beneath the blank mirror was an empty bottle.

Mercy stood in the doorway as if she had never been here before. She knew he would have seen the whisky and she was afraid she really was becoming an alcoholic.

Where is she?

She took him to the bedroom and they stood over her for a moment. What remained of her blood had settled and her face and arms were waxy and clear and Mercy felt she was looking at the tired dry shell of some animal that had outgrown itself and moved on.

Carter's breathing was shallow and he sat on the edge of the bed. There was nothing in the room but the mattress and a pile of clothes.

Are you OK?

She touched his shoulder lightly. He nodded.

I just don't think I can do anything right now. I can't even carry her with you.

It's OK. We'll call somebody.

You can look in the phone book under Funeral Director. Don't go for one with a fancy picture.

Mercy went to make the call but he couldn't stay with Mara any more. He turned the light out and when he closed the door his hand was shaking.

¤

The cemetery ran in a narrow strip between the exhibition centre and the old school playground. A flint gatehouse with a single window stood at the head of the path. The wall around it had been raised to keep the children out and beyond the blind brick the high-rise flats towered like colossal headstones. The council had tried to persuade Mercy to cremate Mara because they were duty-bound to keep each plot for sixty years and they were desperate to raise cash by parcelling out the land to developers but she could not bring herself to burn her.

The coffin was already slung in its ropes when she arrived with Carter. A subsidised burial entitled Mara to a priest and two grave-diggers but by some oversight there was also a professional mourner, a young man in a dark suit who carried a top hat and gloves but never wore them. He rocked on his feet with expert gravitas and nodded when anyone spoke. The priest shook their hands.

It is a terrible time.

Carter would have spat but his mouth was dry. He had measured a pastor and a curate for their caskets as they lay dying and they had both demanded polished panelled mahogany with solid brass handles and stirrups and the interior lined with silk at their congregation's expense. The closer they came to the God they had preached – if not served – the more they feared their own end. Children were braver.

The priest said a few words about transience and Mercy felt inexplicably reprimanded. When they lowered the coffin it dragged at the earth at the sides and they could see the layers of clay and gravel and the fragments of glass and bone. For two thousand years the city had been built on its own detritus and everything that stood now was carved from previous ruins. They would bury Mara in her own history.

Mercy turned to look up at the rows of blank windows in the tower blocks above and she could see the soft violet light from the televisions flickering on every ceiling and she thought of those soap operas where every death brought redemption or vindication or an unexpected bequest. Mara's dying brought nothing to anyone. The mourner offered a silver box of earth to scatter and she saw it had been dried and sifted – God forbid the bereaved should dirty their hands – but the grave-diggers had already started to shovel the soil and she saw no point.

Carter could feel the old anger rise at the urgency and the insincerity of it all but when he stared down at the casket as it disappeared under the earth he could not tear his eyes away. It was the first funeral he had attended since his father died that he had not arranged or supervised and he was shocked at how the loss of control left him vulnerable. Without the ceremony he so cherished what was there but a body in a hole in the ground? He wanted to vomit as he watched the grave close over and he begged the men to be gentle as they stamped the earth down with the heels of their boots but he knew it was not Mara he hoped to comfort but himself.

¤

Fairburn sat on the bench in the square waiting for Lucas and he stared at the reflection of the orange street-lamp in his toe-caps. The man in charge of his monthly polish – two pairs of black brogues and two of brown – was on holiday and there was something cloudy about the finish tonight. The superficial brilliance was there but the deeper lustre was gone. Some-thing in the saliva, he thought; perhaps the new man was a vegetarian. Smokers were best because their phlegm was full of nitrogen. He checked his watch: exactly midnight.

Lucas walked up kicking conkers. His deck shoes had not been polished since he had bought them and his wax jacket from the Outback Store had been artificially aged. He sat on the wall but before he had gathered himself to speak Fairburn whispered in a French accent:

My uncle's truffle pig has lost his sense of smell.

What the fuck are you talking about?

I thought you might want some kind of code if we're going to meet like this.

It's just a park. Somewhere we can talk.

Fine. Call me Smiley.

Tell me something, Smiley. Did you tell Mara I was coming?

I haven't seen her since our evening together.

She was gone when I got there. I found her stuff. Mayman was asking after her.

I thought he was under your hat with the bread and butter.

Nobody loves a smart-arse. I told him about you.

Fairburn glanced at him. Did Lucas see fear? He tried again.

I've got a business to run. I don't know if I can really help you any more. I was thinking I should just put you two in touch.

Fairburn hated dealing with the police. They patronised, they interfered, they misunderstood everything. There was no crime. He rubbed his eyes.

What do you want me to do?

I sent some friends to see Carter but he's not talking.

Maybe he didn't like your friends.

Maybe he'll like you better. Maybe you can talk to him in Spanish.

Italian.

Lucas wanted to hit him. Maybe when all this was over he would.

Go and get him to tell you what the fuck's going on. Don't kill him.

What if he's got nothing to say?

Then you can kill him.

Fairburn was unmoved. For Lucas death was the ultimate weapon – a vital territorial tool – and yet there was something

186

clumsy about the way he wielded it. Fairburn tried to imagine killing a man and he knew Lucas might be dangerous because he was impulsive and petty but Fairburn himself would be lethal because he had no instinct of restraint.

Lucas gave him the address and he hesitated a moment before he walked away. He wanted to put his arms around Fairburn and tell him everything would be fine if he'd just play the game but he was beginning to see it was already too late.

¤

Carter lay naked on his back across Mercy's broad bed, his legs twisted in the sheets and his arms spread wide. He felt her hair trail across his chest as she turned and leaned forward to kiss him. Their breath was slowing now but the room was still fiercely hot and she put her forehead to his.

My God, am I sweating that much?

We both are. Perspiring.

Glowing.

They laughed. The insistence of their need the previous night had given way to a more tender passion. He reached up to touch her and he could hardly believe she was there. Still there. She spread herself over him and he kissed her between her breasts.

You're so beautiful.

She sat up and rubbed her cheeks. She smiled at him but he could see some spell had been broken.

So beautiful.

He put his hand to her face to draw her down but something in her held back. She thought of all the times she had heard that. The photography tutor in her first year at art school who flattered her looks and then her talent until she turned him away and then he failed her term paper. The art director at her first editorial spread for Vogue who said her beauty was rarer than she knew and that it would be a gift from God to be allowed to kiss her until she discovered that God had already given him the new receptionist and the personnel manager that same week. Michael Winterton with his hands smelling of gravy and his giggle. And she thought of all the men who had ever said they loved her. Perhaps some of them had told the truth in some way she had never understood but she didn't know why their ghosts had come crowding back into this room tonight to drive away the man she lay with.

He doesn't love you. We love you.

They liked each other and they trusted each other and right now they needed each other but they were sharing a part of themselves that each had guarded for so long that neither of them really knew if it could be given any more.

Carter was still awake. He was too hot and the memories of the last few weeks flickered at the edges of his mind like a soundless storm at the horizon. He tried to focus on the deaths and the burials and the threats and on this extraordinary woman whose bed he shared but when he turned to them they slipped away like shadows. Perhaps that meant it was all over now. Mercy would grieve for the death of her friend but she would harden again and gradually their lives would return to normal. And yet he thought of his life alone among the dead and hers with its restless reinventions and he tried to imagine what could be more normal than two people asleep in each other's arms.

He walked naked through the unlit rooms wondering what kind of home Mercy would make for herself here. It was a labyrinth of corridors and hidden entrances and he was afraid he might lose himself and never surface or see her again. He came to the drawing room she had destroyed and it was like the heart of the earth. An abandoned world.

The floor glistened with the gems of glass that had fallen from the mirror. He saw the broom against the wall and he picked it up and began to sweep the room clean in long straight lines as best he could with his awkward shoulder and when it was done he closed the boxes and stacked them again and set the chairs upright. He gathered the horsehair and the down and put it in the hall and he found cushions to cover the worst of the damage to the seats. He could not hang the curtains with one arm but he folded them and he opened the windows to the clear night air. He put the broken chains of the old chandelier in the bucket along with the bottle and carried them to the kitchen.

When Mercy found him in the morning he was asleep on the sofa. She made coffee and held a cup under his nose until he shook himself awake.

You must be frozen. If I'd known you liked tidying up I could have given you a maid's uniform. They left them all in the cloakroom.

She put the cup in his lap and he yelped. She kissed him.

Where did you go?

You must have really missed me.

I sleep like the dead.

They don't snore.

He winked at her and she found it gauche and charming.

I've never had a complaint before.

I shan't ask.

He took the coffee and she thought she must have misunderstood him.

I know I live in a brothel but I'm quite a nice girl really.

I know you are.

Why did she care what he thought? Did he imagine she'd never slept with anyone else? She resented him for judging her and it hurt all the more because she wanted him to be here. Why had he slept on the sofa? The ghosts surrounded her again.

He doesn't love you. We love you.

She stood up quickly, confused.

Have a bath if you want. I'll wash it out.

She took his cup and crossed the hall. Carter suddenly doubted everything. He had hoped they would spend the day together. They would walk through the park and have breakfast in some part of the city he had never visited and he would ask her all about it. And they would talk about new things, not Rose or Mara. His arm was freer now he had slept. Mercy walked in with his clothes and put them on a chair. She didn't look at him.

Do you need a hand getting dressed?

He shook his head. Was her life so easily restored? He had buried her bodies and kept her safe from the man who had killed her friend and maybe she had just taken him into her bed to put it all out of her mind. He struggled into his trousers but it took him five minutes to get the shirt on and he wished she would come and help. He could hear her cleaning the bath. A normal day. He had got it all so wrong. He tried to persuade himself that it had never been meant to be more than this – that getting laid twice for a burial was better than a tear-stained note of thanks or a bottle of brandy – but it still felt wrong. He didn't want to sleep with her if he couldn't have her for ever.

He went to say goodbye but she was making the bed and when he left she didn't even kiss him.

¤

Carter sat at the kitchen table and stared at his hands on the pale wood. They were almost healed now. He was glad to be free of that strange oppressive heat and darkness but his own house was empty by comparison, unformed. Not a home at all. He thought of Mercy in his arms and of her hot mouth and her cool fingers and he could still smell her hair on him. In two nights she had given him back everything he had tried for so long to keep from himself. He had begun to take chances with his life again – to live it, not measure it out – but she had handed him his clothes and disappeared to clean a bath.

He imagined her here again. They would hang pictures and he would show her how to frame her own work. They would have breakfast in the morning, not at midnight. He pushed his chair back and went to the drawer to find the invoice book. He turned to a fresh sheet and tucked the carbon paper behind it. Every entry was a burial. Each life inexplicable and irretrievable but every death just a few words on a page: a kind of wood, a kind of lining, a number of men to carry the coffin. He tried to remember the date and he counted back to All Souls' Day. Why had she come into his bed that night? Because he had risked his life for her? What life?

When he was seventeen and in his last year at school he had adored Anna Hallett. She sat two rows in front of him and he knew every strand of her dark hair as she leaned her head from side to side. On the days when the heating was overpowering the teachers would prop the door open with a fire extinguisher and he would watch her face reflected in the wired safety-glass of its window. He had no experience of the manoeuvres of dating and he simply asked her one day if she wanted to see a film with him and she was so surprised she said yes.

She barely reached his chest but she was bright and pretty and they made each other laugh. He always took her

191

somewhere proper – to a pub with tables by the river or the better cinema – because he wanted to show he cared for her. He had never had anything to care for before. She liked him well enough and one evening she took him back to her house and they kissed for an hour in the kitchen in the dark. They touched each other through their clothes and she could feel he was hard for her but there was so much tenderness between them and somehow it could not be translated into the mechanics of sex. Not there with the breakfast things already laid out and her swimming costume drying on the radiator and the cast photograph of the school play still on the fridge door. He kissed her goodnight one last time and as she held him she whispered *But you can say we did it if you like.*

He had never learned to pity himself and he was furious that Mercy had slept with him because she was sorry for him. Sorry he had tried to help her. Sorry he loved her, if that was what it was. He held the book of invoices with his left hand and filled it in with his narrow designer's script. It hurt his arm to write but he had learned never to mix business with pleasure.

When he heard the knock at the door he went to the window. He saw the spotless dark grey overcoat and shined brogues and he didn't think it was going to be trouble but there was something about the way the man stood that didn't look like he wanted to bury a body. He knew he should put the jacket on but it would have taken too long so he draped it over his shoulders.

Carter Stark?

He nodded. Fairburn was arrestingly good-looking.

You're an undertaker.

I organise funerals. Make coffins. Whatever you need.

You make them here?

Carter nodded. Normally he could gauge what his visitors wanted from him – comfort, efficiency, reverence – but the man gave nothing away.

May I see?

Carter stood aside and he watched him as he walked around the benches and the stacks of wood. He had known when he filed Rose's death certificate that they would send the inspectors again but council officers couldn't afford shoes like this. Fairburn stopped at the rack of inshaves and drawknives and reached out to run a finger along a blade.

You still use these?

Carter took one down and showed him how to hold it to shape a handle or a tight curve. He could tell from his questions that he knew about wood but he wanted to know why he had come.

Do you have a workshop?

I have some chairs.

Carter had visions of genteel poverty but he meant he had a set of twelve rare pieces by Gostelowe with cabriole legs and splat backs. Fairburn was disappointed that the workshop was just a carpenter's studio, a place where coffins were made with no more ceremony than chests or cupboards. He hadn't expected blood-stained sawdust or skulls in the corner but it was all so ordinary. Even Carter. He drew back the cloth on a low table and put his hand to the smooth steel. He thought it was a work surface but the metal bore no marks of cutting or joining.

A cooling board.

Fairburn had spent his first pay cheque – a whole week's wages – on a shellac seventy-eight of *Death Walk Among Us*:

> **Come to my door he dont knock but once**
> **Dont say but one word Death walk among us**

Take the one you hate take the one you love
That man so greedy cant never get enough

Close her shutters down put a lock on the door
Dont need no bed when you got a coolin board

Took her hand to mine Lord just as cold as stone
Never know you miss her till you see her gone

Close her eyes so she cant see me cry
Well you know we walk this world and then we die

No point to fight no point to make you fuss
We aint never finished till Death done with us

He thought of Rose cold under that sheet in her tight black dress and she turned to smile at him.

Never know you miss her till you see her gone—

He let the cloth fall.

I do all the traditional designs in any wood you like or I can try something more unusual. I've buried people in cars and boats and cigars and even a football boot. But I've put my shoulder out so I don't know how quick I'll be.

Fairburn thought of Lucas and his inept violence but he could tell already that Carter was not a man who would be made to talk with threats. Not that Fairburn cared much who had taken Rose or even whether Mayman would pursue the case but he wanted to know what it would take to make the man crack. He remembered Bruno's chisel heavy and cold in his hand and how that immense marble base had sheared at a single blow. Carter seemed implacable but everything has its plane of fracture.

¤

Mercy knelt in the bath as she lit the candles by the taps and the flames swayed as the steam rose around them. She had done nothing all day and she was restless. She softened the kaolin with water in an old mortar and she pinned her hair up and smoothed the mixture on to her skin. Forehead, left cheek, right cheek, throat. She turned to the mirror and her dark eyes stared back at her, brilliant behind the pale mask.

She had wanted Carter to stay. To climb back under her quilt or to sit with her on the balcony and drink coffee. To talk about everything or nothing at all. He had stood and watched her make the bed but he was already dressed and when he left he didn't even kiss her. Did he expect her to sleep with him just because he had buried Rose? She would rather have paid him in cold cash than acquit herself this way.

She had fucked men for less but she had always been careful to show that she took as much as she gave and she had twice thrown a lover out of bed because he bored her. But she was twenty-nine and she was tired and she didn't want to have to be on her guard any more. The first time she had kissed Carter there was no cautious bargain: only trust and desire. She used to love the old painted board at the flower stall opposite her art school:

> *Because you love her*
> *Because it's your birthday*
> *Because he bought the ring*
> *Because she found your keys*
> *Because it's Tuesday*

Because he's Carter. She lay back in the water and thought of him beneath her and her pulse quickened again. She loved the way he had entered her without hesitation or questioning, taking her and holding her as if whatever he needed must be also right for her. And it was, and she wanted him there right now in the bath in that hot flickering darkness. To be used by him and to use him for that. But she did not dare hope he might love her for the things she wanted to believe – that she was beautiful, and good, and that she would never again have to try to be anything but Mercy.

The water had grown cold and when she sat up to reach for the tap she saw herself in the mirror again and the mask was dry and it had hardened into a thousand tiny pieces.

In her dream the phone rang.

Alabama Slammer?

It was Rose.

Southern Comfort and amaretto one-to-one, half a shot of sloe gin. Lemon juice. Highball glass. With my eyes shut.

Long Island Iced Tea?

Tequila, vodka, gin. Rum. Light rum. Coke and lemon. Highball glass.

Pretty good. Red Light?

Red Light. Don't know. I can't believe I don't know.

Vodka, cranberry, ginger ale, orange slice—

You made that up.

Sounds good, though?

Not with that name.

Let's have a party. It's been too long.

In the morning she sat in bed and watched as the line of sunlight that forced itself between the curtains swept across the carpet like the hand of a watch. At dawn it had fallen on the shoes she had dropped in the corner and as it grew brighter and colder it had crept to the chair with her clothes on it. Soon it would touch the foot of her bed. She felt her life hurrying to catch up with itself and before long it would reach her and pass her and race on into the future while she lay there watching.

The hall was dry now and as Mercy gathered the keys they left pale shadows of themselves in the carpet. She did not have the patience to hang them back on their hooks so she laid them out in a line on the dado rails and they stretched from the front door down the hall and into the corridor below like a golden chain drawing her down.

She hadn't opened these doors since she bought the place. This was where the real work was done. Upstairs there had been the quiet ring of ice in heavy glasses and the crackle of a fire; conversation was hushed and manners impeccable. Louise Parrish would broker the deals and steer the men instinctively to the girl who would serve them best but down here – in the underworld – was where they came alive.

She stepped into the first room. The bed was made but she knew if she turned it down there would only be the counterpane and the pillows; nobody had ever slept here. There was a chair for clothes and a bedside table. Two towels on a rail and a little sink in the corner. A bottle of unscented oil and condoms in the drawer. It would be the same in all of the others.

She stood in the doorway as the men came down the stairs with the women.

It's not easy to park around here. *Will she blow me without a rubber?*

It's busy tonight. *I want to come on her face.*

That's a lovely dress. *I hope she's a screamer.*

They all had something they loved to do or something the girl must do to shape herself to their fantasy. The girls themselves were nothing. Get on your knees. Leave the stockings on. Don't use your hands. Bend over the chair. It was heartbreaking to see two people entwined and crying out and never even looking at each other. Who did they dream they were with? After a while she saw the men collapse gasping as they rid themselves of something or yielded to it. *They don't make love, do they? They don't make anything.* She thought of Mara brushing out her long dark hair every night and waiting for the men to come to her. She could not stop the waiting and the men could not stay away.

She closed the door and stood in the silence. Rose was right. She would throw a party here in these empty rooms and Tanya and Brittney and all the others would bring their men and her own home would be a brothel once again. And the men would come – because they always did – and one of them would be the killer.

PART THREE

Carter's shopping list was identical each week and every Monday afternoon he would walk to the high street with his canvas bag. The first of five stops was the butcher. Despite the homogenisation of convenience stores and supermarkets and fat-free bacon and chickens with their heads removed Marsham's had survived with its wooden floor and moulded tiles and its black and gold glazed sign. Carter loved the ranged trays of sweetbreads and hares and spatchcocks and noisettes rolled and tied. He only ever bought sausages because he would have no idea how to cook anything else but he was happy to support a man who sold food that had actually walked the face of the earth.

Miles had Carter's order ready before he came in but his visit to Mercy and her lunch with him had thrown his larder into disarray and he wasn't sure if he ought to explain why he only needed four pounds instead of five. He wanted to know if Mercy ran her life like this but he doubted it.

He sometimes stopped for a sandwich at Jack's on the corner but today it smelled like rain and he turned for home. He had adapted his weather instincts to life in the city and where farmers look to a darkening sky and scent the grass he would watch the wind curl the iridescent rainbows of oil in the gutters or listen for the gulls calling upriver. Not that he cared if he got wet: it just reassured him to know.

*

When Carter reached the alley he saw the overcoat and wondered how long he had been waiting. Fairburn stood up and brushed a leaf from his trousers.

I was passing.

This part of the city was a mile from the elegant winding streets of the financial district – surely that was where Fairburn worked – across a no-man's-land of goods yards and viaducts and parking lots. There was nothing for him here.

Come in.

Carter realised he was desperate to get back to work. Everything in his life had been shaken loose since that night on the river and he needed something to draw him back into the old routine. Fairburn followed him in. He held the leaf in his hand.

Sometimes you find them and only the veins are left. Like lace. Bones.

The tips had dried and curled around themselves like a hand clutching at air. Carter wanted to put the food in the fridge but he had learned to be patient with these conversations.

Is that what happens when you bury a man?

Carter shook his head.

We decompose. That's desiccation.

Fairburn held the leaf high and let it fall but he caught it with his other hand and put it in his pocket.

What happens when you die?

It was cold in the workshop and their breath hung in the air. Carter wanted to say *You go to heaven*.

Depends what kills you. A plane crash? You wouldn't have a body left. If you fall through a plate-glass window you'll bleed to death and your brain will run out of oxygen if there's nothing left in the arteries to take it there. Most deaths are pretty uneventful. Some sit there in bed saying their goodbyes and their breathing just stops.

How do you know they're dead?

Check the pulse. Cornea reflexes. I'm not really a patholo-gist. Actually, you go blue pretty quickly. You can see it in the mouth and the nails.

Fairburn pushed back a cuticle.

If you're really not sure you can hook up an EEG and if the line is flat, that's it. Just like in the films. When the brain stem goes, you go. Consciousness, breathing, blood pressure all collapse. Irreversible loss of function.

He saw his father sitting at home with his pint glass wait-ing for the factory gates to swing open. Irreversible loss of function.

Fairburn had lost his bearings. It was all unbearably prosaic. Death had distilled Rose into the essence of his desire – his very will – but for Carter he supposed she was just another body. He wanted to ask *What did you do with her?* and he wanted to hear how she had lain in this room and where she had been buried and he was jealous of Carter because of the time he had spent combing her hair and folding her hands but he knew he could show nothing yet. He was just feeling his way.

He saw the old printing press and he turned to it. A stack of papers lay on the galley each with the same text but leaded and justified in a dozen variations:

> *To the one we are the savour of death unto death;*
> *And to the other the savour of life unto life.*
> *And who is sufficient for these things?*
>
> II Corinthians 2:16

Above the cases of type was a shelf lined with blocks and he picked one up. Ink had crept into the grooves and the image was hard to see but he flattened the back of his hand and forced the shape into his flesh and for a second before the blood rushed back into the skin he saw Death in his dark robe embracing a young girl. Her dress was thrown open to the waist and his cold hand had forced its way between her legs. Her eyes were closed and she kissed him with a terrible hunger.

Do you send this stuff out with your condolences?

If I hear a funeral director's going bust I go to see what they're throwing out. The bailiffs just want the phones and the chairs.

Fairburn stared at the block.

Oro supplex et acclinis –

Carter wanted Fairburn to leave now even though he could not say what had made him uneasy but he moved around the room as if searching for something beyond the gauges and planes and cramps. As if there was something here to be discovered that not even Carter could see.

What do you want?

Fairburn could hear the fear. Not the fear of violence – Carter had welcomed Mayman's snoops and Lucas's strongarms and still he opened the door to strangers – but the fear of something deep within Carter himself.

Nobody likes to talk about their own funeral.

Why would I give a shit what happens when I'm dead?

Fairburn's anger flashed darkly and he tried to imagine what he would feel if Lucas made him kill him. He turned back to the blocks and took another. He reached inside his coat and found a folded piece of paper and he pressed the stamp hard to it but the image was faint so he lifted it to his mouth and breathed on it for a moment. The warm air softened the ink and when he pressed again he saw a crowd gathered at the gallows. The man had already dropped and his head had fallen to one side and his mouth hung open. The grandmothers in the front row had put their work aside and the young women at the back climbed on each others' shoulders to stare at the swelling in the dead man's breeches.

A big lad.

They all look like that in the engravings. They sold thousands.

He put the block back on the shelf.

Any violent death brings an incredible rush of blood. An erection is one of the more notorious side-effects.

Fairburn stiffened.

I have some pictures of caskets I made.

He could see he was close to Carter's fault line now and he enjoyed the thought that he might steer him deeper into that fear. If he wanted to make a coffin, then let him. Carter took an album of photographs from the shelf and began to turn the pages.

I don't care how it looks.

He hesitated.

What kind of wood?

He wanted the kind of wood that was in those breeches.

Cheap. Show me something.

I haven't enough here. I'll have to go to Richardson's but I've missed them now.

What time is it?

Carter looked out of the small high windows at the darkening sky.

Five.

I'll come back when you have the wood.

I need to take your measurements.

It's not for me.

Not for you—

Carter was helpless and angry.

We'll go to the timber yard in the morning.

Richardson's, on Marsh Way—

Ten o'clock.

Fairburn patted his shoulder as he left and Carter felt the hand brush his cheek. He was so happy to see him go that he didn't even stand up and only when he went to close the door did it occur to him that he had forgotten for the second time to ask his name.

¤

Lucas still didn't know how to make a cappuccino. He stood at the bar as the last few girls arrived. It was three o'clock on a Monday afternoon and everyone resented this interruption to their week apart from him because he only had to pull on his trousers and a shirt and walk down two flights of stairs. The women sat on the floor or on the bar stools and Carmen was asleep on the sofa with her cowboy boots on the arm and Lucas was going to yell at her but he looked around the room and decided he would let it go this time. He hated this room in daylight.

He had introduced another management first: employee enfranchisement in the sex industry. He had read an article in a newspaper he found in a sandwich bar that described how American companies allowed their workers to participate in the greater success of their business and this married neatly with his own experience as a petty thief and gang member where he had learned through years of bickering that inequality is the first cause of unrest. Pursuing this to its logical conclusion, he had brought in a policy where the girls pooled their earnings and – after he had taken fifty per cent off the top – split the rest according to the number of days they worked. The girls were furious but the only time they could find to protest as a group was out of hours. Lucas had assumed sisterly solidarity would support a just redistribution of wealth but he had not counted on the jealousy and self-interest of forty smart women who worked considerably harder than he did for their wages. Star performers (the naturally gorgeous and outrageous) and specialists (bondage and schoolgirl) earned almost three times as much as the straight girls who had not found a loyal following. The less popular knew that Lucas gave them to the first-timers or the difficult clients because he made more money with the others from the regulars. And they each had their own technique for screwing extra fees or tips from their visitors and untraceable income was the most desirable kind. So much for worker participation.

Lucas was starting to think he should ask for a refund on his business school fees but the girls had reasons of their own for wanting a meeting. Chrissy spoke first.

Where's Tanya?

They all knew he had beaten her. All pimps put their girls under the manners from time to time and even Brittney had disappeared after she took Tanya to the hospital but she had called Chrissy to say she was working on the south coast.

Tanya's fine. She knows she's welcome back here any time.

Although it didn't sound like she'd be doing a lot of business with a black eye and her jaw wired shut. Most of the girls knew they were safe enough if they continued to earn and not cause trouble, which was fine by them except that it was nearly two weeks since Rose had been killed and Lucas didn't appear to have done anything about it.

We want to know what happens if he comes back. Or someone else.

Lucas still didn't really know what had happened that night. Perhaps he would have to put Fairburn under the manners, too.

Some of you know a copper by the name of Mayman. He's been here a few times helping us look into it.

He seems awful careless with his parking.

The room burst into giggles but Lucas couldn't see who had said it. There was nothing he hated more than the sound of women laughing. Chrissy waited until they were quiet again.

We all know the cops are here all the time. They must be able to do something.

Lucas shrugged.

They want to fuck me just like they want to fuck you.

The dream came to him again abruptly. He had gone to pee and he found himself lowering the seat to sit and when he looked down at himself he saw he was a woman. Or half a woman. His chest was slim and muscled but between his legs was a tangle of dark hair and as he splashed into the bowl he touched himself. It was so soft. The door opened and he saw Mayman in uniform with handcuffs and truncheon hanging from his belt and he came and lifted him and carried him to the bed.

That was all he could recall. All he dared recall. He looked at the women ranged around him in the room and he wondered what it would feel like to be filled by a man like that and he was jealous.

We want to be safe. We can't work unless we're safe.

They had discussed this before. Lucas had offered to put hidden cameras in the rooms but the girls knew that instead of recycling the tapes he would offer them to touts who would copy them and put them out with ridiculous titles like *Cathouse Capers* and *Boudoir Bangers #3*. Or that he would keep the more interesting ones for future reference. But if anyone was going to start blackmailing clients it would be the girls – it was their only insurance against violence and they didn't want Lucas to break their monopoly.

They talked it over for a while and eventually they settled on a panic button hidden behind the headboard. Lucas wrestled with the maths of cost per room times number of rooms plus cabling and a central monitoring system – he didn't want the whole place emptying just because some enthusiastic client slapped a girl's arse a little too eagerly – and he could see it running into the thousands.

I'll organise it but I won't write the cheque. You'll have to come to an agreement among yourselves about payment in kind for the lads that put it in.

The girls were outraged. This time Jessica spoke, a German with a boyish figure popular among the older men. She had been with Lucas since he started up and with Louise Parrish for seven years before that.

I am a professional and we expect you to be professional too.

She looked around at the others and they shouted their agreement.

No more favours. Not cops and not plumbers. If we worked like they worked you'd be out of business in a week.

He wanted to tell her to shut up and sit down but he knew it was true. A younger girl spoke without looking up.

There's a guy who comes who just always asks for me and he sits on the end of the bed and tells me about his wife and his boss and his brother-in-law and all the crap about how he hates his life and it's so pathetic. He doesn't want a girl, he wants a shrink.

They had been waiting for her to say it.

You know? I don't mind banging like a barn door so long as they don't depress the shit out of me first.

I just don't think we should have to sleep with the ones we hate. We find ways to wriggle out of it. Nicely. That's what I did before I started here.

They whooped with delight and Lucas felt his heart sink. Someone else shouted out:

And you can tell that arsehole Sandburg to go fuck himself. I heard he sells riot gear in Indonesia. If he lays his hands on me one more time – I mean, he fucking *kills* people.

The room collapsed in a chorus of anger and complaint.

Christ alive, Lucas thought. Whores with a conscience. Where would it end?

¤

Mercy stood in the corridor in front of the yellow door and she could feel the building shudder as the trains pulled out of the station far below. When she knocked the letterbox lifted and she saw small eyes stare at her and then the door opened and Louise Parrish waved her in.

I'm Nan today. My best role.

Her granddaughter hid behind her legs. She wore a blue negligée with gold fur trimming over jeans and a sweat-shirt and a pair of matching mules and her lips were red.

Give us a twirl, Caitlin.

She looked up at Louise and took the hem of the dress and curtsied but when Mercy smiled at her she turned and ran and she nearly fell in the heels and then they heard the bedroom door close.

Louise leaned against the sink while the kettle boiled. Mercy sat.

I found Mara.

Louise smiled. Her contacts were still good.

Did she tell you anything?

She told me what happened.

She told Louise how she had found her and taken her home and how she had woken the next morning to find her in the bath but she didn't understand.

She cut herself with my scissors. She locked herself in the bathroom, the room with the gate—

Louise took Mercy's hand and Mercy squeezed it but she couldn't cry any more.

It's not your fault.

She knew it wasn't her fault but she needed to hear it. She wanted her to say the words again and again until there could be no more doubt.

She stood and went to the window and she looked out over the city. The sun had moved behind a low broken cloud and its silvery light fell here and there on the green water of the river and the great parks and the rows of houses on the far hills. Silent streams of cars coursed through the valleys below and the railway lines stretched away to infinity. Aircraft filled the sky, banking into their approach or unravelling their trails of condensation high above. They all moved towards their own horizon but Mercy just circled her own life and every day it seemed the world grew smaller. She wanted to stow away, to be taken somewhere far from here where her past would not recognise her.

I want to open the brothel again.

Louise reached for a cigarette and she fumbled with the lighter.

I'm going to turn the house into a club. I want you to help.

She turned away.

I know you think I'm crazy so let's make this easy for both of us. I am crazy but I want you to help me set it up. I want to know about the girls and the rooms and the drinks and what to say when they come and what to charge and how to make them feel like we're going to take them to heaven and never bring them back.

Louise stared at her through the smoke and she waved her hand around her at the bare pipes and the unpainted walls and the furniture under dust-sheets.

I ran the best salon in this city for twelve years—

The ash fell on the table and she brushed it onto the floor with the back of her hand.

This is where it got me.

Mercy wanted to tell her that she didn't care if it failed or if it cost her money or even if she was arrested just so long as every man those girls had ever seen would come.

I don't ever want to go back there.

Maybe she was right. Stow away. Move on. Head for the horizon. She stood and went to the door but Louise didn't get up.

I know you loved her. She was a good girl. But I helped you find Mara and now—

She didn't want her to say it.

Now I think it's enough.

It was her fault.

¤

He sat by the printing press for a long time. His eyes had grown used to the darkness and he didn't want to switch on the light. He hadn't taken the food upstairs but it was so cold now it didn't matter. He wasn't even hungry. He moved along the racks of tools straightening them and hanging them in their proper order as if this in itself would restore the pattern of a world that became more obscure as every day passed. He could not rid himself of the feeling that Fairburn had reached deep inside him – had held his heart in his manicured fingers for an instant – and even as he turned back to those things in his life he had learned to rely on, he saw that they had been transformed. He could not go back now and he pushed forward like a man lost in a dark wood who believes the path must loop back on itself and bring him to the place he left long ago.

He looked at the blocks Fairburn had touched and he no longer saw the integrity of a world that made its peace with Death but a vision of hell on earth where Death danced among us without purpose or meaning. Death was not an angel who walked in our shadow from cradle to grave but a clown and a vandal who would not even trouble to learn our name before he pitched us down a flight of stairs. He clamped the mechanism and inked the rollers and when he lifted the image from the bed it glistened on the heavy paper. The young woman in the arms of the skeleton no longer kissed him passionately but screamed and pushed him away frantically as he thrust his fingers into her.

He put it back on the shelf and he saw that Fairburn had taken the block of the hanged man. Only the paper lay on the case of type with its pale impression and he picked it up. The crowd were laughing now as the body swung and the hang-man's assistants would come to cut him down and drop him into an open grave in a sack filled with quicklime.

He folded the cover back. It was a programme for a per-formance of Mozart's requiem. It was almost too dark to read but the last sentence caught his eye:

> *Although it has become habit with me always to fear the worst in all things, I realise – now that I confront it – that Death is the true purpose of our life. Over the last few years I have become so close to this greatest and truest friend of Man that his face no longer fills me with terror and I find in him peace and solace. And I thank God that He has granted me the good fortune to be able to learn that in this lies the key to our truest happiness.*
>
> Letter from Mozart to his father, 4.iv.1787

¤

Mercy had kept Rose's bag behind the bar in the big drawing room but she had not yet dared open it. Her own backpack was a distillation of her life, a store of secrets both banal and intimate, and she never let anyone else touch it. Her mother had been terrified that her husband would see the sanitary towels she carried for emergencies even though she kept them in a quilted wallet inside the zipped pocket of her handbag and as a young girl Mercy had learned this urge to privacy. She used to hide condoms in an old tin of throat pastilles; one was daring but two was thrilling. Nowadays she didn't care who saw these things but she was intensely secretive about address books and diaries and contracts and ideas for projects and tokens from friends and lovers. Like most models she was more afraid to bare her soul than her body.

She spread the contents on the green baize table and when the bag was empty she held it upside down and shook it. A mist of crumbled eyeshadow and flakes of tobacco drifted to the floor and she could smell the rich pale leather. Hairbrush. Spare knickers (two pairs). Cigarette packet (empty) and cigarette packet (unopened). Lighter and matches. Powder compact and lipstick and eyeliner. Toothbrush and paste. Breath freshener spray. Travel alarm clock. Lip balm. Hair grip (broken). Coins green with corrosion. The purse contained twenty pounds in notes and change and an uncashed cheque for thirty more and four months of receipts and old tickets. No condoms and no sanitary towels. The diary was a week-to-a-page from the science museum but the address book was bound in calfskin and her name had been embossed in gold.

And the lady's name, sir?

Rose.

Any last name, sir? Or an initial?

Just Rose.

She opened it and flicked through the pages. Most of the entries looked like clients but she recognised a few old faces.

Some were listed by their first name and some by their last. Some were grouped together. How on earth would she begin? *I hope you don't mind me bothering you at home but I'm a friend* – most of them wouldn't even know she had died. *You didn't happen to be a colleague of hers at work recently? I'm trying to find out* – it would be ridiculous. How do you ask a woman if she sleeps with men for a living?

She opened the purse and spread the receipts in a thick layer on the floor. She would build up a picture of her life over the past few weeks. Where she had gone and who she had seen. She sifted through them, amazed at how much and how little they told her. The same sandwich every day for a week. A book about natural-health remedies. Moth balls. A bus to work every day and a taxi home every night. Two hundred and thirty pounds on a pair of shoes. And then on September 28 a bottle of champagne and at the bottom Brittney's name and mobile number.

She dialled and hung up twice before she waited for the ring. She would only have one chance to persuade her to help but she was afraid of what she had said that time they had met at the cafe on the corner. *We should get on.*

Brittney?

Who is this?

It's Mercy. Rose's friend.

Oh, hi. How are you.

Not even a question.

I'm OK. I found Mara—

And then she had let her kill herself.

I need to ask you something.

Silence.

I know how to find this man and I'm going to do it. I need you to help me get in touch with the others.

The other who?

The other girls.

We're not sisters.

Can I tell you about it?

She could hear her turn the music down.

I'm not in the city.

I found a receipt for a bottle of champagne.

Are you an accountant?

Mercy laughed and Brittney joined her.

No. I just meant. You know. From a friend.

Brittney knew they had drunk it from cups and had toasted each other and made a wish but she couldn't remember what she had hoped for.

I'm going to start a salon of my own in Louise's old place and I need someone to help me get it ready. Make it look good.

I thought you were an artist.

I am. But I need girls.

She tidied the receipts into an old envelope and put everything apart from the diary and the address book back in the bag. She went to the kitchen to see what was in the fridge and saw the stack of letters that had arrived that morning. Normally – in her real life, her life before all of this – she would begin the day with a fierce coffee at the bar and open the mail and sort it into piles to be referred to Richard or her accountant or to be answered herself. Even the morning after a show she would force herself to do it as a way of proving that she was on top of it all. A smart businesswoman. A good girl. But for the last few days she had let it build and the longer she left it the more overwhelming it became. She took an apple and decided she would open anything written by hand. The rest would have to wait.

There were two invitations and a wedding announcement and a pre-paid lightweight letter from a friend in New Zealand and she read it quickly but when she put it down it was gone from her mind already. Richard had sent her a personal note with a few of the better reviews from the opening night but most of the reactions were to the staging of the party, not the work. There were a couple of postcards forwarded from collectors who had bought her earlier pieces and a second letter from Richard himself:

Chaos HQ / Friday

Mercy mine:

Connor Fairburn, mysterious millionaire collector and man-about-town (but married, I had S check), has made what I can only describe as an OFFER WE CAN'T REFUSE on one of the unprinted pix from your contact sheets – he's desperate to find something nobody else has seen. I bet his mother told him nothing was ever good enough for her little boy but he's offering 6 figs for 1 print (we keep the neg) and he says YES to the press. Need to know by the end of the (this) week. Tell me we're not going to say no???

Yr. agent / adviser (& best friend of your bank manager)—

R

The last was a simple brown envelope written in a formal hand and when she opened it a square of lined paper fell to the floor.

CARTER STARK, UNDERTAKER
Professional services rendered:

Casket:

Weymouth pine	....
Fixings ditto	....
Plain linings	....
Materials & labour	£250 – 00

November 5th

She read it again to make sure she hadn't misunderstood it and then she tore it carefully into pieces. She was shaking. Why couldn't he have just disappeared, sent nothing, said nothing? Enough men she had known had done that and she had grown used to it.

She went to the fridge again for a glass of wine but the bottle was empty.

She walked down the hill to the late-night grocer. It was bitterly cold but the sky was clear and not even the streetlights could dim the stars. She tried to be rational. He had taken a professional risk and he had worked hard to have everything ready in time. Two hundred and fifty pounds was a bargain – a single one of her pictures would have cost more to frame than that. He had no money. And she had told him to send it. She had even given him her address. She thought of all the times she had found ways to slip a man her number but demanding an invoice for a coffin was the best yet. She asked herself what was the point of years of cultivating her sexual liberation if she was going to let a struggling carpenter hurt her this way but the rhetoric was disingenuous and she knew it at once.

She saw him crouching beside her on the jetty, carrying Rose from the van, climbing the hill with the wooden cross on his back, cutting the bread fried in the pan, crushing ice at the sink, kissing her as if he would devour her. She had never shared so much with any man. They were already beyond secrets and she saw it was not each other they shied from but themselves.

¤

She hesitated outside Carter's door. She always came here at night but at least this time she hadn't brought a body. She had left the car running with the headlights on so she could see her way in the alley but even an undertaker would surely be asleep by now. She had found a cash machine and wrapped the money in the bag from the store where she had bought the vodka and she had decided to drop it through the letterbox. She didn't want to seem like a coward but she wasn't sure there was enough left to be brave about. She forced the brass flap up and let the package fall to the floor inside and she walked back to the car.

Carter was sitting on the bonnet. He looked tired.

I'm getting a lot of visitors who don't care to announce themselves.

Hello, Carter.

Do you need a receipt?

It's cash. I thought it would be easier.

He nodded.

I didn't think you'd be up.

I got a commission.

Great.

She didn't want to stay if this was all they had to say.

It's too cold for small talk.

You can come in.

She shook her head.

Come in. I want to show you something.

They climbed the narrow stairs and he put the plates to one side and they sat opposite each other.

Do you want some of that brandy?

Maybe I shouldn't. It got me into trouble last time.

He picked at a knot in the table top. She wanted the vodka in the pocket of her coat and she thought of the empty whisky bottle he had found but if they were beyond secrets they were beyond worrying about that so she pulled it out and stood it between them. He reached out and felt it was warm from the heated car. He brought her a glass and he went to the fridge for a tray of ice and cracked it to loosen it and she poured herself what she imagined was a modest measure. He took the requiem programme from the shelf and passed it across to her.

Come up and see my etchings?

Look at the letter.

She stared at the hanged man.

Has he got the most amazing hard-on?

Any sudden death will do it—

He tried to turn the page but she held it.

There's hardly a man in the crowd.

It was true. He hadn't noticed until now. She wanted to ask him if he'd ever seen one on his cooling board but they had misunderstood each other enough and she didn't want to stray into that territory. She started to read. Carter watched her and he reached for the vodka and tipped a mouthful into the cap and drank it down. Eleven years on the wagon and it was like an electric shock. Mercy handed the booklet back.

Good?

He thought she meant the alcohol and he was ashamed but she hummed a bar from the *Lacrimosa*.

It's a monumental piece.

I wasn't there. A man came yesterday and asked me for a coffin. He wouldn't leave his name. He came again today and left that.

He realised how ridiculous it all sounded and he tried to laugh.

It must be his idea of a practical joke.

He went to the cupboard and brought another tumbler. He held it for a moment because it was something to occupy his restless hands and he knew he dare not take that step backward but he wanted to drink with her and he poured himself a shot. He didn't taste it at once but swilled the liquid around watching it climb the sides and then he took a sudden sip. Already the fear and doubt that had pursued him since they had buried Mara were beginning to dissolve. He took a handful of ice and slid it into the glass and he lifted it in a toast but she didn't raise hers so he drank to thin air. He wanted to kiss her. That was all he could think about. He knew if he took her now and crushed his lips to hers that the world around them would fall away for ever. He smiled and took her hand and she felt it was cold from the ice. She didn't meet him but she didn't resist.

Carter—

She had never seen him like this.

I'm glad you came.

He was struggling to explain so much but this was all he could say and he hoped she could see what the words really meant. Having her here was all he wanted. When she was with him he was different – more powerful and more alive – and he was desperate to believe it was the same for her. He reached for the bottle again but Mercy covered her glass.

I'm driving.

You know you can stay.

She wanted to stay and it was all too complicated but when she tried to confront whatever it was that stood between them there was nothing there. She had been hurt by him and she had thrown up her cool practised defences but the great walls she had set around herself no longer protected her. She had hidden behind them and they had shut her in. And she saw with a piercing simplicity that if she could build them she could tear them down and she leaned across the table and kissed him and he felt her fuse with the alcohol coursing through his body.

*

They were breathless already. He had held her to him for so long that she pushed him away to come up for air and they stood panting for a moment. Carter drained the last of his glass and put his arms around her again. He wanted to carry her to his bed and she let herself fall into his embrace but as he took her weight the pain tore at his shoulder and he cried out.

She took him by the hand and drew him to the bedroom. They sat and kissed again and then they lay down and kissed some more and their hands strayed to each other's face and arms and they touched each other's fingers touching themselves. She wanted to see him naked beside her and they undressed each other clumsily, turning their shirts inside out with the buttons still fastened. She reached out to hold him from head to foot and she loved the warmth of his long body against her. She wanted no more talking now. She brought her hands to his belly and stroked him and she loved to hear his breath grow faster as she took him in her mouth and she searched for his hand and felt it tremble. She teased him like this for a long while but he would not grow hard so she kissed him lightly and lay her head on his thighs.

Eleven years I haven't drunk—

We have all the time in the world.

She wanted him but it was perfect just to be here and her body calmed itself. She pulled the blanket over their legs and she watched him fall asleep. She had done nothing to make him need her but if he wanted her in his bed just the way she was and if he loved her after everything they had seen and done together who was she to deny it?

¤

The long lanes of timber stretched away on all sides like a map of the world:

AMERICA	Maple, Walnut, Redwood, Butternut, Hickory, Alder
FAR EAST	Rosewood, Teak, Kauvula, Ebony
OCEANIA	Blackwood, Jelutong, Silky Oak
EUROPE	Birch, Elm, Boxwood, Oak, Ash, Hemlock, Yew

When he was a child his father had told him stories of these extraordinary trees. The cedar of Lebanon, so sturdy that insects could never harm it and whose vital oils were distilled for scent. Rosewood, its dark flesh streaked with purple but which rotted from its core as it grew. Sequoia, three hundred feet tall and broader than a house. The only other image of America Carter had seen then was the skyline of Manhattan and behind those vast towers he imagined the redwoods stretched in a single forest clear to the Pacific.

He was slow today. He hadn't slept and he thought it might be the vodka after so long without alcohol. A dozen years ago as his liver collapsed under the onslaught of a bottle a day he had never experienced a hangover because it only hits you when you stop but he knew his body bore the scars. It was past ten already and if Fairburn didn't come soon he would write the whole thing off. He had almost convinced himself that the commission was a hoax and he had tried all night to think of a way to call his bluff and he had brought the programme so he could look him in the eye as he handed it back. *It's a monumental piece.* He thought if he confronted him he would give himself away somehow and then he could dismiss him but he began to see he didn't actually want that.

He crossed the yard to the softwood racks to find something simple but dignified. Hoop pine, he thought – the plain-sawn sapwood, if they had a good lot in. He knew pretty well how much he was looking for although he still needed measurements. Would he be given them or would he be driven to meet some elderly relative close to death? His man – he would ask his name today – looked like he had his clothes made for him and his family would be used to the feel of a tape across their shoulders. Carter always preferred his father's old cloth Rabone to a steel rule.

The timber was laid out in corridors that stretched away to the back of the dark warehouse and he stood beneath the tall cradles turning the planks to find matched cuts. He spun them and flipped them and dragged a few into the light to check the colour. When he had enough he went to look for a yardsman to mark the chit and as he walked out he saw Fairburn watching him. There was only one way in and he had been working near the doors and he knew he could not have come in while he was there. He must have been waiting.

What's this?

Hoop pine, plain-sawn. I know you wanted to keep costs down and it's a tidy batch.

He had been wrong-footed. He wanted to challenge him but he was apologising already.

I saw something by the gates for nine pounds a sheet. Tell me what you think.

They walked together and Fairburn took his arm. He seemed excited. Carter pulled out the programme.

You left this.

Thanks.

He didn't take it and he didn't even look at it. Carter couldn't put it back in his jacket – it would be a step backwards in some way he couldn't quite fathom – but there was nowhere to throw it and he didn't feel comfortable letting it fall on the gravel.

Fairburn reached into a pocket and held out an envelope:

Carter hoped it might be a drawing or a reference for a design but it felt like money. It was thick, too. Even if it was only tens it would be a thousand pounds. What was he expecting of him?

Can't have you working for nothing.

It's too much.

If it's a good job I shan't mind. I know you'll do a good job.

Now Carter had both hands full and he didn't know what to do with either. They crossed the yard in silence and Fairburn tried to remember what Bruno said about the Eskimo and the polar bear. That somewhere beneath this perverse unyielding professionalism lay the real Carter and all he had to do was hack away the fragments that hid him.

You must have seen a lot of people die.

Carter had washed and dressed hundreds of men and women but he had only ever seen one at the moment of his death. He had found out the name at the trial. Russell Emerson. The spinal cord had severed instantly and the sound Carter had heard was just the air being forced from his lungs as he collapsed onto the wooden floor. They say our lives hang by a thread and he knew it was true: he had heard it snap.

They reached the gates and Carter saw the sign:

INTERIOR SIX-PLY 8' x 4' £9 /SHEET

He wouldn't put up a shelf with it. It was strong enough but it wasn't a craftsman's material. Why would a man who was happy to give him a thousand pounds before he had even started try to save fifty by using factory-patched furniture board? Whoever – whatever – was going in here was worth Fairburn's money but not his respect.

I thought something like this.

He patted the sheet.

It's—

He had no idea what Fairburn wanted any more. He made a last bid to dissuade him.

I'm sure I can get a deal on the pine if it's the money you're worried about.

Fairburn laughed.

Thanks. But you know—

He lowered his voice to make Carter complicit in the secret.

It's going straight in the ground, and then what? Six foot of wet earth. It's not for the mantelpiece.

He picked at a corner of the board and it came away in his fingers. Carter could smell Mara's grave and he thought he would be sick and he desperately wanted to hand back the money and walk away but now he dared not. Something drew him on now. He could not make it out but he could not deny it. He wanted to spit but he swallowed the rising bile.

If you really want the ply then it'll be a traditional design.

If you say.

Fairburn saw a taxi and he ran out into the road. Carter hadn't seen an empty cab pass this way in five years.

I still have to know the size.

Fairburn climbed in and shouted over his shoulder as he slammed the door:

How big are you?

Tall. Taller than the average—

He was already pulling away and Carter ran after him and Fairburn mouthed behind the glass *Measure yourself.*

The driver asked him where he wanted to go but his mind was blank. Rooms appeared in his head, the landscape of his life – home, his office, his club, his shoemaker or his tailor – but he could not imagine himself in any of those places any more. He saw his bed and his armchair and his desk but they were objects quite separate from him now. Evidence of a self he could no longer inhabit. Nothing held him to the world any more and the only room that existed for him was at the brothel but he was afraid to go there. Afraid his desire had finally outrun him and that he no longer had the strength to confront it.

He must have asked the cabbie to take him to his office because he found himself on the pavement handing over a ten-pound note as Eleanor stepped out for a nicotine break. She was shielding the lighter from the wind when she saw him and she snapped the cigarette in half as she tried to push it into her coat pocket.

Mr. Wilmot and the surveyor were in reception for half an hour. For your ten o'clock.

Have they gone?

She nodded and he was relieved. She walked in behind him but he gestured outside.

Finish your smoke.

He stood in the lobby for a moment but he could not face the slow climb in the lift and the messages and the soft hum of the phones and the diary with the letters clipped to the pages and he walked to the end of the corridor into the mailroom. The photocopier was churning through a sixty-page cost analysis and he watched the collating-trays fill with statistics like a random-number generator. When the boys returned to bind them they found him at the franking machine in his shirtsleeves weighing the jiffy bags and keying in the postage.

¤

Carter reached the workshop still holding the programme and the envelope and as soon as the door was closed he tore it open.

He could tell from the colour that they were fifties and he counted quickly to a hundred. Five thousand pounds. He had never had that much in the bank let alone held it in his hand. But there was something unsettling about red notes: blood-money. What did Fairburn want from him?

He wanted to go to Mercy and ask her what she thought but he still felt ridiculous after his confession the previous night. He stood for a while with the money in his hand and then he put it in the drawer with the whetstones. The boards would be with him by tomorrow and he no longer had a choice. The only way he would ever find out what was really happening would be to start the work and see where it led but the idea of beginning a commission without plans or any sense of the funeral itself unsettled him.

He took down Liddell & Erskine: *The English Burial 1215–1918* to look at the coffins he had copied in the past. The straight-tapered casket with its peaked lid like a treasure chest; the solid case hewn from a single trunk with an adze; the simple wedge; the early rounded shoulders that followed the shape of the cross. He had made all of these but none of them was right for what Fairburn needed. Even the most austere and primitive of them said something of the solemnity of a burial or of the dignity of its owner. What he wanted was a box quickly built and easily forgotten. He read again of the hasty funerals for Wellington's troops as they fought their way across Spain and how the villagers had ripped the doors and shutters from their own houses to make coffins so the battalions could bury their dead before they struck camp and marched east. That was what he needed: a crate.

He took the pad of graph paper and sharpened a pencil into his cupped hand and began to sketch the dimensions. The exact length was not critical in something as simple as this but he wanted the proportions to be right. It didn't take him long and when he had finished he stared at it and he was shocked at how brutal it was. He had spent years persuading his visitors that a burial was not just eternity in a box but what he had drawn was exactly that.

He reached for the Rabone in its leather case and he realised the last time he had been measured he was handing over his civilian clothes to the prison medical officer. He tucked the lip under his boot and unwound it as he stood and he held it with a thumb to the top of his head but he couldn't bring himself to mark it.

> *Six months before his death Mozart became possessed with the idea that some of his enemies had given him Acqua Toffana, and had calculated the precise time of his decease – 'for which,' he would exclaim, 'they have ordered a Requiem. Yes, it is for myself I am writing this.'*
>
> *Musical World*, Sept 15 1837, No. LXXIX

He stood there with the tape raised but he could not look.

¤

He sat upstairs on the bus and as it passed the foot of the bridge he looked back at the curve of the river. Night had already drained it of colour. The broad floodlit façades of the north bank crowded the waterfront and the derelict wharves and warehouses of the south stared back at them from a different world and between them the water lay like a wilderness. The dome of the grand cathedral was bright in the distance but the broad ranks of offices and galleries had forced their way past and the golden cross – three hundred and sixty-five feet above the streets – was lost in a landscape of air-conditioning vents and satellite dishes.

He swung his feet up on the steel handrail of the seat in front and lay his head against the glass to gaze up at the night sky as the buildings sailed above him.

As he climbed the hill he passed Brittney and Tanya but they didn't recognise him. Tanya's jaw was still in plaster and she wrote something in a notebook and passed it to Brittney. She stopped under a street-lamp to read it but Carter was too far away to hear.

He was hot from the walk as he pushed the heavy brass bell and as he waited he could hear music. He put his ear to the door but Mercy opened it straight away. She wore an old chef's apron with a T-shirt the wrong way out and yellow rubber gloves and no make-up and she had tied her hair with a duster. She conducted the orchestra with a scrubbing brush as she curtsied and kissed him on the forehead.

Good timing.

She handed him a cloth and a bottle of window spray.

The girls said yes!

He had laid her out on the freezing jetty and he had been with her when they buried Rose and Mara and he had seen her grieving and laughing and afraid and exhausted but he had never seen her carefree and right now she was more beautiful than she had ever been. He closed the door behind him and he hoped it would never open again.

She turned back along the corridor singing with Orfeo:

> *Vieni, segui i miei passi,*
> *Unico, amato——*

He stood under the arch as she walked backwards, beckoning.

> *Come and follow in my footsteps*
> *My beloved—*

He was sure the heat would crush him. He watched as she moved among the shadows and she floated before him.

> *— My beloved, on whom alone*
> *My eternal love is fixed.*

As she crossed the hallway and started down the stairs to the lowest corridor the darkness crowded in on her. The walls dissolved and she hung before him, a tiny distant gliding figure. Her voice had faded and he watched her lips move, soundless. He felt her eyes on him begging him to come with her but he could not. Twenty paces but he could not take himself there. He was suffocating and he struggled to stop himself falling and he leaned against the wall and he noticed he was crying. He heard her call his name and in that instant he knew she loved him and the joy of being loved pierced his heart and a lifetime of denial collapsed inside him. She ran and it seemed she would never reach him and by the time she threw her arms around him and cradled his beautiful strong head in her gloves he was sobbing in great gasps.

Oh my Carter. My poor Carter.

He sank to his knees. She pulled the gloves off with her teeth and spat them onto the floor as she stroked his hair.

I love you.

He held her tight to him but he could not look at her.

> *Ma un sguardo solo—*
> *È sventura il mirarti.*

It is for me. I knew it was for me.

Mercy hesitated. She was gradually finding a way back to her own life and she didn't know if she had enough strength for both of them. Everything was so fragile. He took her hands and shook them like a child trying to make her understand.

You don't die when your heart stops and they close your eyes. You're not dead when they light the candle and sit by your bed all night. You're not dead when they lay you in the coffin. But when they bring the lid and you hear the hammer—

She put her hand to his mouth. His lips were dry and she could feel the stubble on his chin.

I can drive those nails home in three swings.

You're not going to die.

My whole life is death.

She tried to kiss him but he turned away and she tasted salt and sweat on his cheek.

Every time I carried someone to their grave I buried Death. But who buries the undertaker?

Stay here and help. You don't ever have to go back.

He didn't want to tell her he had taken the money. A fortune. It terrified him.

I love you.

He had never spoken those words before and already it was like a parting. She held him tighter.

You're not afraid to die. You're afraid to live.

He was afraid of all the things he had done and had not done and of all the things he had not allowed himself to want. He was afraid of waiting and afraid of not waiting. For so long everything had had some consequence beyond his comprehension but at last he saw that Death was not God; not the judge but only the timekeeper. Death would end his life but it could not take it from him.

She took his face in her hands and something in him gave

232

way. He turned to her and they were so close now they could see their reflections in each other's eyes and they watched themselves kiss. Happiness flooded back into her. He took her by the waist and she fell back beside him as he struggled out of his coat. She pulled it from him and he tore her apron free. He wanted to wrap himself in her – to feel her in every pore of his body – to melt into her in that ferocious heat – and he was filled with the incandescent energy of a man trying to live an entire life in a single breath. His new hardness was rooted in his very backbone and it sprang free as she forced his trousers down around his knees and he lifted her back on her hips as he pulled her pants aside. He touched her with his fingertips and she bit his lip and held it and she was wet but he wanted her dripping and he wiped the sweat from his eyes and rubbed it into her. She threw her arms around his neck and he rocked her back and pushed into her in a single arc as she fought to breathe. She forced herself back against him and he twisted her hair free of the duster and pinned her head back as he kissed her throat. She cried out and he hesitated as if to ask *Shall I stop?* but she gripped him with her nails and he closed his eyes as he readied himself for their final falling. He had frightened himself with the power of his desire and he had seen the same fear in her but they had taken each other beyond the point where they could shy away and he had learned tonight that if you love you must trust. They were fighting life and death and if they could only hold tight enough to each other as they tore down their own defences they would free themselves from all fear for ever. He shouted her name over and over and she thrilled to hear it and he felt his thighs bruise as he delivered himself into her and when it was over he cried again and she tasted the hot tears in her mouth as she brought him to her.

They lay there for hours listening to the building settle as the heat ebbed and after a while they began to shiver and they dragged themselves from the corridor into her bed half in sleep.

¤

The thick carpets and hangings were designed to bury the sounds of the world outside and the girls had been knocking and calling for ten minutes before Mercy woke. She answered the door in Carter's overcoat and Chrissy laughed.

I see business is brisk.

Seven of them waited outside and Mercy hardly recognised them in their jeans and sweatshirts as they stood smoking and talking. Only one wore make-up and Mercy saw she must have come straight from work. It was nine. She brought them in and told them where the cloakroom was but they were old hands. They hadn't been there since Louise was arrested and they were curious to see what Mercy had done with it and when they saw the nail varnish and conditioners in the Correction Room they laughed and congratulated her.

Brittney had rung everybody she knew and they had agreed to call others in turn but nobody had wanted to come on a weekday morning and most were doubtful that they would ever catch a killer this way. They were beginning to think it was just Rose's bad luck – one of the risks of a dirty business – and they were tempted to let the whole thing go until Brittney promised them a decent share of the takings.

They had brought whatever they could to help. Helen (a hundred and fifty pounds an hour for uniforms and fantasy play) had limescale remover and a gallon of bleach. Julianne (mainly girl-on-girl) hated fingerprints on paintwork and had come with cream cleaner and white spirit. Mel (oral without) brought her own vacuum cleaner that washed carpets. By the time Mercy came back with coffee in three mugs and five glasses they were already at it. Maybe they were just used to working hard or maybe they had learned that cleanliness is next to godliness in a profession where the filth is in the mind or maybe they just did it because they knew how it had been when Louise ran it but the air was filled with the scent of spring morn and alpine mood. Mercy drew back the curtains and opened the windows and everywhere she was amazed at how light the rooms were.

Carter woke eventually and walked into the corridor without dressing and three women greeted him without a second glance. Mercy laughed.

Looking for your rubber gloves?

She took his hands and kissed them and he kissed hers as they held him.

¤

Carter walked with a long stride in the cool sunshine of a November morning as he turned into the yard and found his key under the fallen slate. The fierce clear daylight had shortened the shadow of his fear and he was eager to start work. He went to the drawer to check the money was still under the whetstones although he knew he must not spend it until Fairburn had seen the coffin. He didn't know when he would come again but he did not doubt he would and he let himself enjoy the cautious circling. It was like staring into a mirror and waiting for the reflection to move first.

The boards lay against the far wall and as he took one to the sawhorses to mark it up he tried to remember what Farragh had taught him about plywood. Usually he would lay out different timbers for each part – planks and mouldings and trims to be measured and prepared for their own use – but this was like working with huge sheets of paper and he began to see in it a fine challenge.

He was free in the work now, letting the rule and the saw find their way as the lengths fell sweetly under his hand and when all the panels were cut they lay together as if pressed from a template. All his life's happiness was in these details. It was enough for him if a door swung silently or a table stood solid and he believed everything else in the world could be perfected in increments from these correct beginnings. And if the coffin was for him? He would make it with such patience and love that it would be a monument. The marking gauges and try squares would hang untouched on their racks and he would finish it with nothing but a saw and a plane. It would be the summation of his work and for the first time in his life he would call himself an artist.

¤

For three days Mercy fetched polish and bleach and chocolate and beer and cigarettes and takeaways and batteries for the radio and vast amounts of coffee, milk and sugar. Every time she came home there would be three more volunteers who had to be fed or a room that must be painted or a light that needed a plug and she would drop her shopping on the hall table and head out once again with a fresh list. She drove the girls home at all hours of the day and night to every district of the city and she took them to the brothel for their shifts with Lucas and she put them up in the few rooms that had sheets and pillows beneath the bedspreads and she struggled to memorise the names which all ran together like a mantra: Donna, Patti, Maddy, Tammy, Jamie, Haley, Tracy, Katie, Kelly, Lily, Lulu.

She was surprised at how many had wanted to help and some came every day but there was a distance to them that she could never bridge. She worked alongside them whenever she had time and she would try to tell them how much it meant to her that they were there but they never really wanted to talk and they would answer without catching her eye. They had known Rose and liked her but they were not here because of her memory and not even for revenge but for their own safety and she sensed that her love for her friend was an embarrassment to them. A weakness. And she was afraid that weakness would make her vulnerable just like Rose.

On Saturday morning she was sitting in traffic on the airport road taking two of them home and Kelly was skipping through the radio stations as they waited for the flyover to clear. The soft drink sign bubbled silently beside them as the jockey introduced *Cut and Run* and Kelly leaned forward with her arms on the back of Mercy's seat.

What is the cut?

What cut?

Management. The house. Yours.

Mercy hadn't even thought about it. She had taken out a few thousand pounds for essential repairs and alcohol and clothes for herself and she had no real idea of what else she might have to cover. But she didn't see why the girls should pay, especially since they had already given her a week of their time restoring the rooms.

Lucas takes fifty and all we get is the rubbers.

Pounds?

She squealed with laughter at the thought.

Per cent! Half!

Mercy had no idea what they earned and the thought of brokering the deals and arranging fees was more than she could face.

You're just going to have to find your own men and make your own deals. If you think you're getting into something you can't handle you can come and find me but whatever you make is yours.

Kelly turned to Paige in the back seat.

Do we pay to rent the rooms?

All you have to do is bring me those men.

They shrieked again and leaned over to hug her and she stalled the car.

The men were her biggest worry. The girls were supposed to call their regulars and let them know that a new club was opening on Sunday night and that they were invited to an evening for intimates but she was beginning to worry that their sexual skills were not matched by their social graces. She knew she would only get one shot at this and she had to have every man in the city who had visited Lucas in the last few months. Brittney and Tanya had taken Rose's address book and they were supposed to add to the list but they had already called a few men – including Rose's godfather and her elder sister's first husband – who were definitely not clients and they were starting to lose their enthusiasm.

When word spread that Mercy didn't want a percentage the girls relaxed and a few new faces even arrived with buckets and brooms. She began to enjoy having them there. She took eleven of them to lunch at *Pig in a Poke* and on the way back they crowded in to the local chemist and bought two hundred and forty regular condoms and a hundred and twenty fruit-flavoured. The pharmacist counted the packets carefully into brown paper bags and as he took the money he asked:

Is it rag week?

Haley turned to Donna and whispered too loud:

Not if I can help it!

They fell into uncontrollable hysterics.

That afternoon she answered the door to Louise Parrish. The track suit had been replaced by a dark skirt and jacket and Mercy thought she saw the sheen of lipstick.

Welcome back.

She stood aside as Louise walked in. A few of the girls washing the windows ran to greet her and Mercy could tell she was pleased. She knew all the names.

You've a lot to do.

Mercy didn't want to tell her how bad it had been four days ago. She let Louise talk as they wandered through the rooms and she barely recognised it herself.

They won't sit in these side rooms if the bar's still open. How many do you expect?

We have forty girls tomorrow night.

Louise tried to imagine it. She had never had more than twenty.

You'll have to use the two upper bedrooms as drawing rooms and have separate drinks on the side tables. The men won't like to be crowded. Take the chairs from here and put a few at the top of the stairs. That's always quiet. What happened to the mirror?

One of the girls had cut a panel of silk from the lining of a curtain to fill the empty frame.

I sent it to be re-silvered.

She hoped she wouldn't notice the chandelier.

Who are your bartenders?

Brittney has some friends who don't work Sundays.

Do they know what they're doing? These people are going to spend up to a thousand pounds in three hours and if they ask for a champagne cocktail it had better be good.

Three drops of bitters on a sugar cube, shot of brandy, top up with champagne. Flute.

They work at Elbow Room.

Very good. For all I know they do this anyway but you must tell them to water the spirits. You can't do it with the beer but the last thing you want is men too drunk to come. They stay all night. Are you lighting the fires?

The sweep was here yesterday and the girls all came to shake his hand when he'd finished. He was about seventy and he came up to here on me and he thought he'd died and gone to heaven.

Louise laughed.

You've thought of the important stuff.

We'll get there.

How are you getting your men?

The girls have made some calls.

She shook her head.

They're the best in the business when they're on their backs but I wouldn't even let them answer the door when I was here. It's a skill all of its own.

Brittney has Rose's book. It's all we've really got.

Louise took the folded lined paper from her pocket.

Sorry about the writing. Caitlin copied it for me at a penny a line but nobody gets the real book. It's my pension.

There must have been five hundred entries and beside each one was a telephone number, the dates of the visits and the girls.

It's no guarantee they were ever at Lucas's place—

Mercy still didn't believe Louise liked her but perhaps she gave it because she believed she owed it to herself or the girls or even just to these familiar rooms. Not so long ago she would

240

have handed the list back out of pride but now she just took it and hugged her.

You must only introduce men to women – never other men, even if they look lost – and you don't call anybody by their name. Just kiss them and tell them how glad the girls will be that they're back. The rest will happen by itself. The birds and the bees.

¤

The last wash of blue beyond the courtyard wall had faded and the wind had died and the coffin waited in the silence. It was finished. Carter sat unmoving at the foot of the stairs and the light from the kitchen fell around him on the cobbled floor. He had swept the room and put away the few tools he had used and his work lay ghostly pale across the sawhorses. It was faultless – simple and strong and light and perfectly proportioned – and when he ran his thumb along the joints he could feel no edge. It might have been carved from a single piece. He had been tempted to lie in it but he knew it would fit him perfectly and for the wedge to support his head he had chosen a length of English oak; Fairburn could not grudge him that.

He went to the little shelf to fetch the *eau-de-vie* and took the two tumblers and placed them on the step beside him and filled them to the brim. The meniscus quivered as he put the heavy flask down. He kept the liquor for the friends and relatives of the dead and he would always pour a glass to leave on the lid the night before the burial but tonight he saw he was both the mourner and the mourned. He drank the first down in a single shot and felt it grip him. He took the second more slowly trying to sense what it could have been distilled from but it tasted of nothing, hot and white. A spirit.

As his body abandoned itself one last time to that terrible nullity he felt the memory of it – the inertia of deep unending drunkenness – had never left him. For so many years alcohol had drawn itself like a veil between him and his life but tonight he could no longer tell which side of that shroud he stood. Whether it hid him or the world. He opened his mouth to shout for Fairburn as if his voice would carry across the city but no sound would come and he realised he was already dead. He lifted his hands to his face and he could not tell whether it was his fingers that were cold or his cheeks. He wanted to look in the mirror to see if his eyes had grown dull but he was too tired to stand and he poured again from the flask. Perhaps he would pretend nothing had happened. He would go to bed and in the morning he would dress and take the offcuts to the bins at the end of the alley and have breakfast at Jack's and wait to see if anybody spoke to him. Now the frosts had come the decay would be gradual.

He was not afraid but he was angry. Death had courted him like a lover – confidentially and solicitously, as though he were the only one in the world he cared to take – but now he spurned him. He had turned his back and already he was making his way across the city striking his deals with the next man and the next again. Did he never stay to admire his trailing wake of grief and fear?

He longed for Fairburn to claim the casket but he did not know whether he would strike or embrace him when he came. He was powerless and fury raged in him as he saw that all the rites he had devised and directed were charades, the frantic vain rhetoric of a man pleading for his own life. Nothing he had made or trusted had endured and nothing had been able to withstand Fairburn's grim seduction.

*

The room was too dark now even for shadows but years of work at the same benches echoed in him and the hammers and rasps and try-squares fell under his hand as he took them unseeing and piled them in the old tea chest. He did not bed them in sawdust or wrap them in greaseproof paper but merely let them drop haphazard in the crate and if the blades and rules and points rang as they fell together he did not hear it. He cleared the racks and the shelves and emptied the drawers and the boxes and the cabinets until nothing was left to show that this place had ever been his. He would leave it as he found it and as he opened the doors to the yard to let the coffin pass he could hear that even the silence had changed.

¤

Mercy slept as late as she could but by early afternoon Brittney's friends from Elbow Room had begun to unload the crates of glasses and alcohol and after she had shown them the bar she ran a bath. She hung her dressing gown across the gate and climbed in and crouched as the water cooled and finally she settled back and floated for a moment in the silence.

She washed her hair and let the conditioner sit while she stripped the polish from her nails. She shaved her legs and under her arms with a fresh razor. She used the orange bran soap on her face and the sandalwood on her body and she softened her hands with the aloe and borage.

She spent an hour there and when she stepped out the room was warm and pale with steam and she left the towel on the floor to stand before the long mirror and she watched the water run from her hair over her shoulders and across her belly and down her legs. The silvery lines seemed to draw her body out forever and she moved closer. She was radiant. She ran her hands from her throat over her breasts to her thighs and she thought of Carter and that heat inside her. She stared at the hair between her legs still dark from the bath and she reached for the scissors and cut it back until just a shadow hid her. Nobody could doubt her as a whore now.

She put on a dark backless dress, black tights without pants and her favourite heels. Perhaps she had forgotten that Rose had worn exactly the same the night she died. She had to be breathtaking for the men but also for herself because if she allowed her confidence to slip for a second the illusion would be gone. She must be invulnerably beautiful but she knew too that she would have to abandon her defences utterly in order to draw him and to sense him when he came to her and she must discard all the diffidence her work had taught her. She must let herself become the woman she had never dared believe in. It was more liberating than any political statement or any shocking image she had ever made but she had to remind herself that soon she would be alone in a room with the man who had killed Rose. If there was a second of self-deception – a single false step – he would seize it and turn it against her.

¤

Carter had parked the van under the railway bridge and dragged the coffin through the deserted streets and now he knelt with it on the jetty as he had with Mercy hardly a month before. Night had overtaken afternoon without pausing for the quiet colours of evening and the banks of dark windows at the water's edge reflected neither stars nor cloud and in the valleys and the shadows around them great clocks translated the dizzy hum of electric motors into the invisible swing of counterweighted gold hands. Seven o'clock. A minute before. Two minutes past. Far below him the river looked tranquil enough but he knew that even now – just before low tide – the current would be running strong. He finished the last of the liquor and threw the flask into the darkness but before it had even righted itself in the waves it was lost from view.

He lit the hurricane lamp and spread the canvas roll and took a straight gouge and he began to carve his name on the head of the casket. He had already pencilled it out and he was careful to sharpen the blade every few strokes because he knew the plywood would splinter once the layers were exposed. He had all the time in the world but it was quick work and when he was finished the crossed grain of the plies gave the letters an extra depth and it looked well. He had asked his father once to write his name on the side of his favourite yacht on the high shelf but he had told him the hull was too small. *But it's only a small name.*

He put the hand bell in his pocket and took the lamp in his teeth and he knew he could carry the coffin on his good shoulder but he couldn't manage the lid at the same time so he stood at the edge of the jetty and let it drop. It fell end over end spiralling past the massive timbers that shored the city walls and sliced into the mud eighty feet below. A headstone. He lowered himself over the edge of the ladder and felt his way down the rungs and the further down he went the colder the metal grew. The thick cladding of rust flaked free in his fingers and he was surprised that it had outlasted a century of tide and storm. Twice he nearly slipped and the alcohol had dulled his reflexes but eventually he stood at the bottom and the sounds of the city high above faded to nothing and he let the coffin fall and dragged it over the shingle to the water's edge.

¤

The brothel was fuller than Mercy had dreamed possible. She had grown used to the girls in sweat-shirts and jeans scrubbing carpets and now as they moved through the rooms catching eyes and greeting guests in their evening clothes she was astonished. Some were elegant in dark skirt and blouse and their promise was only whispered but others followed a more brazen tradition with dresses cut high to the naked thigh. The message was shockingly carnal and when Brittney came to the bar to order a spritzer every head turned in her wake. She blew a kiss to the bartender.

Do I get one on the house?

Are you going to return the compliment?

She threw him a V and laughed.

Busy night. We reckon we got two hundred and fifty.

Six each.

In your dreams. They won't all get lucky.

You wouldn't even notice one more.

Not if it's you I wouldn't.

Mercy was a stranger in her own home. She had never seen any of these visitors before but they moved and drank and spoke as if they came here every night of the week. There were dark suits and pressed jeans and silk shirts open to the third button and monogrammed handkerchiefs. There were clips of folded fifties and pockets full of creased tenners and Swiss francs and even credit cards; Tanya had the Visa verification call-centre on automatic redial on her mobile. There were folded squares of cocaine and tablets of Viagra and hip-flasks of thirty-year-old single malt – *older than you, my dear* – and everywhere they mixed with the bland fellowship of men at a row of urinals pretending they aren't exposing themselves to a stranger while they talk about unseasonal sunshine. Everyone knew that the drink and small talk and murmured compliments would end with stifled cries in the rooms downstairs and the delicacy of the approach was all the more enticing because the outcome was inevitable. They knew what was on offer and what was expected and it became a simple matter of arranging the price.

Plenty had already asked after Mercy and she had steered them gracefully to other girls but she wondered what it would be like to stuff two hundred pounds into her pants and unzip a stranger. She hoped Carter would come soon. She made her way across the crowded hall to check the other rooms and Chrissy found her and put her arms around her.

Rose would be proud.

A man in a leather jacket put his hands on their hips as they stood together. He was shorter than both of them.

How much for the two of you? Right now.

Chrissy turned.

More than you can afford.

I'm loaded, pussycat. Put a hand in my pocket.

She could see the rolled notes and she slid her hand across his flies.

Too bad we only fuck the poor.

She kissed Mercy on the lips as she walked away. With Lucas standing guard she would have regretted it but here she was free.

See you later, gorgeous.

Some of the men had already disappeared with their regulars and the others who had divided their numbers by the total of remaining girls were moving from flirting to more urgent negotiations. Mercy knew she should be looking for Rose's visitor but under the influence of sex and alcohol nobody really seemed a killer. Was the young man who had stood at the top of the stairs alone for twenty minutes a psychopath or just overwhelmed by guilt because he had met a father he knew from the car pool? Were the handcuffs whose silhouette showed beneath the flannel trousers destined for a girl chained to the bed or for the man himself begging to be forced to the ground by a four-inch stiletto? It was absurd. These suits and ties were no different from any in the bar of a decent hotel in this same neighbourhood and she knew it would be the most unremark-able of these pleasant faces that wanted to take a girl and split her lip or stand over her to urinate angrily.

She found Brittney at the top of the stairs.

The baldy by the door. He's talked to all of you but he hasn't chosen anybody yet.

He's haggling. There's no way he's been to a place like this before.

The one who won't drink?

He's one of mine. It's not him.

Has anyone asked for anything rough?

Maddy got tied but she told Tanya and she waited in the next room. Too full for that now, though.

I know. I never knew you could get rich from this game.

You should have taken a cut.

Madam Mercy.

Sounds good.

It sounded like a student theatre piece and she began to think this whole thing was a ridiculous vanity. Had she thought he would walk in with crazy staring eyes and black leather gloves?

Have you talked to the others?

Nobody's gone down with anybody we hadn't seen before. If he's here he's not getting laid.

¤

Carter put the lamp and the gouges and the bell aboard the coffin and set it afloat and waded in up to his waist. The river was no colder than the air around him but it drew the warmth out of him in an instant and he shivered violently. He pushed further out and he could feel the current begin to tug at him but the ground was firm beneath his feet and he was not afraid. He kept the casket at arm's length and it began to rock as it reached the deeper water. He could see the light flickering inside and now he held it only by the tips of his fingers and the water reached his chest and enough of him was submerged that as the swell rose he felt himself lift clear of the bed. He turned to look back at the shore and he knew he had only to walk back but he could not. His headstone was sinking sideways in the mud and he could hear the soft sucking as it wrenched itself free.

A wave lifted him again and the coffin pulled away and he watched it spin in a lazy arc until the tide took it and it began to pick up speed as it moved downriver. It swayed in the shadows and for a moment it disappeared. Carter struck out after it kicking and flailing but as he swam he had to close his eyes and when he stopped and tried to raise himself to see he was too far from the shore and everything was black. He trod water panting and spitting and he turned himself back and forth and then he saw the twin towers of the great drawbridge in the distance and he knew he was already moving east and for a second he saw the glow of the hurricane lamp again.

He reached it at last and he tried to throw his arm over the edge but the casket tilted under his weight and struck him across the temple and he knew he would have to risk rolling it towards him for long enough to climb in. He was desperate now and swallowing water at every breath but somehow he heaved himself up and tipped himself over the side and he fell into it on all fours and fumbled for the lamp. He held it above him but all he could see was the reflection of the flame in the dark surface.

He was drifting now, cold and drunk and exhausted. He had no idea what he would do or where the river would take him. He passed the huge unmanned barges full of timber and salvage tethered to the bed far below and he hoped he might swing broadside into one of the chains that lay taut against the falling tide and climb free but soon he was in open waters and he knew there was nothing between here and the sea. He unrolled the pouch and drove a chisel into the lip of the casket at his feet and hung the lamp from it. If he lay still it was steady enough and he looked up at the embankments sixty feet above him and the shadows of the taller buildings that grew above them. He had not thought that the roof of the city was so full of colour with the red of winking aircraft warnings and the violet of the railway station arch and the high blue curve of the marine registry. He passed flood drains and hidden tunnels and walk-ways and moorings and steps that climbed to nowhere and he was on the underside of the world staring up at its roots. Granite parapets stood at the peak of the coarser walls and below that the stone was black and green with oil and weed and below that again lay the hard compacted rubble and brick of the deeper bank braced with sunken pillars and buttresses until it sank into the formless mud and the river itself. He wanted the tide to ebb for ever and draw him down to the core of the earth.

¤

It was late now and the fires had sunk low and Mercy wandered the rooms trying to avoid the glances of the men who remained.

They would be lucky to get a cab now let alone a kiss but the girls were delighted. Most were still downstairs turning the last tricks of the night and she knew they had done well and that they had drawn such a crowd that they had been able to choose who they pleased. She had no real experience of selling sex but she knew a good party when she saw one and Haley had said that even Tanya with her jaw wired shut had turned a healthy profit giving hand-jobs in the store room.

She went to sit at the bar. Either the killer wasn't in Louise's book or he had come and nobody had recognised him but these girls had fine-tuned their instinct for risk and they were careful to remember the faces on their danger list. If he had been here they would have known. She had been certain she would see him tonight and she thought of Rose and Mara together with him in that room and she understood then that what she wanted was more complex than revenge. And she saw that for the first time in too long she had failed and now she was utterly lost.

Kelly joined her with her shoes in her hand. The baby hair at her temples glistened with sweat. She was radiant.

Nine-fifty in five hours. I don't want to get greedy.

She leaned over the bar kicking her heels in the air and whistled at the bartender.

Campari and orange half and half with ice. What do you want? On me.

Mercy thought of her hug in the car.

Whisky. Thanks.

They raised their glasses.

Cheers, me dears. Let us know if you ever decide to do this for a living.

She downed it in two long draughts and whistled for another and she saw Mercy's desolation and she took her hand.

You're so brave. We really wanted to help—

Mercy looked away. She felt an improbable tenderness towards these girls now but she knew this was just a wild adventure for them and that they had their own lives and that their reasons for coming tonight were nothing to do with her. Kelly kissed her and ran to catch Paige in the hall and she turned to the staff behind the bar and told them to start collecting the glasses.

The whisky was good and she was off-duty now and she went behind the counter to look at the label and fill her glass. There was a champagne bucket of melted ice on the bar and she took a handful and held it and it ran cold on her wrist.

I'll have one of those.

She looked up and she knew the face. He wore the same suit and he was as attractive as he had been in her imagination.

Connor Fairburn.

He looked like he had only just woken and showered.

Your agent introduced us.

She blushed. The thought of Richard making his terrible puns about all these girls was more than she could bear right now. How had he heard about this? She hadn't even thought about what would happen if someone she actually knew turned up. Presumably they would be as embarrassed as she was but Fairburn didn't seem surprised to see her.

I'm sorry I'm late.

Who had invited him? She looked around for one of the girls but the rooms were empty.

Do I get a whisky or shall I help myself?

Sure. Sorry.

She rinsed a glass and poured a shot. She pushed the drink across the counter and he took a creased note from his wallet.

I've no idea what they charge. Don't worry about it.

He laid the money down but she wanted him to go home so they could both pretend this hadn't happened. The evening was over and though she liked him she wanted her house empty again and she wished Carter would come.

I bought one of your pictures.

They haven't been selling well. Not that I should tell you.

Death. Not good on the coffee table.

She laughed but she was flattered.

I didn't think your agent was going to say yes but I sent him the cheque anyway.

She hadn't thought about the show for weeks and the note Richard had sent was a dim memory. She would call him tomorrow. Now that this madness was over her life would slide back to normal soon enough.

I don't give everyone my card. I was hoping you'd call so I could show you some of my stuff.

Stuff. The adrenaline of the evening was wearing off and she was dizzy with the noise and the tension and the whisky. She wanted to say *I'd really have loved to but my best friend was killed and I had to steal her body and bury her in the woods and I found a witness but she slit her wrists in my bath and then I fell in love with the man who made her coffin and someone tried to kill him too and now I run a brothel so I've been pretty busy* but she just said:

We should do that.

Kelly and Paige waved from the hall as they left. She wanted to know which picture he had bought and then she remembered Richard had said *He's desperate to find something nobody else has seen* and her heart missed a beat. He picked up the twenty-pound note and smoothed it flat with the ball of his thumb.

Did he show you the contact sheets?

You were right; there were hundreds. It took me over an hour to pick one.

Fury and humiliation tore at her and she wanted to call Richard right now and tell him how he had betrayed her. If she could not control the way she showed herself to the world then what would be left for her? The shots she had rejected flooded her mind and she was mortified to think that he would hang a picture five feet high that she had censored behind a scribble of chinagraph. Nobody must ever see her like this but she dare not admit it and she was too proud to ask which he had chosen.

Are you doing something with whores?

The word sounded bitter.

Doing?

For another show. People find it fascinating. Prurience and outrage, our national pastime. You should look into it.

He folded the note in half along its length and stood it on its end.

Are you shocked?

Why should I be shocked?

To see what these girls do just for money. To see me here.

Why are you here?

The word was out – the murmur—

He gestured around him.

—a new club.

She thought of his wife and she resented him coming like this. She didn't want to be a part of his secrets. He was trying to draw her into something and she tried to fight against it.

I want the ones who don't do it because they need the money.

She felt her anger rise. He held his hand above the counter and crushed the note.

It's a man's first fantasy. The woman who fucks strangers because she likes it. She's the whore.

Why are you telling me this?

Why are you selling me a picture of yourself pretending to be dead when you still want us all to want to fuck you?

As he cursed he flicked the crumpled ball onto the floor behind the bar and she knew at once that he had come. She looked around her but they were alone again and the fear she had waited for began to fill her.

You killed Rose—

He turned to her as if something had resolved itself in his mind. His mouth was neither open nor closed and a tiny drop of spittle hung at the corner of his lip and for the first time since she had known him he was not flawlessly beautiful.

I never touched her.

Mercy tried to think what Mara had said. *Make her shut up. Shut her up.*

I wanted her more than anyone I ever had and I never touched her.

He could not see why Lucas had been so afraid of Mercy in her vulnerability and her anger and of Carter, naive and headstrong. He wanted her to laugh with him at the stupidity of it all but he knew their counterposed mutual grief was too raw. He wanted to confess everything and hear everything from her and he knew he should be afraid now that she would bring the girls to identify him and hold him while they fetched the police and he tried to remind himself that he would face a charge of murder but he did not really believe it. How can you murder someone you adore?

¤

Lucas lay on the leather sofa with a tumbler of vodka and he could see where Carmen's cowboy boots had marked the arm. The room was dark and the fire was not lit and he was drunk but instead of making him forgetful and unfocused the alcohol had made him angry. He knew that every single one of his girls was using this Sunday night – when the brothel was always closed – to help at a new club nearer the centre of town but he dared not show his face there until he knew for certain what was up. He had not decided yet whether to put the girls under the manners one by one if they tried to jump ship or simply to reclaim his territory by burning the new place to the ground. All he knew as he lay staring at the ranks of bottles behind the bar was that he had spent his whole life building an empire he could call his own and he could not afford to let it collapse around him now. He still had fifteen months left on the lease and twenty-four thousand mono-grammed cocktail napkins in the store-room and without those little initials lying on the bar he himself would cease to exist.

Tina had told him that the girls had been talking about it downstairs for over a week but none of his professional acquaintances had heard anything so he had sent Fairburn to take a look. If any of his lot recognised him as Rose's visitor and called the cops then so much the better: he could only hold Mayman for so long and if Fairburn could not get any sense out of the undertaker then maybe it was time to bring the matter to a close by giving Fairburn the push instead. Coppers loved a happy ending, he knew, by which they meant neat if not actually correct. A victim, a killer, a conviction. Catharsis in triplicate.

¤

The coffin began to pitch in the faster water. Mile by mile the city unravelled itself in a floodlit chain of pumping stations and hoists and holding tanks until fences and asphalt gave way to open sand and darkness descended.

Carter reached down for the hand bell and began the lazy cadence and he paused to listen to the sound race back from the sea wall and then he rang and rang again until the triplet measure ran over itself and the world was lost in the echo. He could smell the salt from the marshes now and the swell was rising and soon he knew the waves would break over him. He wanted to stand and he tried to get his legs under him but the casket lurched and water poured over the side. He kneeled and steadied himself but he was spinning in the current and it threw him to the other side and he sank lower again. The lamp went under and Carter tried to snatch it up but the chimney shattered and he lost his grip on the smooth wood under his feet and pitched sideways.

The shock of the fall and the cold winded him and as he fought for air he knew his lungs were filling with water. Mercy had chosen to drown – to suffocate – because if the body was found quickly there would be no damage to the face but he did not know what would become of him. Would he sink here at the mouth of the old docks or drift to the coast to lie hidden in the reeds for the crabs and the gulls? Would Death take him by the hair and drag him to the shore or would he roll with the tides forever?

He struck out for the coffin again but it was on its side now and he saw the gouges slip from the canvas pouch and drop below the surface. He took a final breath and dived down after them. They hung before him not so heavy in the water as they were in the air but they were soon beyond his reach and he watched them melt away in the darker channel below. He twisted onto his back to see the clean square line of the casket as it floated high overhead. The twin beams of the lighthouse swept the waves and the pattern folded and unfolded far above but he was sinking and the horizon shrank around him. The bell tumbled past his face and the brass flashed in the darkness like lightning to a blind man and a tremendous heat flooded his body. He knew he no longer needed to hold his breath and he let the bubbles explode out of him winking and swelling as they rose. He swam among them with his arms outstretched and his hands were huge in front of him and he reached up to the silvery skin of the sleeping world as if blessing it.

¤

Fairburn rang the night bell at his office twice and they waited several minutes on the pavement before the security guard stepped out of the stairwell and crossed the darkened lobby. He shone the torch in Fairburn's face for a moment before he recognised him and reached for his keys.

Who's here?

He didn't know his name.

Nobody, sir. Me.

The clock above the stairs read a quarter to two. Fairburn held the door for Mercy.

Can I get something for you?

We'll be in my office. You can wait down here.

They walked to the lift and Fairburn turned again.

We'll be fine. You let me have the keys and you can go.

I'm supposed to be here till eight.

That's all right.

I'm not allowed to leave the building, sir. In the contract.

The building's mine and so is your contract.

The keys hung from a chain looped around his waist and he tried to slip it free but it caught in his belt. Mercy didn't want to be here alone but she had staked everything on finding Fairburn and now she had him she dared not let him go. She had wanted to shout for the girls to help as she sat with him at the bar but if the police had come what could they have done?

258

There was nothing to connect Fairburn to Rose's death any more and once they had seen the kind of party she had thrown she would have followed Louise Parrish to jail. Everything she had done added up to nothing and even now – here with the man she had been desperate to find – she was powerless. She signalled to the guard to stay but he knew Fairburn was married and he did not want to catch her eye. Discretion was another clause in his contract.

The lift came and Fairburn pressed the button for the upper floor but the doors would not close and the guard walked back.

When the alarm's on you have to use the key.

He slid it round the chain and pushed it into the slot. Fairburn pressed the button again and the doors began to close but he held them with his foot until the man was gone.

Mercy stood beside him in the carpeted silence as the green numbers began to flash softly in front of them. Raw fear had exhausted itself and a strange indifference had settled and her actions were no longer decisions but instincts. The instincts of a self she had not yet learned to trust.

The steel doors opened but the office was dark. The city lay at her feet beyond the massive glass wall and for a second she thought she was outside and she dared not step forward. She could make out the shape of the river between the buildings that skirted it and the silhouette of the great triangular tower floated towards her as the moonlit clouds moved around it. Fairburn walked out into the darkness and he remembered that the lights were controlled from Eleanor's office downstairs. He turned back and twisted the key in its socket to hold the doors open and when his eyes had grown used to the shape of the room he crossed to his desk. The street-lamps layered their sodium glow across the ceiling and his shadow rippled as he walked.

Mercy had no idea where she was or what Fairburn did here but she watched him as he went and when he reached for the parcel she knew at once what it contained. He brought it to her and in the soft cool light from the open lift he tore the paper free and laid it on the floor.

It was not the photograph she had dreaded where she lay plain and swollen and her mouth hung open and when she saw it she hardly recognised it but Fairburn's eye was unerring. What had barely been worth a second glance when it lay two inches square on a sheet with a dozen other shots had a power all of its own when blown up three feet across. It must have been the final picture of the evening and perhaps she thought the photographer had finished the roll because she had half-raised herself from the worn boards and she reached out and her eyes met the camera and she stared back at herself as if to say *You cannot touch me*. It was not a model portrait but it was riveting and she could not tear her eyes from it. She wondered why he had chosen it and she could not know that it reminded him of Rose and that look he could not drive from his mind. That promise.

Is this who you think I am?

I don't know who you are.

Is this who you want me to be?

Who do you want to be?

She did not think he was drunk but he was stumbling over his words. He tried to get back to that room with the low chair and the sickly light but this time the face that stared up at him was not Rose.

What do you want?

What Rose wants. What she wanted.

She wanted me.

He was desperate to believe it. Mercy shook her head. He took a step closer and he held his palms to her as if to say *How could she not?* and Mercy forced herself not to back away. He asked again:

What do you want?

I want to know what happened.

You know what happened.

I know what Mara told me.

Isn't it enough?

Mercy remembered the cold hands.

What did she tell you?

She could hear Mara as she wept but when she spoke her own voice was filled with violence. Fairburn was under her spell and he followed the contours of her words as if they were a language he did not speak and when he thought of Mara he realised he no longer knew what she looked like.

When Mercy fell silent and Rose lay dead it was as if she had made her own confession and when she looked up Fairburn's eyes were closed and he thanked her.

What if everything she told you is true?

Mercy knew now that it had been the truth but she had thought it would be different when she stood before him. That it would mean something else. That it would exist in some more solid way and that it could therefore be denied in that way. She felt as if she had carried something precious in her hands day and night over an unimaginable distance and now she had arrived and she looked down to see she held nothing.

Fairburn walked to the window.

I didn't want her to die. Accidents happen and they happen to those that deserve them and those that don't. I don't know any more than that.

He shrugged and turned away.

But you know more.

I know you killed her.

She did not dare to believe that Mara had been right. That

Rose had not been killed by anger and spite but by urgency and the recklessness of lust.

I didn't kill her.

You took her to that room and you undressed her and tied her—

She was a whore!

His fury rang against the wall of glass.

She was there every night waiting for us to come. For me. Do you think I was her first?

Mercy could not see his face. He spoke to the city spread below him.

Maybe you didn't know she was a whore. Or maybe you knew but you didn't know what those women will do for their money. She took my money and she agreed to everything I asked.

To be choked to death?

She stepped towards him.

You don't buy—

Are you so shocked?

He laughed in the darkness.

Maybe you're not shocked. Maybe you like the sound of no but the feeling of yes.

He turned to look down at her photograph on the floor.

Is that what you like?

She stepped onto the picture and ground her heel into her own face beneath the glass and it shattered and the heavy print paper buckled.

Don't dream your dreams on me!

He looked at her in the dark dress and he saw her anger and her wild courage and he took her by the hair and forced her back against the wall and kissed her but she turned her face aside. She tried to push him away but he had knocked the breath from her and her eyes flashed with fury and he was hardening again. He was strong and Mercy could still feel the whisky in her and she knew she could not fight him for long. He took the hem of her dress in his hand and pulled it aside and stared at her. Mercy thought of Rose and tried to imagine a thousand men who had seen her friend like that and still she had given them nothing of herself.

Wait.

His arm was across her throat and she could hardly get the words out.

Let me—

He kept a hand to her chest and she kept her eyes on him as she slipped her shoes off. She would not break that gaze.

Nothing you could pay me would buy me but you can fuck me if you dare.

Are you a whore now?

I'm nothing that you know.

He let his arm fall and she swung the shoe at him. The heel caught him below the eye and he raised his hands to his face and she ran at him and he crouched but they fell together and his head hit the floor and he cried out. He struck out with his arm and her cheek flashed in agony but she was up before him and she kicked out with her bare feet. He rolled on his hands and knees and tried to stand but he fell against the steel doors and the broken glass lay all around and he felt himself bleeding through his silk-lined trousers as Mercy dropped on him. He reached up to pull her over but she had his arm now and as she forced his head down she heard the shards grate on the marble and she hesitated for a second because everything in her training as a model told her that a face must never be scarred. He lay to one side and she saw the shadow of blood beneath the fragment of glass that had pierced his cheek like a tear and in her fury she hit out again and again—

Don't dream your dreams on me!

He tore at her hair and she screamed as he moved beneath her and she knew all she could do now was run. They struggled together in the mouth of the lift and the chain hung down beside her and she stood and tried to rip it free but his hands were already at her legs. She turned the key and the cabin light went out and she twisted it the other way but there was nothing but darkness and against the brilliant backdrop of the city his shadow rose up on all fours and then the doors slipped free and they closed at his throat. He tried to loose himself but he could not raise his hands and the lights flickered on as she watched him writhe and the doors slid open. His head dropped but he was ready to come for her. She punched the buttons again and again and the doors closed once more but she knew they would not hold him and she tore the key free from the slot and the lift died. Without power the doors would not move and she could hear him fighting for breath but he could not speak to her. She moved to the back of the cabin and waited for it to be over.

Fairburn looked up at her and the darkness came on him in waves and he felt that final monumental surge of blood swell between his legs as he lay on the cold stone floor. He was no longer here but in that room again and he looked for Rose on the bed but she was already gone. Death's conquest crouched with her dress thrown open to the waist and he reached out to touch her and he saw his hands were nothing but bones.

PART FOUR

The sky was lightening and thin cirrus unwound from the horizon as colour crept back into the land. The rushes stirred as the breeze awoke and as the tide turned once again the fresh water ebbing and the salt water rising hovered in equilibrium. Carter lay in the reeds hidden from the winds and gradually he felt his breath return. He was numb with cold and he was too tired to care if he was alive or still dead but as the shorebirds began to call he stood and stared around him and everywhere the wetlands reached away to nowhere. The sun had just risen free of the sea and the marshes were flooding with its weak warm light. It was barely dawn but already everything was touched by it. He had never woken outside a city sunk in the shadow of its own valleys and he was transfixed by the bright serenity of this empty world.

To the north lay the estuary and the pale shapes of the sandbars and further off in the deeper channel a freighter crept out to sea. He watched it until it was gone and the sun climbed into the clear air and the water was darker now as the reflection melted away. Twenty miles to the west lay the city he could not see but he turned and followed his faint shadow across the grass.

¤

Mercy watched that same dawn spread through the gap in the doors and the glass around Fairburn's body shone in the cold sky light. She had not slept but hours had passed and she was cold and stiff. Her scalp was bruised and her cheek pounded when she moved her jaw but she was safe.

She knew she could not carry the body by herself and she must get help before the new guard came at eight. She had wound the chain around her wrist and she found the key and powered the lift again and when the doors opened Fairburn slipped sideways as he had when they fought but the sound of his falling was utterly different. The glass was still in his cheek but he had not bled. She could not bring herself to touch him so she stepped over his body where it lay on her torn face and walked to his desk.

She called Carter but it was barely day and she was about to cut herself off but she knew the sound would have woken him already and she waited for him to answer. At the twentieth ring she hung up and she wanted to know where he was and she was angry and then jealous again until she remembered this would be the third time she had brought a body to him and she was glad he was not there.

¤

The grass whispered around him as he pushed on through the shallows. The creeks and ditches had dissolved the land in a patchwork of sunken fields and he dragged himself across the marsh on his hands and knees. He could no longer feel his fingers and his feet had swollen in his boots and he knew he must find somewhere to sit to take them off.

The sun had swung south and it was no longer at his back

but he pushed on and he saw the river curve across him now and he would have to follow it around. He skirted the flats and the tide raced to meet him across the rippled sand and he saw the wall of a sheep-wash long abandoned and he rested there for a moment as the sea rolled in. The double bows were still fast and he could hardly curl his fingers to grip them and when he pulled his feet free the laces and the seams were printed deep in him. He left the boots on the wall and when he reached the headland he turned back and they were barely visible above the rising tide.

¤

Mercy watched from the window and she saw the white van reverse the length of the one-way street. It was nearly eight. She went down to let them in and she could tell Brittney and Ross had been arguing as they drove.

Not in the back of the van.

I can't take you home. Gary's back.

You're taking the piss.

She took them back up with her and when they stepped out into the office the bickering stopped.

Christ almighty.

Brittney stood over the body and she looked up at Mercy and she nodded.

I saw him leave. I didn't know it was him. Did he come?

At the end. I didn't know where you were.

Are you OK?

I'm still here.

She wanted Brittney to hug her but she went to the window and stared down at the city as it stirred.

Unbelievable.

Ross sat at Fairburn's desk and opened the drawers and Brittney called across to him:

I'm not fucking picking him up. You're going to earn this.

Mercy tried not to think about the trail of bodies she had left and about the questions she would have to answer. She was afraid.

We have to go.

Ross dragged Fairburn by his feet and his hair trailed behind him. As the doors closed he blew in Brittney's ear and whispered:

Ever done it in a lift?

He parked the van in the alley where nobody would see them and Brittney went in first and she could hear the cleaners in the bar and she knew if they had started that Lucas would be asleep. The Shadow Suite was last from the end on the lower floor and they laid Fairburn on the bed with his head to the door and Mercy wondered if it was true that he had never touched her. She stood and listened for a moment – she didn't know why – but all she could hear was the vacuum cleaner upstairs.

She drove Brittney home and when they pulled up they said goodbye in the car so she wouldn't disturb her boyfriend.

He's mad if he doesn't get eight hours.

Mercy wanted to sleep for the rest of her life.

What do you think he'll do when he finds him?

Waste disposal.

We could have the police there before he's even awake.

I've been thinking about it since we left.

Mercy held out her hand for the phone but Brittney shook her head.

If they put him away they'll close the place down and the girls will be back on the streets like they were when they took Louise in. It's a bitch.

Mercy thought of Louise being hustled down the steps after twelve years and she thought of Kelly laughing and kicking her heels at the bar and she thought of herself alone again in her bed in that empty room hidden from the world and she opened her bag and held out her keys.

What's that?

I don't want to go back.

Home?

It's not home.

She dropped them in Brittney's lap.

I don't think Louise would take over but you could make her an offer for the furniture. I'm sure you'd get a loan approved if you found a bank manager who liked what you had to offer.

Brittney laughed.

Or run it yourself. Looks like you made more by yourselves in one night than in a week with Lucas.

You're crazy.

Not any more. You'll easily cover the mortgage and the bills.

She stared at her.

Try it for a year. After that I don't know. All I do know is I don't want to go back.

She held her hand out for the phone.

Come on. I've always wanted to call the cops.

¤

Mercy sat in her car outside Carter's house. She had thrown all the chocolate wrappers into a plastic bag under the seat and put all the cans and bottles in another for recycling and she had sorted all the cassettes into their rightful covers and even allowed herself to throw away the cases to three she had not seen for a year. The engine idled and she was warm but she wanted to get out and breathe real air for a moment.

It was past six already and she left the headlights on as she had before and as she closed the door she saw a man walk under the arch and she ran but it wasn't him. He carried a plastic bag and as he came closer she read:

M & J Marsham
✺ *Family Butchers* ✺

Not here?

Not for two hours.

Nobody buries on a Monday, he told me. I thought he could be laid up.

I thought I was going to see him yesterday.

Neither of them wanted the conversation.

If you're staying will you keep this?

She took it and she realised she had no idea how long she had planned to wait but he waved over his shoulder and then he was gone. She put the bag on the step and sat beside it and the yard was calm. No windows overlooked her and the backs of the houses framed a strip of moonlit cloud and even the traffic had faded to nothing.

She knew now that she loved him and she was almost ready to believe that he wanted her too but she needed to know why he had not come. She was afraid to be betrayed but she was more afraid that if Fairburn had found her he must have found Carter too and perhaps Carter had not been so lucky.

She thought of him reading the letter and laughing and she did not believe she would ever rid herself of this trail of violence.

When he came up the alley he was quiet and she was asleep against the door and the first thing she saw were the feet. The mud had long since worn away but the grime of the roads and the fumes had streaked them and at the heel the blisters wept a darker grey. She stood and when she saw him she could not imagine what had happened. His shirt and trousers had dried but they had loosened and the jacket had pulled apart at the seams and he looked like a man who had been sewn into his clothes as he walked. His face was raw from the sun and the wind and his hair was white with sand and salt and as she leaned up to him she didn't know where to hold him that would not hurt.

Did he come again?

He shook his head. He hadn't spoken for a day and a night and his lips were bleeding and she stopped him.

He's dead. We left him with Lucas. He did come.

Carter put his arms around her and she whispered to him: I'm OK. I think I'm OK.

She ran a cool bath and helped him climb in and she warmed it gradually until the heat crept into his bones. He lay back and closed his eyes and she poured water through his hair again and again until at last it ran clear but he was already asleep. She knelt on the floor with her arms in the tub to warm her own hands and as he lay there she told him how Fairburn had come and how he had died.

*

The butcher's bag was on the table and she cut six links and put the rest in the empty fridge. The pan was already on the stove and butter was in the dish and she had seen him take the plates from the cupboard and the bread was stale but it would be fine when it was fried. There was nothing else on the shelves but they would take care of that tomorrow.

When the food was on the table she roused him from the bath and he came in trousers with a towel around his shoulders. She poured water into the tumblers and set them down and he waited for her but she put the pan in the sink to soak and wiped the counter and wrapped the bread and put it back in the cupboard. He had never tidied away before eating but he would learn to be patient. He cut the sausages with the side of his fork so he could hold her hand and he could hardly believe that after all this time he was still starting breakfast at midnight.

¤

The moon was high and its light fell clear through the water. The tide ran fast in the lower channels and small stones were lifted downstream as they shook free from the bed. Rocks and sunken timbers lay like shadows of themselves. Everywhere was the low roar of the river and when the hand bell rolled end over end in the racing current the clapper swung but it made no sound.